Before Allie realized what was happening, he reached out, caught the back of her neck in his hand and hauled her to him.

He bent his head and covered her mouth with his in one fluid move, so fast, so effectively, her mind spun.

She moaned. Or was that him? She couldn't be sure, but she rose up on her toes, falling into him as she matched his kiss. Every synapse fired to life as the emotions of the day—terror, panic, uncertainty—melted under Max's touch.

When he lifted his mouth, it wasn't by much. When she blinked open her eyes, it took a moment to focus, and as she looked at him, it wasn't humor she saw on his whisker-roughened face, in his curious brown eyes. It was her own confusion and uncertainty reflected back at her.

He barely moved, and the heat of his fingers brushing her neck may as well have branded her as his. "Suffice it to say this is something we might need to pursue once we work our way though this nightmare."

* * *

Be sure to check out the other stories in this exciting miniseries!

Honor Bound—Seeking justice...and falling in love

* * *

If you're on Twitter, tell us what you think of Harlequin Romantic Suspense! #harlequinromsuspense

Dear Reader,

It's funny how we as writers deal with the characters in our heads. Sometimes we struggle to help them become who we need them to be. Other times, the character bursts onto the page pretty much fully formed and rather demanding. Such was the case with Dr. Allie Hollister. She's the quiet one of this trio of friends, the analytical one, and some might say the coolest of the bunch. She thinks a lot. Perhaps too much.

A difficult childhood was made worse by the murder of her best friend twenty years ago, but it was the bond she formed with Eden and Simone that helped make her the woman she's become. Allie's a fighter, especially when it comes to the people she cares about. When Hope Kellan, one of Allie's patients, disappears, she finds herself at a bit of a loss. But it's her unexpected attraction to Hope's uncle Max that really throws her.

Allie isn't the only person Max threw for a loop. In my preplotting notes—and pictures—I thought I knew exactly who he was, what he looked like, what his temperament would be. Max, however, wasn't having it. The hero I'd imagined as a polished, sullen, lost soul of a hero turned into the Max who showed up—quirky, scruffy, with one of those grins that you can't help but respond to. And Allie most definitely responds. Oh, and so did I.

For the first time in Allie's life, aside from her two best friends, she finds she has someone else willing to fight for her—and with her. Even better? She has something else to fight for: her own happily-ever-after.

Anna J.

GONE IN THE NIGHT

Anna J. Stewart

HARLEQUIN®ROMANTIC SUSPENSE

Recycling programs
for this product may
not exist in your area.

ISBN-13: 978-0-373-40231-1

Gone in the Night

Bestselling author **Anna J. Stewart** can't remember a time she wasn't making up stories or imaginary friends. Raised in San Francisco, she quickly found her calling as a romance writer when she discovered the used bookstore in her neighborhood had an entire wall dedicated to the genre. Her favorites? Harlequins, of course. A generous owner had her refilling her bag of books every Saturday morning, and soon her pen met paper and she never looked back—much to the detriment of her high school education. Anna currently lives in Northern California, where she continues to write up a storm, binge watches her favorite TV shows and movies and spends as much time as she can with her family and friends...and her cat, Snickers, who, let's face it, rules the house.

Books by Anna J. Stewart

Harlequin Romantic Suspense

Honor Bound

Reunited with the P.I.
More Than a Lawman
Gone in the Night

Harlequin Heartwarming

Recipe for Redemption
The Bad Boy of Butterfly Harbor
Christmas, Actually
"The Christmas Wish"

Visit the Author Profile page at Harlequin.com.

For Allison Brennan

Never farther than an email away,
you've always believed.

Chapter 1

Dr. Allie Hollister rounded the circular drive of the Vandermont home and parked behind two patrol cars. This part of El Dorado Hills might be considered one of the more affluent areas of the Sacramento Valley with its mini mansions, lake views and lush acreage, but at six in the morning, the winding roads and sporadic street lamps did not make for a relaxing drive.

It didn't help that she was suffering the aftereffects of a champagne-heavy dinner at her foster siblings' new restaurant last night. No doubt she'd used alcohol to compensate for the fact Eden and Simone, her two best friends, hadn't been able to come with her. Not even two cups of coffee and a painkiller put a dent in the pounding in her skull.

"Dr. Hollister." A fifty-something uniformed deputy with wary "I've seen everything" eyes and a too-tight lip line strode down the paved walkway and offered his hand once she'd climbed out of her mini-SUV. "I'm Deputy Sutherland. I appreciate you coming out. When Mr. and Mrs. Vandermont weren't able to immediately get in touch with Hope Kellan's parents or uncle, they insisted we call you. Not the end to their daughter's sleepover they were expecting, I'm sure."

"Don't worry about it." Between her suddenly attentive mother and finding herself embroiled in the opening of the cold case concerning her best friend's murderer twenty years after Chloe's death, it wasn't as if Allie slept much these days. Right on cue, her cell phone chimed. Allie glanced at another text message. Obviously she wasn't the only one who couldn't sleep. Compared with yet another update on her parents' upcoming anniversary celebration—how many reminders did she need to bring potato salad?—suddenly making the trip up to the foothills didn't seem so bad. Not that Allie was thrilled one of her most challenging patients—nine-year-old Hope Kellan—had started what Allie had planned as a quiet Sunday at home with a jarring bang. "I'm just sorry Hope's recent proclivity to running off had to take this turn. Shall we?" She pocketed her phone, hugged her arms around her torso and wished she'd worn more than a thin sweater over her pastel-pink pedal pushers and matching tank. Her mind was all over the place these days; she couldn't seem to concentrate to save her soul. As someone who prided herself on keeping an eye on every aspect of her life, she was not coping as well as she'd like.

She aimed her gaze at the oversize glass-and-wood front door, quickly determining that her entire house would probably fit in the tiled atrium. She knew of the

Vandermonts in passing; Matthew Vandermont was a big-time lobbyist while his wife was one of the top real estate agents in the region. She also knew they'd both come from very humble beginnings, which explained their dedication to providing the numerous scholarships at various private schools, including their daughter's.

"Mr. and Mrs. Vandermont are with their daughter and her friends in the sitting room. Just there, off to the right," Deputy Sutherland said. "My men are still trying to get a feel for the property. It's more extensive than we expected, but we should be able to get an organized search underway soon."

"How extensive exactly?" Allie stopped just outside the doorway to get her bearings. The home was elegant but with homey touches, family mementos, framed certificates of achievement, and photographs from vacations, events and gatherings that included not only the Vandermonts but their daughter's friends, as well. *Warm*, Allie thought. *Welcoming*.

"There's at least four acres of wilderness leading down to Folsom Lake," the deputy explained. "And I do mean *down*. No fence line to speak of and the property lines are a bit skewed given recent construction projects. No telling what direction the girl might have gone in. I was about to call in reinforcements and have them bring up the search dogs to help."

"Hope," Allie said as diplomatically as possible. "The girl's name is Hope and you're right. More officers can't hurt." Self-doubt crept in around Allie's practiced interaction with law enforcement. Had she misjudged Hope's recent excitement about this long-awaited sleepover with her three best friends? Or had Allie been so distracted during their last session that she'd missed warning signs the little girl planned to run away? While Hope had become increasingly withdrawn in the months since her parents' contentious separation had turned into a vicious custody battle, her spirits had lifted considerably with the arrival of her uncle Max. Other than her three best friends, talking about her hero firefighter uncle was the one thing guaranteed to bring a smile to her freckled face. "I'm sure your team will find her safe and sound," Allie replied in an encouraging tone. "Hope is a smart girl. If she got lost, she'll know enough to stay put until someone finds her."

"At least we aren't having to deal with harsh weather," Deputy Sutherland agreed. "I'll go make the call. You all right with them?"

Allie peered into the sitting room that glimmered in the same glitz and glamour as the outside façade. "I'll be fine, thanks. Mr. and Mrs. Vandermont." Allie set her bag on the floor by the door. The sitting room was decked out in hues of gold and white. The lush carpeting, glass coffee table, enormous French glass doors leading to a backyard with a pool and that large expanse of land reminded Allie of the house Simone, one of her own best friends, had grown up in. Sophisticated, rich. Isolated. But again, where Simone's house had all been for show with nary a hint of emotional attachment, here she saw a celebration of family. As detached and remote as Simone's parents had been, the Vandermonts exuded concern and warmth as Allie approached them. "Thank you for calling me. I can only imagine how worried you must be."

The last words nearly froze in Allie's throat as she focused on the three girls sitting between the handsome couple. She'd seen photographs of the girls, of course.

Mercy, Portia and the Vandermonts' daughter, Willa. Hope talked about them incessantly during their sessions, something Allie herself could relate to given her own relationships with her two best friends. But seeing the three of them here, together, without Hope…

She had to remind herself to breathe.

"Hello, girls." Allie didn't recognize her own voice as she rounded the table to crouch in front of them. Willa, all thick blond hair and debutante blue eyes, clung to her mother in a way that made Allie question who was comforting whom. Mercy, a strawberry blonde, conveyed a familiar edgy defiance that Allie could see masked a good amount of fear. And then there was Portia. Allie blinked as she took in the girl's slight frame, pale complexion and a pixie cap of dark, dark hair. Allie touched the edge of her own cropped cut. Unease bubbled inside her. "I'm Dr. Hollister, but you can call me Allie. I've heard a lot about you."

"We know who you are," Mercy told her as Mr. Vandermont tightened his hold on a trembling Portia. "Hope talks about you a lot. She likes you."

"I like her, too." Allie couldn't shake her apprehension. Having the three of them look at her as if she held all the answers had her relying on her years of education and training as a psychologist. That was hard enough. But, together, they also reminded her of one of the worst days of her life.

Allie took a slow, deep breath and pushed the past where it belonged: out of reach.

Keeping everyone involved calm and focused until Hope was found was the order of the day. That, and finding Hope, was all that mattered.

"The girls are the ones who suggested we call you,"

Mrs. Vandermont said, her round, kind face easing Allie's mind. With blond hair, a clear genetic connection to her daughter, she was dressed in gray yoga pants and a T-shirt, pedicured red toes stark against the white of the carpet. It was evident by Mrs. Vandermont's expression that she was focused on the girls—all the girls. "Thank you for driving all the way up here. I'm sure we're overreacting and that this is just a matter of Hope getting lost—"

"Please don't give it another thought, Mrs. Vandermont." Allie held out her hands to Mercy, who, as far as Allie could tell, was trying her best not to rely on the support her friend Willa was attempting to provide. She squeezed Mercy's hands tight in a silent gesture of understanding. "I'd always rather have someone overreact than assume. Deputy Sutherland is going to be bringing some additional help to search for Hope."

"I should make some coffee, then." Mrs. Vandermont squeezed her daughter's shoulders before she pushed herself to her feet. "That would be all right, wouldn't it?"

"More than all right," Allie said. "Girls, would it be okay if I talked to you about what's happened in the last day or so? Just in case there's something the police officers need to know."

"Dad?" Willa leaned over to look at her father. "You can go help Mom. We'll be okay."

Mr. Vandermont glanced at his daughter with more appraisal than disapproval. "Are you sure? Mercy? Portia? You, too?"

"We're sure." Mercy let go of Allie's hand to wrap a solid arm around Portia's frail shoulders. Portia twisted her hands together and gave a weak nod.

"I won't ask them any questions," Allie explained at the hesitant expression on his face. As a certified children's therapist trained to treat kids who had been or were going through traumatic experiences, she wasn't allowed to pose any. But she could give them an opening to talk. In Allie's experience, listening was the most important thing she could do. "I promise, if we run into any issues, I'll come and get you."

"All right." Mr. Vandermont kept his blue eyes pinned on the three girls as he raked restless hands through his hair and followed his wife out of the room.

Allie stood up and walked the few steps to the padded straight-back chair at the end of the coffee table. She needed some distance; she needed to see how they were with one another, on the off chance something was going on here other than a friend who had wandered off. "Hope has been telling me about this sleepover of yours for a while," Allie told them. "She was very excited about it. Were you all, as well?"

All three girls nodded.

"It would help if you could tell me everything you did. What time you all arrived," Allie said, nudging the conversation where she needed it to go.

"Around five," Mercy said. "Hope was late, but that's because she'd gone to the movies with her uncle before he dropped her off. He stayed for a little while, talked to Mr. and Mrs. V. and then we had pizza for dinner."

"We don't order pizza very often. Mom doesn't think it's good for us," Willa interrupted. "But it was for my birthday, so she made an exception."

"Did it have mushrooms on it?" Allie asked in almost a whisper. "My friend Eden hates, and I mean *hates*, mushrooms. And you know what? Whenever we order it, we make sure to order with mushrooms. Just so we can watch her pick them off."

Willa and Mercy both laughed a little. "I don't like peppers," Mercy said with a watery smile.

"Vegetables on your pizza means it's healthy." Portia's eyes filled. "That's what Hope always says."

Simone said the same thing. "I bet you watched a movie."

"That one where the girls go chasing ghosts with lasers and stuff," Mercy said as Willa sniffled. "Mr. V. fixed up the tent over by the trees so we could feel like it was a real campout. Her mom made us s'mores in foil for dessert."

"Campout?" Allie's heart stuttered to a stop. "You slept outside last night?"

"Uh-huh." Mercy nodded. "We thought it would be fun and different. Mr. V. even went out and got us a tent—"

"This was a last-minute decision?" Allie's thoughts threatened to race, but she pulled back, tried to distance herself. "What made you think of that?"

The three girls glanced uneasily at each other. Finally, Willa shrugged. "We all agreed, but it was Hope's idea. She said she'd seen something about it online and that it sounded fun."

"It was fun," Portia whispered. "Until it wasn't." Willa and Mercy nodded, but Portia's big brown eyes shifted to the floor.

"What is it, Portia?" Allie leaned forward, letting the other two girls take a bit of a lead. "I promise, anything you say here, none of us will be mad. We all just want to make sure Hope is found safe. Okay?"

Portia didn't look convinced.

"Por." Willa reached across Mercy's lap and held out her hand. That Portia immediately grabbed hold conveyed the strength of friendship among these girls. "What's wrong?"

Portia's chin wobbled. "I heard Hope get up. I should have gone with her, but I didn't want to. It was cold." The last few words came out in a sob. "I'm so sorry! I should have been her friend and now she's missing and it's all my fault." Tears spilled down her cheeks as Willa tugged on Portia's hand. Mercy moved to the side as they settled Portia between them, hugging their arms around her.

"I didn't hear her." The alarm in Mercy's wide eyes told Allie she wished she had.

"That's because you were snoring," Willa said.

"I do not snore!" Mercy countered and brought a trembling smile to Portia's face; the goal, Allie realized when she caught a silent exchange between Willa and Mercy.

Allie barely heard them over the roaring in her head. For the first time in as long as Allie could remember, the security she found in her clinical world crumbled. She clenched her fists to cling to the trained detachment that allowed her to do her job. Words that should help them seemed to have gotten trapped somewhere between now and twenty years ago when another nine-year-old had disappeared. During another birthday campout.

Chloe.

Allie squeezed her eyes shut, snapping them open again when she heard Willa speak.

"None of this is your fault, Portia." Willa hugged her friend close. "We should have all gone, just as we promised." Willa turned pleading eyes on Allie with a pained expression that might haunt Allie for the rest of her days. "We made a pact when we first met. We're sisters. Where one goes, we all go. Except we didn't. And now one of us is gone."

Allie stared at the three of them, huddled so closely together she couldn't determine where one ended and another began. Her own arms ached from her tightened fists. Her throat burned from trying to swallow. Her skin had gone icy, as if she wasn't ever going to be warm again, and yet part of her, the tiniest part, clung to the thin thread of hope that this situation wasn't what it seemed to be.

"Are you all right, Dr. Hollister? Allie?" Mercy asked as Allie rose to her feet and walked to the French doors.

Allie heard her as if from a vast distance. "I'm going to go see where you all were sleeping last night. I'll be back in a few minutes." She pulled open the door, stepped out onto the patio and walked quickly around the pool. She could hear the girls calling her from inside the house, but she didn't stop. Not as she hopped over the low-lying bushes. Not as she slipped and slid her way down the slight hill to the clearing ahead. She could see the outline of the red-and-blue tent situated beneath an outcropping of healthy pine and willow trees.

Her breathing came in short bursts, as if she had to remember to inhale. The brisk morning air felt tainted with gloom, the heaviness pressing down on her as she kept her eyes pinned on the tent, resisted the pull into the past. She started to run, as if she could leave the memories, the sensation of panic behind. But she knew the emotions had settled inside her chest another early morning twenty years ago.

She skidded to a stop at the edge of their campsite,

her toes damp from the early-morning moisture. Four cloth folding chairs, water bottles stored in holders, the gooey remnants of the foil-wrapped s'mores lay amid wadded-up sleeping bags peeking out from the zippered tent flap.

An odd keening erupted into the air and only as Allie turned in a slow circle, did she realize the sound came from her. She covered her mouth. Haunting little-girl whispers and giggles echoed through time and sent chills racing down her spine. "Not again. Oh, God, please, not again." She bent double, her stomach rolling as she dropped down to the ground. "This can't be happening." The date. What was the date?

"Dr. Hollister!" Deputy Sutherland, along with a handful of deputies, followed the same path she'd taken moments before. "Dr. Hollister, are you all right?" He hurried over and grabbed her by the arms to haul her to her feet.

"No." His demanding question pierced the fog in her brain. Now wasn't the time to break down. Now wasn't the time to lose control. She needed to get a hold of herself. Disconnect. Separate herself from the nightmare unfolding around her. *Hope*, she told herself. Hope was all that mattered. And yet... "Is there any sign of Hope?"

"No, ma'am." An officer who introduced himself as Deputy Fletcher shook his head. "We're about to expand the search. My officers already went through this area—"

"She won't be here." Allie shook her head and only then did she see the concern on the older deputy's face. "She's gone."

"Gone? You mean you think she went down to the river?"

"No, that's not what I mean." She took a step back, focused on the tent.

And the solitary plant situated on the ground.

Violets.

Allie walked forward, knees wobbling. Every impulse coursing through her urged her to discount the pot and spilling flowers. *A coincidence*, she told herself, but as she, Eden and Simone had learned in the last few months, there were no coincidences.

She took a shaky step forward and then another.

Every cell in Allie's body screamed out as she remembered that night, the following days before their friend's strangled body had been found.

In a field of violets.

Allie touched a hand to the hollow of her throat. "Chloe."

"Hope," Deputy Sutherland corrected. "Dr. Hollister, if you think we need to be searching elsewhere—"

Allie shook her head, got to her feet and pulled out her cell phone. She pointed at the deputy while it rang. "You need to get your team back here, but no one should touch anything. Not a thing, do you understand?" Allie's hands shook. When the deputy didn't move, she shot into command mode. "I think we're standing in a crime scene. I'm a special consultant with the Sacramento PD, Deputy. I also work extensively with the FBI, so believe me when I tell you you'll want to do as I suggest. Now."

"Ma'am." The hostility was expected; clearly he wouldn't appreciate being told what to do in his own jurisdiction. "What exactly is going on?"

Allie held up her hand to silence him. "Lieutenant Santos? It's Allie Hollister."

"Allie?" The shock on the other end of the phone didn't surprise her, nor did the distinctive sound of rustling sheets and murmured voices. "Hang on. We had a late night with the kids."

Allie pressed her lips tight and wrapped her free arm around her waist.

"Ma'am?" Deputy Sutherland's tone strained to the point of snapping. "Would you please tell me what's going on?"

"Hope didn't run away," Allie whispered. She returned her attention to the potted plant, resisting the pull once again to fall solidly into a past she'd been trying to climb out of for two decades.

"Allie?" Lieutenant Santos came back on the line. "This can't be good news if you're calling me before seven on a Sunday. What's going on?"

"You need to get Cole and Jack and get up to—" she recited the Vandermonts' address, grateful that she could request two detectives who were friends "—as soon as you can. One of my patients, who was staying overnight at a friend's house, went missing in the last few hours."

"That's out of our jurisdiction, Allie. As much as I'd like to help—"

"Hope Kellan is nine years old. She was camping with her three best friends. Now she's missing." Allie's eyes burned. "But this isn't just about Hope." She took a deep breath and uttered the words that would turn her nightmare into reality. "It's about Chloe Evans."

Chapter 2

Max Kellan missed a lot of things about Florida. Late-night boat parties, fire-emblazoned sunsets, that ocean-tinted smell that wafted along the shoreline after a summer rainstorm. Humidity? That obnoxious gift of nature didn't come close to making his list, not when it meant his morning jog required a before-sunrise start time. Too bad that in the weeks since he'd moved to the upscale suburb of Sacramento, California, he'd been unable to reprogram his brain to allow for mid- to late-morning runs.

His feet pounded in familiar 7:00 a.m. rhythm as he focused on his breathing, felt the cool morning air wicking away the sweat building on his face and arms. His lungs burned in that familiar five-mile, pressing-himself-too-far kind of way.

Pushing his limits, embracing the aches and pains, forcing himself to feel reminded him he was still alive.

Having spent most of his thirty-three years on the strict, self-imposed routine that acted partly as life-preserver, Max didn't feel inclined to abandon the regime. Yep. He'd had more than enough change to even think about ditching his schedule. Working out cleared his head, helped keep it clear. It had been a rotten six months. Max ducked his head in a useless effort of avoiding the wave of depression that threatened him. Near as he could tell, the only good thing to come out of the last year was his brother's suggestion he make a fresh start of things.

Leave it to Joe to tell him the truth: that he'd wallowed too long. It was time to get up off the mat and fight back. But what to fight for? That was the question. What did an ex-firefighter do when he walked away from everything he knew? Come out to California, obviously. Plenty of space for him to live his life, Joe had said. A life on his own terms for a change.

With strings attached, of course.

Max grinned. As if he'd ever call his brilliant, beautiful, willful niece Hope a string. He'd been crazy about her from the day she was born. She was his video-chatting buddy, his email pal; they even competed against each other in that online game about birds destroying pigs. The few weeks during the summer she'd come out to visit him were what he looked forward to most. It didn't matter how bad a day he'd had—seeing Hope's face, hearing her voice, put everything in perspective. And now he got to see her every day.

If moving out here made his niece smile again—even a little—what was packing up his shattered life compared to that? The visible change in Hope since her parents' less-than-amicable separation physically hurt him. His niece needed security, familiarity. With her father's hectic travel schedule and her mother's lack of parental interest, Hope needed reminding just how much she was loved.

All the things Max and his brother had growing up. Until they didn't.

Taking up residence behind a country club had never been in Max's plans. He was as blue collar as they came. His kid brother had gotten all the brains and earned his status by turning his ideas into a freaking fortune. Who was Max to complain when his new digs came with an amazing, inspiring jogging view?

He rounded the corner, picking up the pace as he headed for the driveway, his body already humming in that way it had when it knew he was nearly done with his daily overexertion. Coffee. Max's blood pumped in anticipation. He needed coffee, stat.

He gave a cursory glance to the sedan parked on the street in front of one of those dinky wannabe SUVs. As if his appearance had triggered their release, two people climbed out of the sedan and approached him. He stopped jogging, planted his hands on his thighs and bent over, took slow, deep breaths to bring his pulse down to normal. He pushed his too-long hair back when it fell over his eyes. "Can I help you?"

Cops. The blazer one man wore wasn't the only giveaway, nor was the badge on the waistband of his jeans or the uniformed deputy right on his heels. Despite this guy's congenial expression and California-boy good looks, Max had spent enough time around the police to identify one from thirty paces.

The deputy behind him, however, appeared barely old enough to shave, with that fresh-faced blue-eyed optimism still shiny and new. Max tilted his head. He'd give it another year, two tops, before he tarnished. He shifted his attention to the woman shuffling about as she climbed out of her car.

She barely reached the detective's shoulder. Jet-black hair that curved over her ears and brushed over concerned brows, along with the pale pink pants and shirt reminded Max of those flitting-fairy animated movies Hope was so nuts over. Not his type, Max told himself, trying to recall the face—and figure—of the last woman he'd dated. Instead, all his mind could come up with was this smiling pixie of a woman.

"Joe Kellan?" the seasoned cop inquired.

"My brother's on a business trip." Max didn't have as easy a time catching his breath as he usually did. Probably because his pulse was beginning to hammer in an unsteady rhythm. "What's this about?"

"You'd be Max Kellan, then." The detective scanned the area as he approached. Between the steady hand on his badge and the serious tone in his voice, Max's skin prickled.

"That's what my driver's license says, Officer." Grudging respect didn't mean he didn't enjoy ribbing the boys in blue. He planted his hands on his hips and let his gaze return to the woman as she joined them. Any thoughts he might have had about aiming a smile at her faded as he caught the uneasy glimmer in her eyes. Wow. Max took a sharp breath. He'd never seen such dark eyes before, eyes that reminded him of the deepest dives he'd taken in the Keys.

"I'm Detective Jack MacTavish. This is Officer Bowman and Dr. Allie Hollister. Do you mind if we go inside?"

Doctor? Max's smile vanished. "Not until you tell me why you're here." Cops and doctors on the doorstep first thing on a Sunday? Alarm bells Max hadn't heard in months, had hoped he'd never hear again, clanged in his head. "Is Joe in some kind of trouble? Did his plane—"

"As far as we know, your brother is fine," Detective MacTavish said. "We've been unable to get in touch with him or his wife. We've also been trying to reach you for the last few hours—"

"Yeah, my cell phone's charging. It's insi—" The words he planned to speak vanished from thought. "What is this about? Wait." He searched his memory, eyes pinned to the woman's face as she very lightly, almost imperceptibly, flinched. "Dr. Hollister. I know that name. You're Hope's shrink."

"I'm her therapist, yes." Dr. Hollister's eyes narrowed in a way that told him she didn't appreciate the moniker. "Please, Mr. Kellan—"

"Max. It's Max. Tell me what's going on." His heart picked up speed, racing faster than it had at any time during his jog. His entire body went cold.

"Please." Dr. Hollister took a step toward him. "Let's go inside so we can talk. It's about Hope."

He dug in his pocket for the house key. Once inside, he managed to hold out until they had closed the door behind them. "Tell me."

He leaned against the wall and stared blankly at the three people in his brother's foyer. He focused on Dr. Hollister, daring her to blink, to look away. She didn't blink. Nor did he see anything other than cool detachment in her stoic expression.

"Your niece has been missing for at least four hours. The Vandermonts contacted us when they realized she was gone from their property. We've been searching ever since," Detective MacTavish said. "We still have people searching for her as we speak."

"How could she have disappeared?" He bent double, bracing his hands on his knees as his stomach rolled. "Are you sure? How can you be sure? The Vandermonts were home when I drove her up there last evening." Everything had been fine when he'd left. Hope had been so happy and excited, she'd run off without even saying good-bye.

Good-bye.

"Let's go sit down, Mr. Kellan. Get you something to drink to calm your nerves."

"I don't need to sit down." His spine stiffened against the fear coursing through him. Hope missing? How was that possible? He pushed off the wall, walked to the kitchen and poured himself the coffee he'd been looking forward to for the last mile. Once it was swirling in the mug, all he could do was stare down and feel himself fall...falling...

"What are we looking at? A kidnapping for ransom? A stranger ab—" He dropped his chin to his chest, unable to complete the thought. He needed to find some logic here, something to grab onto like the plans made to combat a nasty out-of-control fire. But where was logic when a child was missing? When there wasn't anything other than complete and utter panic.

"We're considering every possibility," the detective told him, but he found the statement far from reassuring.

"My brother—"

"Mr. Kellan. Max." Detective MacTavish stood across the counter from him while Dr. Hollister remained just inside the doorway, those eyes of hers scanning the room like a laser beam. "I realize this is difficult, but we need to know if you've heard from your niece since you dropped her at the Vandermonts' yesterday evening."

"Um, yeah." He pinched the bridge of his nose. "She sent me a text message before she went to sleep. It's our routine." Max spun in a circle. Where had he left his phone? "Here." He pulled it free of the charging station and handed it over. "There's a picture of her with her friends. I think they were eating s'mores. It's all over her——" He couldn't think. Why couldn't he think? He stared down, transfixed, at the grinning image of the only person who brought him a modicum of joy these days. "I need to call my brother."

"Please." Detective MacTavish nodded, but Max could tell the cop was humoring him.

Max dialed, clenching his teeth so tight his head ached. "Voice mail. Typical. Joe, it's me. Call me back. Now. It's about Hope. She's…" He scrubbed his hand across his forehead. Missing? Dead? Gone? His chest hurt from breathing so hard. "Just call me back, man. Please." He clicked off, let out a sound that might have been a laughing sob. "Can you believe my brother's invented some of the most advanced technology on the market and half the time he forgets to turn on his cell?" He tossed the phone on the counter, barely noticing when the detective picked it up. He needed to move, to think. To do something, anything.

"You haven't heard from Hope since she sent you that picture?" the detective asked.

"No. You said you're considering everything. That means she might have gone off." Was she out there? Alone? God, he hoped she was alone. But she could be freezing. Hurt. Scared. "I know there's some pretty thick wilderness around the home. I didn't think it was anything—"

"Again, we aren't ruling anything out," Detective MacTavish said. "We have sheriff's deputies searching the property around the Vandermont home. We also have officers going door-to-door in case anyone saw anything or anyone suspicious in the area in the last few days. Do you have other contact information for your brother besides his cell number?"

"Yeah." Max returned to the mug, watched the steam swirl up but still couldn't bring himself to drink. "Yeah, he wrote it down and stuck it on the message board." He walked around the detective to the recessed desk, pulled the paper off the corkboard. "He's been working on a merger with a Japanese company interested in his latest invention, app, something I don't understand." Joe with all his big ideas that always paid off. Out to change the world, make it better. For everyone. For Hope.

"Do you know where we can find Gemma?" Dr. Hollister asked.

"She said she was going to a spa until Joe got back." Because his morning wasn't going bad enough, now he had to think about Hope's mother. "Joe wanted her to go with him, thought maybe they could work out some of their issues. She refused. Big knock-down, drag-out fight the night before he left. Nothing violent," he added when he realized the impression that statement would make. "Joe would never hurt either of them. But things have been difficult between them. As I'm sure *she* knows." He glanced at Dr. Hollister, who gave a nod of agreement. What was wrong with the woman? She knew Hope; she'd been treating her. Why did she look as if she didn't want to be bothered to be here?

"Do you know what spa Mrs. Kellan was going to?" Detective MacTavish asked.

"Honestly, I don't pay much attention to anything Gemma says." Max blinked. "And no, before you ask, I haven't heard anything from her since she took off. She knew she wouldn't have to worry about Hope with me around." Guilt walloped him in the gut.

"I'd agree with that assessment," Dr. Hollister said as she flipped through something on his phone. "Gemma isn't the most hands-on parent, but if she stayed local, I'd lay odds on the Camellia Day Spa off Fair Oaks Boulevard, Jack."

"We'll have one of our officers work on tracking her down," Detective MacTavish said. "May we have your permission to search your cell phone and the house? Maybe there's a chance someone picked her up and dropped her off here late last night."

"Search whatever you want," Max said. "Hope hasn't been here. I'd know. I don't sleep much." Maybe never again.

"Hope told me you're living in their guesthouse," Dr. Hollister said as she returned the phone to the detective.

"Officially, yes, but I moved in here when my brother left so I'd be close to Hope. The guest room is on the other side of the stairs. You're wasting your time questioning me." But he knew they had to. How many child abductions led to relatives or friends of the family? Frustration began to swirl. "I should be out there trying to find her." He couldn't just sit—or stand—around and wait. He needed to be *doing* something.

"We are doing that, believe me." Detective MacTavish left the room with a gesture that he'd soon return.

Max stared at the doctor, anger boiling inside him as he pushed aside those warm, fuzzy feelings that had descended out on the street. The last thing he needed in his life again—in any capacity—was a useless doctor. "Stop looking at me like I'm a specimen under your microscope, Doc. I won't lose it completely." He gripped the edge of the counter, leaned over and squeezed his eyes shut. "Not yet, anyway."

"I haven't used a microscope since college." She walked over and picked up his coffee, carried it over to the sink and dumped it out. She searched the cabinets, pulled out another mug, one of the ones Hope used for her hot chocolate, and filled it with coffee. "Here. Drink."

He wrapped both hands around the white ceramic, his eyes falling on the cartoon princess frolicking with her animal friends. "Why did you do that?"

"To give you something of hers to hold on to." Dr. Hollister pressed her hand over his for a brief moment, long enough to warm him in conjunction with the coffee. "We're going to find her, Max. We've got a lot of smart, dedicated people who are going to help us. Jack and his partner? You won't find better. We just need you to be here when she comes home."

"Easy for you to say, Doc. I bet you don't feel what I'm feeling."

"You'd be surprised what I feel." Her faint smile was anything but bright. "And it's Allie, please. Doc sounds a bit clinical."

"All doctors are clinical." He sounded harsh. He didn't care. Couldn't let himself care. The only thing that mattered was Hope. "What if she's run away again? She's been doing that lately. It's one of the reasons I moved out here."

"If that's what's happened, we'll find her sooner than later."

"But you don't think that's what this is," Max countered, daring the doctor to claim otherwise.

"She's well aware she can trust you," she said after the briefest of hesitations. "I've seen a marked improvement in her since you came to stay. She's spoken about you often during our sessions. She loves you. Worships you, as a matter of fact. Her hero uncle Max who fights fires and saves people. I think I actually saw stars explode in her eyes talking about you one day."

"Twist the knife deeper, why don't you." Max drank more coffee, surprised at how soothing the jolt of caffeine felt. The last thing he needed to dwell on was Hope out there waiting for him to find her, which he couldn't do as long as he was stuck in here. Not that leaving was an option. What if a call came in…

His arms shook as his muscles clenched. "For the record, I don't fight fires. Not anymore, anyway."

Detective MacTavish reentered the kitchen.

"What?" Max's spine went stiff.

"Crime scene unit is on its way. My partner is working on getting some FBI assistance while he's up at the Vandermonts' home. We want as many agencies on this as possible. The more we blanket the valley, the sooner we'll find her."

"Tell him to request Special Agent Eamon Quinn," Allie said. "He's out of the San Francisco office, but he's one of their top experts in cases like this." She flinched, as if afraid she'd said too much.

"Cases like what?" Max demanded.

"Missing persons," Allie said quickly. Too quickly.

"Before this goes any further," Detective MacTavish said, "I need to ask you something, Max."

"Ask away." What was it with these people that they were treating him with kid gloves? "I don't have anything to hide."

The detective glanced at Allie, who gave an encouraging nod. Max reined in his temper. Damned doctors always thought they knew best about everything.

"Given the custody fight over Hope," Detective Mac-Tavish said, "do you think it's at all possible that either your sister-in-law or your brother could have taken her without telling you?"

"You have got to be kidding me." Max set the mug down with a clack. "Seriously?"

"Very seriously. Allie's filled me in on what she can—"

"Did she?" Max sneered. "Stretching those confidentiality boundaries are we, Doc?"

If his words hit an emotional target, he couldn't tell. Not even a flicker of acknowledgment. Boy, she was one cold ice queen. "I told the detective what I could," she said. "That your brother's case has been contentious. Something I've been witness to in court on numerous occasions."

"Joe wouldn't do that to me." Max couldn't shake the sensation there was something more to this situation than he was being told. Or maybe he was overreacting. The last thing he could rely on these days was his own judgment. He'd never done well when people he loved were threatened. Situations like this always threw him into a tailspin and that's when he made bad choices. Life-altering choices. "My brother wouldn't set me up like this or use me. It doesn't matter how much Joe and Gemma might loathe each other, he wouldn't let me think Hope was in danger." The very idea would have made him laugh if he could remember how.

"What about Hope's mother?" Detective MacTavish asked.

"Gemma wouldn't have any problem letting me hang." Max grimaced. "We aren't the other's favorite person. We only get along for Hope's sake. I've never trusted or liked her and she knows it."

"Why don't you trust her?" Allie asked.

He hesitated. No need to air that bit of dirty family laundry unless absolutely necessary. "Because my brother's worth about three-quarters of a billion dollars and she didn't pay him much attention until he hit the Fortune 500." Aggravation built to the point of bursting. Max had long believed Gemma had only had Hope to ensure she would be financially tied to Joe forever. "Search the house, take my prints and DNA, hunt down Gemma, set up your phones or what have you, but I need to do something. I've got training. I can be out there looking—"

"We need you to stay close to home for the time being," Detective MacTavish cut him off. "At least until we can get your brother or sister-in-law back here. You being around to answer any questions we might have is exactly the kind of help we need. Beginning with any friends of Gemma who might be able to help us track her down."

"I'll be here if you need me," Allie's too-soothing voice grated on Max's nerves.

"I don't need you," he spat. "I don't need anything

other than for my niece to walk through that door and prove to me this is all some horrible mistake. So take your niceties and your platitudes and put them to use somewhere else. You find my niece." He moved in on the detective, who straightened to meet him eye-to-eye. "And you do it fast. Or I'm going to do it myself."

Chapter 3

It was strange, Allie thought, how time possessed a vicious will of its own. It sped up when you wanted to stretch out the memories and slowed to an agonizing crawl when all she wanted to do was push forward.

The hours that had passed since she'd sat before three terrified little girls felt like days, days she'd do anything to pretend had been a dream. Now, as she stepped inside Hope Kellan's second-floor bedroom, the reality of the little girl's absence hit her like an anvil.

She watched as the last member of the Sac PD's crime scene unit snapped a metal case shut and left. The tech offered a strained, understanding smile as he did so. Never before had Allie put so much faith in the department she'd worked closely with and in the detectives heading up the case. She trusted them, absolutely and without question.

And yet...

Allie, of all people, knew there were no absolutes in life. Not where children were concerned. Not twenty years ago and not today.

She'd needed solitude; she'd needed quiet. Watching Max Kellan occupy himself with pacing, sitting, standing, and then repeating the pattern, pressed in on her. She understood how he felt; all she wanted to do was go out the front door, breathe in the fresh air and walk until she couldn't walk anymore.

His panic, his concern, tasted bitter in Allie's mouth as she tried not to surrender to the logic of what statistics said about how Hope's disappearance would play out. The first twenty-four hours were vital—forty-eight, if they were lucky—but Allie was a realist; she knew the odds didn't favor a happy reunion. Chances increased by the second that she'd be standing in another field, over another little girl's body.

"Stop it!" She had to say it out loud, so she could hear it through her own ears. It's what Simone or Eden would tell her, but they weren't here. What she wouldn't give for her best friends to be standing beside her. They were her support system, had been from the moment they'd met on the kindergarten playground.

Allie had been trying to stand up for herself against a second grader who wanted the bright blue plastic ball she'd gotten for her birthday, but she soon found herself flat on her back on the cement.

Next thing she knew, Simone Armstrong and Eden St. Claire were standing over her, hands stretched out for her to take. They hauled her up, introduced themselves and then their friend Chloe Evans, who had been standing behind them. Chloe, with her excitement-tinged, wide-green-eyed uncertainty, crooked pigtails sticking out on either side of her head. Her clothes hadn't matched, not even a little, Allie remembered.

That day Simone had helped Allie straighten her new pink dress and sweater while Eden retrieved Allie's ball—before being sent to the principal's office for kicking the second grader somewhere Allie later learned was vastly inappropriate.

They'd been picking each other up off the ground ever since.

Times like this, as she stared at the youthful optimism of Hope Kellan's bedroom, Allie envied people like Max Kellan.

Where other people became jittery and restless when faced with a traumatic situation, Allie pulled into her tiny, tiny shell like a petrified, silent turtle.

Call it professional training or life experience, it was part of what had kept her sane all these years. Today, for the first time, the calmness seemed to be pushing her to the brink.

When her cell phone buzzed, Allie answered without thinking. "Dr. Hollister."

"Well, there's a surprise. I thought for sure I was going to get your voice mail." Nicole Goodale's cheery voice dropped Allie into the quicksand of her youth, exactly the last place she wanted to dwell. "I just wanted to thank you for coming last night to the soft opening of Lembranza. We really appreciate the family support."

"It was my pleasure, Nicole." Allie rubbed the space between her brows. If there was one talent her foster siblings, Nicole and her brother Patrick, had picked up during her three years as one of Allie's parents' "projects," it was Allie's mother's bad sense of timing, unfortunately.

"The meal was fabulous and it was great to see both of you again." Funny how, after more than fifteen years and sporadic contact, Nicole seemed inordinately determined to make up for lost time. Not that Allie minded. Nicole and her brothers were among the few bright spots in her childhood.

"Glad to know we earned your seal of approval. I also wanted to check in and see if everything's okay with you." The concern in her foster sister's voice dropped another weight of guilt onto Allie's shoulders. She hadn't wanted to go last night and had even contemplated cancelling at the last minute, but if she'd done that she never would have heard the end of it, especially from her mother.

"Everything's fine," Allie lied. "I'm just dealing with a problem with one of my patients at the moment. Sorry if I sound distracted."

"I hope it's nothing serious," Nicole said.

"Serious enough," Allie said. "And I hope I wasn't too much of a downer last night at dinner. There's just been a lot going on." Being stalked by the monster responsible for murdering your best friend didn't make for emotional stability. "But it was great to reconnect."

"Seeing you again made us realize how much we've missed you," Nicole said. "And you're right, things have been…" Her voice trailed off and Allie flinched. "It's been a rough few years trying to get Mom settled and, well, the rest of what happened."

She did know. Of the three Goodale kids who had stayed with Allie's family while their mother underwent in-patient treatment for severe psychosis, Tyler had been the youngest and, even to Allie's young eyes, the most fragile. She hadn't been surprised to hear years later that he'd eventually developed the same issues as his mother and been committed to a long-term psychiatric facility. "Tyler was always very nice to me."

Allie shivered and looked down at the pale pink carpet. Tyler had been so considerate, so attentive. Especially after Chloe's death. He'd followed Allie around, offering to help, to talk. He'd paid attention to her, listened to her, which was more than her own parents had done. Sitara and Giles Hollister had been wrapped up in their own lives, their own ideas, and had chalked Chloe's death up to "one of those things the universe gives us as a test of character."

It was only now, years later as a practicing therapist, that she realized the damage they'd done; but walking away completely would have felt hypocritical given her professional dedication to healing families. Besides, no one could work guilt like Sitara Hollister. But Tyler? He'd been her savior.

Whenever Allie recalled the quiet times she and Tyler spent in the ramshackle tree house her father had built, eating peanut butter sandwiches and playing board games, she smiled. A little.

"Well, we all have to move on, don't we," Nicole said. "I'll check in with you again soon. If only to remind you to bring your famous potato salad on Sunday."

Allie sighed. "Ma called you, didn't she?"

"She thinks you're ignoring her texts."

That's because she was. "Yeah, well, I'll answer the next time she calls." Like Allie had the wherewithal to deal with her mother today. "Thanks for checking in on me, Nicole. I'll see you soon."

Allie called on every ounce of courage that had abandoned her the second she'd stepped foot in the makeshift campground at the Vandermonts'. This wasn't her. She didn't flounder. Yet here she was, spinning out of control as if someone had pulled the floor out from under her. Adding her wacky and emotionally scarred family to the mix only made her rotate faster.

Where was the control she'd based her entire life on? Control that had been slipping away from her for months? Ever since Eden had begun receiving her "reminder" gifts. As if any of them had gone a day without remembering Chloe's murder.

Never had it occurred to Allie that Chloe's killer would target someone Allie cared about, other than Simone and Eden. Why would she, given a motive for Chloe's murder had never been uncovered? Chloe's case had simply been designated cold, attributed to an individual passing through who had taken advantage of a young girl out on her own in the middle of the night.

For decades the police and even Chloe's family, who had moved away long ago, had assumed it was a random act.

Except it hadn't been.

Allie should have been more aware as far as Hope was concerned. The physical similarities between Hope and Chloe were part of the reason Allie had been so determined to help the little girl. She didn't need another therapist telling her the dangers of transference. Chloe hadn't been given a long, happy, stable life. Allie wanted that—maybe too much—for Hope Kellan.

And by doing so, she had inadvertently put the little girl in danger.

When was Allie going to learn that whenever she let feelings get involved in any decision, trouble followed? All the more reason to take the offer of a new job, a new start, seriously. Allie's stomach clenched. Moving on would mean leaving Simone and Eden behind—her real family. But they didn't need her as much. Eden was happily married and Simone was practically on her way down the aisle.

Starting over, doing something that scared her both professionally and personally—that was a good idea, wasn't it?

Once Hope is home, she told herself. Then she'd talk about it with them. Besides, they were going to have enough to deal with once the press found out Chloe's case had been reopened recently when Chloe's missing tennis shoe had been delivered to the police. Now, here they were, with another missing girl in frighteningly similar circumstances. Allie could only imagine the resulting spin accusing the police department of endangering valley residents by keeping the information quiet.

Allie shivered. She didn't want to think about how the public—especially Hope's uncle Max—would react to that.

She recognized a time bomb when she saw one and Max Kellan was tick-tick-ticking his way through life.

His life wasn't any of her business. But given his rather shaggy appearance; the long, sun-tipped, dark blond hair that seemed to be in a race to his shoulders; the permanent five-o'clock shadow; his open hostility upon learning of her profession? Allie felt safe in assuming he'd had a difficult go of things lately. Still, there was something oddly appealing about him. Maybe it was the chiseled features of a man who could have stepped out of an action movie. She caught herself imagining how her fingers would get lost in the thick length of his hair. Her reaction to him was curious. Unusual. Which only increased her fascination.

When she looked into those swirling brown eyes of his, she found something familiar, something unsettling that she found in the mirror every morning: the man was haunted.

She also saw a man in need of care and compassion, whether he wanted to admit it or not.

Add all those elements together and sharing her suppositions with Max about Hope's kidnapping could very well set up a reaction of furious proportions.

For now, as far as the connected cases were concerned—as far as Max was concerned—she'd keep her mouth shut.

If she'd expected to find some peace in Hope's bedroom, it was keeping its distance. Allie saw hints of designer elegance, Hope's mother's influence given her penchant for materialistic show-woman-ship. But Gemma's taste extended only as far as the deep layers of pink-and-white striped wallpaper and detailed crown molding decorating the high ceiling.

Hope wasn't a girlie-girl, not completely, anyway. She was a kid who threw herself into all different things, from science experiments to hip-hop dance classes, to horseback riding lessons that had been her mother's idea. She liked playing dress up as much as baseball. She could catch and throw as well as she could decimate the makeup counter at the local store. Despite the sadness and withdrawn behavior that had brought Hope to Allie's office, she'd maintained her spark, however dim; but enough for Allie to gently blow on and reignite.

Allie wasn't so egotistical to believe Hope's transformation was all on her. Max Kellan had played a significant role in pulling Hope out of the darkness surrounding her parents' divorce.

Allie's toes scrunched in her flat thin-soled shoes as if afraid of taking a step farther inside. She pushed past her reservations and forced herself to scan the walls lined with kitten and puppy posters and a boy band Allie had only heard of in some of her other patients' sessions. Like the Vandermont home, Hope's bedroom contained several photographs of the four young girls, all with the biggest, happiest, brightest smiles possible.

Allie could only hope they'd be able to smile like that again.

She wasn't sure she ever had.

Allie walked over to the bay window, sat on the padded cushion stacked high with books ranging from classic children's stories to the latest young adult novels.

"Let me guess." Jack MacTavish's voice had Allie glancing to the bedroom door. "Uncle Max drive you out of your comfort zone?"

Allie managed a slight smile. "Not really. I thought maybe being in her space would help me somehow."

"How do you think he's doing?" Jack strode in and scanned the room in that seemingly casual way he had of absorbing every detail.

"I'd say he's hanging on by his fingernails." Allie got to her feet, realized there wasn't anywhere else to go. She sat down again. "Have you heard anything from Cole yet?" As much as she liked Jack, she'd known Cole Delaney, Jack's partner and Eden's new husband, for most of her life. She missed his solid presence despite acknowledging he was needed elsewhere.

"He's still up at the Vandermont house with the lieutenant, bringing Agent Quinn up to speed. Quinn, I kid you not, arrived by helicopter like some movie super-hero. Cole did say the girls are asking for you. They want to know if there's anything they can be doing."

"There isn't." All they could do was wait. Which was, of course, the most difficult thing anyone could do in this situation. "It makes more sense for Cole to talk to them, see if they noticed anyone strange in the last few weeks. Or if Hope told them something she's been keeping to herself." As if Allie could admit out loud that being around the girls felt like a physical knife to her heart.

Jack lowered his voice. "You think this has been in the works that long?"

"This took planning, Jack." Far longer than Allie liked to consider. The idea that Hope was the one who suggested the campout niggled at the back of her mind.

"You're still convinced this is connected to Chloe's case."

"You saw the flowers." Allie had yet to erase the image out of her mind. "If it isn't connected, why leave it at all? Hope and Chloe could be twins. The red hair, the quirky personality, the friends." Allie felt her breath catch. Only now did she realize how being around Hope eased some of the pain she'd carried most of her life. And now? She scrubbed her hands down her arms. Now it was as if she was stuck in a horrific rerun of the worst episode of her childhood. "I know I'm supposed to try to keep an emotional distance, but I don't think that's possible. We're all out on the ledge on this one, Jack. I'm not entirely sure what to do." And that was her greatest fear: that she'd do something wrong and cost a young girl her life.

"You'll do what you always do. You'll keep us from

falling." Jack squeezed her arm. "You've got a good support system with Eden and Simone. Speaking of which, Cole called Eden and filled her in. She's driving back from Portland. She should be in Sacramento by tonight."

"More like this afternoon given the way she drives. I should call Simone," Allie murmured. "I've been trying to get up the nerve to break her cone of happiness."

"I'd say break away, but then I'd be the one emotionally invested." It was Jack's turn to offer a thin smile.

Allie inclined her head. Jack's ego had taken a healthy bashing a few weeks ago when Simone reunited with her ex-husband, something none of them saw coming, least of all Jack, Simone's on-again, off-again Friday-night date. That Jack rolled with the punches and, in some odd way, had become friends with said ex, Vince Sutton, proved just how nice a guy the detective was. "You need to stop looking so hard, Jack. Your someone is out there. She'll pop up when you least expect it." Or, as was the case for Eden and Simone, when it was incredibly inconvenient.

"Yeah, don't know about that. I'm running out of options." He came over and sat on the window seat beside her. He turned that charming, eye-twinkling grin on her. "Unless you're open to—"

"You really don't need me to remind you that you're like my big brother, right?" Allie said, appreciating the lighthearted banter.

"Ugh." He fell against the wall and clutched his heart as if she'd shot him. "And here I was finally recovering from Simone's 'you're a great guy' and 'it's not you, it's me' speech. I guess taking you for a weekend ride in my new car is out of the question."

Allie chuckled.

"I don't mean to interrupt." Max Kellan's shotgun voice made Allie jump, her face flushing for no reason other than he'd caught her being hit on, however ineffectively. "Your fellow detectives were able to track my brother down. Joe took an early flight and should land at Sac Metro in the next fifteen minutes. They have officers waiting at the gate to bring him home." His amber-specked brown eyes shot disapproval, first in Jack's direction, then in hers. "As you were."

"Now, hang on—" Jack got slowly to his feet. Allie grabbed hold of his arm and shook her head.

"He needs to be angry at something," she murmured. "It gives him focus." On something other than fear.

"Then let it be me. You don't deserve it."

Didn't she?

"Max, I could use your help going through some of Hope's belongings." Allie leaned around Jack. "Are you up for that?" She didn't really need his help, but he needed a distraction and she needed to know more about this man who could prove vital when it came to finding Hope.

"You serious?" Jack's brow furrowed.

"Go back downstairs. Check in with Cole. And see if you can track down Simone and Vince. I'm guessing we might need their input on this."

"More detectives?" Max asked.

"More help," Allie explained and hoped it would suffice.

"While you're at it, see where we are with tracking down my sister-in-law," Max added. With his arms folded across his torso, he resembled one of those Roman statues declaring battle, this time with the well-meaning detective.

"I'll check." Jack glared at Max. "Ease up, hose monkey. Allie's one of the best assets you've got in this."

"Hose monkey?" Allie asked Max once Jack was gone.

"One of the nicer things cops call firefighters." It wasn't until Max looked at her that she saw the reluctant respect glistening in his eyes. "What is it you're hoping to find in here?"

Just like Allie, Max didn't seem in a rush to step into Hope's room; he'd probably feel more comfortable if the room was on fire. "You know her better than anyone. Is there anything that seems off to you? Things that aren't familiar?"

Maybe little gifts she'd been sent like the mementos Allie, Eden and Simone had received over the past few months. Notes. Pictures. Flowers. Every one of them a stark reminder of when they'd lost Chloe and that her killer hadn't been forgotten.

Or that he hadn't forgotten them.

"Hope's a pretty open kid." Max finally moved inside and peered behind the door at the filled-to-the-brim bookshelf. "She's a terrible secret keeper. I don't like the idea of snooping through her stuff."

"If it helps us get a handle on exactly what's going on, I doubt she'd mind."

"What about her laptop?" Max gestured to his niece's desk.

"Tammy, the head lab tech, will go over that. Hope doesn't maintain any social media presence that I know of."

"Yeah, Joe doesn't allow it. One of the benefits of being in on the expansion of the internet. He keeps it as far away from Hope as possible." He ran his fingers along the spines of her books. "I suppose you think that's too restrictive, too controlling." He glanced at her, the accusation clear on his face.

"I can see both sides of that argument, but, as I don't have children, it's not necessarily my place to say." Except in the confines of her office.

"Of course not," Max sneered. "Fixing the messes people make of their kids keeps you employed."

Allie's chest tightened. "Forgive me for dropping all the psychology on you, but that's what we in the business call projecting. And Hope isn't a mess."

"No, but her parents are."

Allie couldn't argue that point. Joe Kellan, Hope's father, avoided conflict at all costs, especially when it came to his wife. Whereas Gemma Kellan knew precisely what buttons to push to get what she wanted. The two were a seriously toxic combination and it adversely affected their only child.

Allie prided herself on being able to read people. It was, after all, a big part of her job. She could walk into a situation and assess the people involved from the start; give her a file and some background and she could, if necessary, get exactly what she needed from them, either child or adult. At the very least she could find a clue as to how to help.

But Max Kellan? Oh, boy. Allie brushed her fingers against the space just her heart. For whatever reason, she couldn't get a good read on him, and Allie didn't do well in uncharted territory. The only thing she could be certain of was that he cared about Hope and he'd do whatever it took to bring his niece home.

And that might just be the most attractive thing about him.

As much as she hated keeping a family member in the dark, openly connecting Hope's disappearance to any previous crime, especially a case as contentious as Chloe Evans's unsolved murder, would only make finding Hope more difficult.

Allie and her friends had lost to this monster once already. She wasn't going to lose again.

If that meant sticking close to an unknown entity like Max Kellan, so be it. She had enough psychological weaponry in her wheelhouse to keep both of them occupied.

"You don't have any affinity for psychologists, do you, Max?" Turning the conversation into something productive could work to her benefit.

"Affinity?" Max pulled out a stack of books and peered behind it before he moved to the next shelf. "In my experience they enjoy putting people on edge. Like the way some of them use big words they think their patients might not understand."

"Nice to know you've painted us all with the same tainted brush." She did some more wandering and zeroed in on the small table behind the closet door where Hope kept a mix of little-girl and big-girl makeup. "Calling me a shrink was my first clue, in case you're wondering. I'm a psychologist, not a psychiatrist."

He snorted. "Like there's a difference. They both mess with people's heads."

She arched a brow, locked her jaw. "Only one is a medical doctor with prescription privileges."

"Noted. I won't come to you for pharmaceutical assistance. You're here to help find Hope," Max said, his tone dismissive when she started to respond. "Not to go rattling around in the empty space between my ears."

"And you seem determined to convince me you're not exactly the sharpest tool in the box." She found his self-deprecating attitude offensive. "Whatever issues you have with your previous shri—um, doctors," she said, almost choking on the unfinished word, "it would be helpful if you set them aside for the time being. We don't need anything else getting in our way."

"Whatever you say, Doc." He stooped down and pushed open the bay window seat Allie had been occupying a few minutes before.

She really should write a book on people's passive-aggressive tendencies. Some used them when making excuses for the paths their lives had taken, blaming everyone other than themselves for their choices. Normally she could ignore this behavior when it was aimed at her. With Max Kellan, however, she found his sarcastic dismissal irritating. "Guess I'll need to find a way to embrace that nickname. What's yours, by the way, Max?" She picked up a beaded necklace off one of the pushpins on Hope's wall.

"My what?"

"Your nickname, call sign, whatever it is you fire boys call it. You all get one, right? Or do you choose your own?"

"We do not choose our own. And we certainly aren't boys."

"Clearly I need to be educated in the ways of the firefighter." She watched the dazed expression vanish from his eyes as he narrowed his gaze at her. "Let me guess. Einstein? Hawking? Hmm." She flicked open the square jewelry box on the dresser. Inside she found a collection of rainbow-colored perfume and makeup bottles. Huh. This one reminded her of one she'd had as a little girl. She picked up the pink vial. "Come on, Max, help a doctor out. What do your fellow firefighters call you? If you don't tell me, I'm just going to keep guessing."

"Entertain yourself all you like, if puzzling me out is going to keep that smile on your lips." He walked around the bed and stood in front of her. Allie lifted her chin high enough that her neck ached. *My goodness, but he is…* Allie swallowed hard. *Tall. And big. So very, very big.* She smelled the freshness of the shower he'd taken, the ever-so-subtle hint of sandalwood and spice from his soap or aftershave. Even fully clothed in something as simple as jeans and a dark T-shirt, she could see there wasn't an inch of him that wasn't toned, controlled. Given what she'd learned about him so far—early-morning runner, tightly wound, protective, judgmental bordering on accusatory—she'd be lying if she didn't admit to herself she considered the man incredibly attractive and intriguing.

She blinked, her hand tightening around the bottle. Now she was the one who needed distracting. "Tell you what. If I guess your nickname, you have to tell me something about yourself absolutely no one else knows."

He moved closer, lowered his voice. "And what do you give me when you guess wrong?"

Allie shrugged, refusing to be put off. "Name it." Her eyes went wide as she realized her mistake. "I mean, um."

He grinned. Not in a flirtatious or playful way as she might have expected or wanted. Instead she suddenly felt trapped in one of those crime novels she was so fond of—caught by someone with a nefarious if not alluring agenda.

"I wouldn't have thought a smart woman like you

would be into dangerous games, Doc. Making an offer like that? It's asking for trouble."

Allie cleared her throat. Was it just her or was it hot in this room? "Maybe I like trouble."

"Or maybe you're just looking for any means to distract me from what's really going on." He put his hands on his hips and stared at her intently. "I'll settle for you answering any question I ask you *honestly*." He stressed the last word. "You were right. I don't trust doctors. Even pretty ones with big brown eyes and a tough attitude. But I do appreciate your efforts, Doc."

Darn. Was that a smirk on his face as he stepped away? She couldn't tell. Allie pressed her lips tight and took a long breath. "Can't blame a girl for trying." She shrugged and played the "aw shucks" card. She twisted the lid on the bottle, lifted it to her nose and breathed deeply. She gagged and covered her mouth.

"What?" Max was at her side in an instant. "What's wrong?"

Allie shook her head, her eyes watering as she tried to breathe around the suffocating, familiar aroma. "Just that smell." The perfume she, Eden and Simone had given Chloe for her birthday a few weeks before Chloe disappeared. What was it doing here? Allie's hand trembled. How had Hope gotten it? "I've always hated it." Her head spun and she swayed, her knuckles turning white around the bottle.

Max moved in, his hands poised to catch her. She held out her arms, shifted her stance as if preparing to defend herself.

He looked startled for a moment, whether at his own instinctual reaction or at her immediate defensive posture, she couldn't tell. Then his expression hardened and he glared, examining her as if she was now the one pinned under a microscope—what Max had accused Allie of doing to him earlier.

"I don't believe you."

That Max spoke so succinctly, so firmly, left Allie even more determined not to let too much slip about the possible connection between Hope and Chloe. "That's not my fau—"

"I don't believe a lot of what's been going on today. There's too much whispering, too much secrecy. You and MacTavish know a lot more than you're saying and I'm betting the FBI isn't too far behind on the information train. Everyone I've run into so far is walking around like they're about to break something and I refuse to let that something be Hope. What's going on, Doc?"

Allie couldn't find the words.

"This is my niece's life we're talking about."

The desperate plea in his voice had her swallowing a softball-sized lump of guilt. He was right. This was his niece's life. Who was she to blame him for reacting like this? Why would he believe her when she said she was going to do whatever it took to bring Hope home? Why would he trust her? Why would he trust anyone? But she needed him to. "For the record, I'm well aware of what's at stake, Max. Don't believe for one second that I'm not."

"Something else is happening here, Doc. Something you're not telling me. Are you going to come clean or not?"

"There's nothing to come clean about," she lied. Would there come a time when she could be honest with him? Why did it matter? "Have you seen this perfume before?" She recapped the bottle and wished she hadn't handled it so much.

"No. But I don't keep up on my nine-year-old niece's perfume habits."

Maybe someone should have. Allie picked up the jewelry box. "I need to get an update from Jack. He should have spoken to his partner by now. Keep searching for anything you think might help."

"I meant what I said before, Doc." Max's voice had her stopping at the door, but she didn't face him. Not again. Not when she wasn't sure she could continue the façade. "I don't trust you. Whatever it is you're hiding, I promise you, I'm going to find out. And I always keep my promises."

Chapter 4

What did a perfume bottle have to do with his niece's disappearance? Max closed the last drawer of Hope's dresser and took a step back, literally and figuratively, as he walked over to the small window overlooking the street. Neighbors had begun gathering in front of homes, speculation running rampant given the lineup of law enforcement vehicles surrounding the Kellan house. He'd seen the Amber Alert flash across the TV screen downstairs, had received the same alert, hauntingly eerie, pop up on his own cell phone screen.

At the window, Max watched as Dr. Allie Hollister exited the house and approached a dark-suited man climbing out of what had to be a government-issued car. Max's mouth twisted. The Feds had arrived.

Dr. Hollister's face broke into a wide, friendly smile as she hugged the much taller, linebacker-looking agent.

Old friends, Max supposed. Maybe more given how she caught the man's pale face between her hands and pushed against his cheeks to make him smile. The man's eyes brightened below slicked-back red hair as he hugged her again. Something twisted inside Max's chest. "Yeah, definitely more."

Dr. Hollister retrieved Hope's jewelry box from the top of a nearby SUV and handed it over, clearly adding verbal instructions because the agent nodded before retrieving an evidence bag from the trunk of his car.

Dr. Allie Hollister definitely knew more than she was saying.

Resuming his search of Hope's room, Max found himself agreeing with the assertion this wasn't a ransom issue. If that was the case, they'd want a fast payout. Keeping a restless and sometimes hyper nine-year-old wasn't easy. Kids were unpredictable, Hope especially so. Given Joe's wealth and how public he was about the money he had, if someone was expecting to be paid off, this whole thing would already be over.

Nor did this seem like some spur-of-the-moment abduction. How could it be given the girls had been camping out on private property? It wasn't as if they were on their own in the middle of the wilderness.

"So if this isn't about money and wasn't random, what is it about?" he wondered aloud. Max had seen enough of the real world to know how powerful emotions like anger and vengeance could trigger someone. Had Joe ticked someone off to the point that they would personally come after his family? Max couldn't see that. His brother made everyone happy, except Gemma, who spent more time gallivanting with her girlfriends—and boyfriends—than she did attending her daughter's school recitals and swim meets. "Unless it is about money." Just not in the way one might suspect. "This is personal." And once this was over, once Max got his hands on whoever was responsible, he'd make certain they realized just how personally he took Hope's abduction. Someone was out to cause his family pain.

Sirens whined in the distance. Tiny explosions of unease went off inside him as the sound grew louder. Once upon a time, that blaring cacophony was a call to action. Now? He couldn't help but wonder if he'd ever hear sirens again and not think of this day. Not think about Hope out there somewhere alone or worse, not alone.

The lumpy stuffed panda bear he'd won Hope at a carnival a few years earlier sagged to one side on top of Hope's unmade bed. Max found himself smiling at the memory of spending over fifty bucks to throw baseballs at milk bottles because she'd had her heart set on that bear.

He picked it up, gripping the floppy head between his hands, imagining Hope curling up with it when she went to sleep at night. *She will again*, he told himself as he started to set it down, but then he stopped. The corner of a small book peeked out from under her pillow. He put the bear aside and picked up the neon-green hardback secured with one of those brass locks that took little more than a solid jiggle to release.

The childlike scribble inside on the first page was dated months ago, and consisted only of one sentence: *Mom and Dad are fighting again.*

Max lowered himself onto the edge of her bed and flipped through the pages. He skimmed the thoughts his niece had confided to her journal. His heart cracked as she poured out her feelings and fears, sometimes taking up pages after one of her sessions with Dr. Hollister, whom Max realized his niece was crazy about. The doc didn't get angry with Hope for talking or saying something she shouldn't. Sometimes they just played a game or drew pictures or whatever Hope wanted to do. Hope felt safe with her.

But Hope didn't feel safe with her mother. Reading the last entry dated two weeks earlier brought Max to his feet. The panic he'd experienced upon learning of Hope's disappearance resurged. The sirens had gone silent, replaced by the staccato sound of doors slamming. Joe.

Max flipped the book shut and headed downstairs just as his brother raced inside flanked by two uniformed officers.

"Is there any news?" Joe asked in that detached, broken way he had when reality was too much for him to handle. "Max? Did they find her?"

"No." Max took a step to the side as Dr. Hollister reentered the house, her tall Fed on her heels. She glanced between them before her gaze dropped to the book in Max's hand. She arched a brow but surprised Max when she focused her attention on Joe by leading him into the living room and gently pushing him onto the brown suede sofa by the fireplace. "Nothing yet."

"Someone tell me what's going on," Joe demanded of her and the detectives as they joined them. "What's being done to locate my daughter? Do you need more resources? Cash? Has there been a ransom—" His voice caught as Joe's face lost whatever color remained.

"We haven't received any calls like that," Detective MacTavish said once he'd introduced himself.

Why was everyone so calm? Why wasn't anyone *doing* anything?

"This is Special Agent Eamon Quinn with the FBI." Detective MacTavish gestured to Dr. Hollister's friend standing by the fireplace. Now this guy, Max realized, he got it. Max could see the anger spiraling behind those intense eyes, the barely restrained urgency as he took in everyone in the room, remaining stoically silent. Maybe the good doctor hadn't been off the mark bringing in her *friend* after all.

"Agent Quinn will be working with us to find your daughter," the detective continued. "Lending every support he and the Bureau can. I'm afraid all we can do in the meantime is wait on the lab results from what the techs examined at the camping site and in Hope's room."

Joe turned dead eyes on Max. For an instant, Max was nineteen again, opening his email to the news that his mother and stepfather had decided life was too short to stay in one place any longer. They'd taken off to travel the world, Joe and Max's stepfather having siphoned off a good portion of Joe's first significant commission check. That same suffocating weight of responsibility and grief bore down on Max now. He knew what Joe was thinking. Max was the one who took charge when it came to these kinds of things. He protected the family. It was the silent accusation he imagined coming from his brother that nearly drove him to his knees. How had he let this happen? Why wasn't he doing anything now?

"Where's Gemma?" Joe asked finally. "Where's my wife?"

"No idea." Max hated not being able to give his brother any answers.

"Heaven forbid she be expected to parent for any length of time," Joe muttered, the stricken expression on his face shifting to hostility. "How long did she wait after I was gone before she took off?"

Max frowned and surprised himself by glancing at Allie for help. She gave him a silent nod of ascent. *Tell him the truth.* "A couple of hours." The words tasted bitter on his tongue. "She said she was going to a spa."

"We checked with the manager at the Camellia Day Spa. She's not there. We're still working on locating her," Detective MacTavish clarified. "It would help if we had a list of places she frequents."

"Joe, you've got the best people working to find Hope." Dr. Hollister—Allie—lowered herself on the sofa beside his brother and covered his hand with hers. "Believe me when I say none of us are going to stop until we find Hope and whoever did this."

"I don't care who did it!" Joe's uncharacteristic anger caught Max off guard. "I just want my little girl back."

"I found Hope's journal in her room." Max bypassed his brother's desperate gaze to hand Allie the book. "You should read the last entry."

Allie took the book and flipped it open. She barely glanced at the page before he saw her jaw clench. Her eyes grew colder as she passed the book to Detective MacTavish. "We need to find Gemma Kellan."

"Why? What does it say? What did she write?" Joe held out his hand for the book and, after a nod from Allie, Detective MacTavish handed it over. Joe's eyes zoomed back and forth. "But she didn't know. I didn't think she knew," he whispered as he flipped the page.

"I thought I was the only one who knew Gemma was having an affair. Oh, no." He lifted terrified eyes to Max. "Hope saw them together."

"And Gemma knew it," Max clarified for the detective when MacTavish looked to him. "She told Hope if she said anything to Joe or anyone else she'd make sure Hope never saw her father again. That she'd take her away forever."

Detective MacTavish's spine went ramrod-straight as he caught Max's train of thought. "Who was this man she was seeing?"

"Hope doesn't say," Max said. "I'm not sure she knows who he is."

"Kent Devlin." Joe pushed to his feet. "He's a former stockbroker working at a financial firm in San Francisco. Married to some real estate magnate's daughter. Just give me a minute." He stumbled down the hall to his office.

"That's not normal for him," Max said.

"There is no normal when your child is missing," Allie said. "Let him work through this however he needs to. And no, that's not a platitude," she added when Max opened his mouth. "It's common sense."

"I was going to agree with you," Max said. "I'm just surprised. He's been known to obsess over his computer and codes and ideas when things get too much to handle. He's not usually so emotional."

"That's because when it comes to my daughter, I'm not a robot." Joe returned and tossed a manila envelope on the coffee table. The fury on his face was tempered only by the fear hovering behind the wire-rimmed glasses. For the first time in memory, Max didn't see the helpless, geeky brother he'd spent most of his life protecting; he saw a father doing what he could to protect the only thing in the world he cared about: his daughter. "I'm betting whatever you need to find Gemma is in there. I hired a private investigator to follow her. She has a routine when I leave town."

"Joe—" Max couldn't believe his brother never told him.

"I hired the P.I. to prove you wrong," Joe snapped. "Except you're never wrong, are you, Max? All these years you warned me about her, told me she was probably running around on me and I didn't believe you. And now here we are. Why aren't you ever wrong?"

The words sliced through Max like a flame-hot blade. "I'm wrong more than you know" was all he could say. He ignored the flicker of interest he caught in Allie's eyes. "Do you know where she meets him?"

"Some exclusive spa in Napa. It's all in that report. I heard enough of the details," he added when Detective MacTavish ripped open the sealed envelope. "I didn't need to read it, too. I didn't give it to the court because I didn't want Hope to find out—" He broke off, scrubbed his hands down his face. "Gemma's been seeing him off and on for the better part of three years. The reservation in Napa is always under his name. I've watched for credit card charges, anything out of the ordinary, and there's nothing. You track him, you'll find her."

"Callistrano," Detective MacTavish read off one of the pages from the envelope. "Membership-only, luxury cottages. Winery on site. Allie? You know it?"

Allie nodded. "That's where Simone and Vince got married the first time. Her family still owns a couple of those bungalows."

That was all Max needed to hear. He took a step back

and then another, keeping his eyes pinned on the doc, then the detective, making sure they were preoccupied. For an instant, he locked gazes with Agent Quinn. There it was again, in those eerie green eyes of his: complete understanding of the situation. But to Max's surprise, he didn't move, didn't do anything but quirk a brow and refocus his attention on Allie.

Max hesitated another moment, glanced at his brother, who was watching him. The guarded expression on Joe's face shifted to relief before he gave Max a quick, sharp nod.

Seconds later, Max was in his truck, cell phone in hand and punching in the spa's name into the search engine app. Shifting into reverse, he gunned the engine and glanced up into the rearview mirror.

The truck jerked as he slammed his foot on the brake.

"What do you think you're doing?" He shoved out of the car and circled around to where Allie Hollister stood, hands on her pink-encased hips, a glare of disapproval on her round face.

"I was about to ask you the same question. Where are you going?"

"To get my niece." Max slapped a hand against the tailgate. "Now get out of the way or get run over." He stepped forward, meaning to loom over her, but Allie inched that defiant chin of hers up even higher and poked a finger into his chest.

"You're only going to cause more chaos for your brother's marriage by going after her. Let the police and FBI handle this, Max. Let them do their jobs."

"They don't know this woman like I do." What would it take for her to understand? "Gemma will turn on the waterworks and she'll use whatever time it takes for them to bring her back here to perfect whatever lies she needs to tell. If she took Hope, if she had someone take her, I'll know. Which means I need to be there when she's confronted."

"And if she's not involved? What are you going to do then? Drive all over Northern California banging on every house until you find Hope?"

"If I have to." Because that would constitute *doing* something. "I can't just sit in that house and wait, biding my time while Hope is out there somewhere. I can't stand around and watch my brother fall apart." He'd witnessed enough families disintegrate over the years. He wasn't going to witness it happening to his own.

Allie's eyes narrowed. "We don't even know if Gemma's at that spa." She took a step to the side. The second her feet hit the front lawn and his path was clear, he took that as his sign to return to the truck. "It might be a wasted trip."

"How about you find out and call me," he yelled over the back of the truck, but she was gone. "Doc? Did you hear me? I said—"

"I heard you." Allie pulled open the passenger door and hopped in. She settled herself in the bucket seat and stuffed her bag between her feet on the floorboard. "You want to do this so badly? Fine. I wouldn't mind seeing Gemma's reaction myself. Let's go."

"You're not coming with me."

"Kinda looks like I am." She clicked her seat belt and gave him a look he thought for sure she reserved for her most trying patients. "You can either get in and drive, or we can both go back inside and wait this out."

"Don't you need to let your boyfriend know you're running out on him?"

"My boyfriend? What boy—" She went from complete confusion straight to amusement. "You mean Eamon? Oh, wow. I can't even fathom that." She actually shivered. "He's a friend, nothing more. Same as Jack. In case you were wondering."

"I wasn't." But even to his own ears he protested too quickly. "Doesn't matter." And yet, he felt a surge of unexpected relief.

"Look, Max." She pushed her hand through that short crop of hair and let out a sigh he recognized as frustration. Finally, a sign the situation was actually having an effect on her. "I know you're angry and you want to blame someone, and striking out at anyone, especially me, feels pretty good. But going into an exclusive members-only spa full bore is only going to a) get you arrested, and b) create more problems for your brother and his marriage than you realize. I can help. I'm going with you. Now get in and let's go. It's a long drive."

Because he didn't think she or her buddy the detective would appreciate Max hauling her out of his truck, he surrendered. Five seconds was all he needed to speak with Gemma. If she had any inkling as to where her daughter was, he'd know in that time.

Soon he'd know for sure.

And it was that hope, and only that hope, that was keeping him sane.

"Your friend didn't sound particularly happy to hear you're on a road trip with me," Max said as Allie hung up from her call with Simone. "I can drop you off at the next exit if you want to have her come pick you up."

"It's not you she has a problem with." Well, not him exactly. Allie cringed. What her prosecutor best friend took issue with was Allie heading off on a spur-of-the-moment—and completely useless as far as she and Eden were concerned—search and rescue jaunt to Napa with a man she'd only met hours earlier.

No matter what Hope's journal led Max to believe, Allie knew Gemma Kellan hadn't taken Hope. That would have taken meticulous planning and patience, neither of which seemed characteristic of Hope's mother. But Max needed something, anything to believe in. Who was Allie to destroy his illusion of getting his niece back soon? Especially when she was going as stir-crazy as he was. It wasn't as if there was anything else she could be doing other than obsessing. So, baby-sitting the frantic, erratic uncle it was.

"At least she didn't call me a troglodyte," Max said.

"I didn't call you one, either," Allie sighed. What was wrong with the man that he seemed to need her to think he was on the bottom of the intellectual scale? "Simone called in a favor and spoke with the manager on shift at the spa. According to her, Kent Devlin checked in ten days ago with a female companion, the same female companion he's been shacking up with every couple of weeks for the past few years. Given the description Simone relayed to me, it's Gemma."

"Great." He glanced at his cell. "Only an hour and five minutes to go. You call Detective Awesome and Agent Attentive at Joe's to fill them in."

"I texted them." Because Allie wasn't up to another "you're going where?" discussion, she'd decided against an in-person conversation with Jack. It was only a matter of time before Jack and Lieutenant Santos upped her police protection, and while Allie didn't know as much as she'd like about Chloe's killer—and Hope's probable abductor—she suspected that was yet another tactic that would push him further out of reach.

She wanted this over. She wanted Hope back. She wanted Chloe's killer caught. She wanted to step out of the haze she'd been living in for most of her life and do what she wanted, not what she was forced to do. If that meant putting her own neck on the chopping block with this maniac, so be it. Geez. She rubbed her fingers hard into her eyes. She was beginning to sound as reckless as Eden.

"Jack reached out to the Napa Police Department," she added. "They'll have one of their deputies waiting for us at the spa just in case we need him. I don't suppose you have a plan as to how you'd like this to go with Gemma?"

"I've got this, Doc."

"I really wish you'd stop calling me that." Allie rested her elbow on the window and frowned.

"Yeah, I know." The quick grin actually had her own mouth quirking in amusement. "Hearing about Gemma's affair didn't seem to surprise you," he said and shifted into serious mode. "You suspected?"

Allie shrugged. "When one partner is clearly more interested in salvaging a marriage than the other, the answer usually involves a third party. How long have you known?"

"That Gemma would be unfaithful? Let's see." Max glanced over his shoulder before swinging over to go around a truck. "They've been married about eleven years, so, eleven years."

Allie turned wide eyes on him. "You're kidding."

"Hard to joke when the bride made a pass at me

before the wedding reception started." He flinched, glanced at her. "Good times."

Allie swore. She shouldn't have pushed so hard for Joe and Gemma to remain in couples' therapy. Maybe she'd been in this line of work too long. Maybe it was time for her to move on. Nothing surprised her anymore. Her phone buzzed, the message from Jack pushing her even more off-kilter.

"Looks like your brother's been calling in favors," she said. "He'll be doing a bunch of interviews both in person and on the internet in the next few hours." She pressed her lips together, looked out the window as the drought-weathered fields and meadows stretched out around them.

"You don't approve?"

No, she didn't, but it wasn't her place to protest. She might have spent a lot of time researching and profiling criminals, but when it came to this particular instance, her objectivity had gone up in smoke.

"Joe's entitled to do whatever he thinks will help get his daughter back." As much as she wanted to believe this would result in a positive outcome, the truth was public attention could very well have the opposite effect and cause the kidnapper, the killer, to panic. There was no predicting what this monster was going to do next after twenty years in dormancy. He hadn't contacted the press since his return; he hadn't done anything to draw actual public attention. Instead, he'd sent her, Simone and Eden reminders—sometimes weekly, sometimes daily—of Chloe's death. He'd reached out to the long-deceased detective originally assigned to Chloe's case. He wasn't interested in notoriety, Allie knew. He was interested in inflicting as much pain as possible on the three of them.

The question was, why?

"But it's maybe not a good idea, right?" Max nodded. "Makes now a good time for you to tell me what else is going on."

"I told you before—"

"And I'm still not buying what you're selling," Max said. "You better start thinking up something better than that, Doc, because if you're right and Gemma doesn't have anything to do with Hope's disappearance, that means I'll be looking to you next for answers."

"Sounds like I could use a lawyer." She glanced down at her phone when it rang. She squeezed her eyes shut and dropped her head against the headrest. "I do not need this right now."

"Is it about Hope?"

"No. It's Sitara. My mother," she clarified. "There's a family… Never mind." She waved away her own attempt at an explanation. "Sorry. I know this seems frivolous. It'll just take a second."

"Life doesn't stop because other people's do. Take the call."

"Thanks." She appreciated his understanding. She flexed her fingers and then tapped Accept, and said, "Hey, Ma. Sorry I haven't texted back. I've been busy."

"Oh, Allie, thank goodness." Sitara's breathy voice had Allie sighing. "Nicole told me you were all right, but I wasn't convinced. Your sisters and brothers are all starting to arrive and I wanted to make sure you had everything you need for the party next weekend. For all the kids and grandkids, we're going to have to get the backyard in serious shape. I just hope the weather people are right and we won't be getting any rain."

"It won't rain." Allie bit her lip as she fell into the familiar cheerleader role. "I'll make sure the salad and gift get there, but I can't guarantee I'll be able to come."

Silence was her only response.

"Ma?"

"You promised, Allie. When we planned this party months ago, you promised you'd be here. Your father and I have never asked much of you, but this we need. One time, I want all my kids together. Do you understand me? If everyone else can find a way to be here, if Nicole and Patrick can put their new restaurant aside for the day, you can do this."

Allie didn't want to hear about the sacrifices her foster siblings were making. "Ma, I've got a case—"

"You always have a case. You owe this to your family. You will be there. Eden and Simone have agreed to come, so you can't use them as an excuse, either."

Funny how Simone had neglected to share that bit of information. Then again, Simone was always trying to play peacemaker between Allie and her parents. "It's not an excuse, Ma. There's a missing girl, one of my patients, and—"

"She's your patient, not your child. I'm sure you can pull yourself away for a few hours to celebrate your parents' anniversary and the family we built."

The family that never felt like her own. Parents who barely seemed to remember she existed. Allie hated the tears that burned her throat. How was it she was almost thirty years old and she still felt like a neglected child around them? Why did she even care anymore? "I'll do my best."

"You do better than your best for everyone else. See that you do it for us for a change."

Allie dropped her hand, knowing her mother had hung up on her.

"That didn't sound fun." Max flicked his turn signal and headed down an off-ramp. "I can't imagine you not being up for a party."

"I wouldn't be up for this one in the best of circumstances." Allie shoved her phone into her purse and kicked the bag out of reach. "Wait. Where are we going?" The sooner they got to the spa and home again the better.

"I need to fill the tank, not to mention find a bathroom. And if you're anything like me, you probably need caffeine."

"I don't need to be coddled," Allie told him, trying not to notice how the sun glinted in the gold of his hair.

"Color me all shades of surprised." He veered off to the right and then turned into the parking lot of a gas station and food mart. He parked, pulled out his keys and turned to her. "We still have a little less than an hour to drive. Let's get some coffee and recharge. I'd like to have you in fighting shape when we knock on Gemma's door."

As anxious as she was to get this trip over with and get back to Sacramento, she agreed that the break— however brief—was welcome. What wasn't welcome was a less-than-hostile Max. The last thing she wanted was to actually like the guy. "Can I get you anything?"

"Biggest coffee they have would be great. And anything with chocolate. I could use a sugar boost."

"He's like Eden but with testosterone," Allie mumbled as she considered her friend's far-from-ideal eating habits. She grabbed her bag and climbed out of the car. Once inside the market, she was thrilled to find a wide selection of fresh fruit and snacks. She bought a container of grapes, two coffees, and an oversize bag of chocolate-covered blueberries. Evidence of his perfect physique aside, Max could probably do with the antioxidants. Up at the counter, she added some bottles of water. Spotting a small picnic area outside, she set her purchases down, dug out her phone and texted Eden, who let her know almost instantly she was stuck in traffic about two hours outside Sacramento.

Allie suggested Eden call Simone for the details of the morning, but noted that she'd meet them at the boat—Eden and Cole's home—as soon as she was back in town. Allie frowned, considering the surrounding view of mountains and meadows far from comforting, as she sent another message.

Did you find anything on your trip?

More than I wanted to. Will explain tonight. Not what we thought.

Not what they thought? Moments before Allie's stomach had been jumping around the promise of food, but her appetite vanished. Not connected to Chloe? she texted back. But that wasn't possible. If Hope hadn't been taken by the person responsible for Chloe's death, how would Eden explain the very specific plant that had been left? The similarities between the girls? Connected came the response. Didn't go dormant. Found other cases. More tonight.

Allie swore, clenching her cell phone so hard she was afraid she'd shatter it.

"News about Hope?" Max asked.

Allie yelped, jumping as she spun and found Max standing behind her. "Wow, you're like a cat. I need to put a bell around your neck." The open hostility she'd been dealing with ever since they met seemed to have melted away. Maybe it was that he was away from reminders of Hope. Maybe it was because he felt as if he was acting instead of waiting. Or maybe she was getting used to his focused presence. "Let me guess, your nickname was Figaro? No, Tiger. Cougar?"

He grinned and the expression tilted her heart. "Not even close. Guess that makes it my turn. I've got a question and remember, you have to answer honestly." He reached around her and picked up the bag of blueberries. "Good choice, by the way. I love these things."

"Thanks. So go ahead and ask." *Ask anything you want, just not about the case or Hope or...*

"How many brothers and sisters do you have?"

The sweet grape she popped in her mouth turned sour. Talking about her family was never a fun subject, and she was happy to have a sort of truce in place with him. But a deal was a deal. She'd guessed wrong. She owed him the truth. "At last count? Twenty-seven. How about we get on the road? I've got an appointment to keep in Sac."

Chapter 5

"Wait."

Max stopped, fist poised to knock on the pristine white door to bungalow number seventeen. The buildings spoke more of Cape Cod than West Coast specifically, with the white plank decks and gravel paths. Allie's delicate hand locked around his forearm. "What?"

"Just—don't go in there guns blazing, okay? I know—"

"No offense, Doc, but you don't know." How could she when he didn't know what he was doing himself? He could be—he hoped he was—feet away from his niece. This nightmare of a day could soon come to an end. Besides, if Allie wasn't going to be straight with him, he wasn't inclined to make things easy on her. "And now isn't the time to speculate." He rapped his knuckles against the wood and sent her a warning look that had her rolling her eyes and stepping back. She shoved her hands in her pockets, continuing to disapprove from a distance.

"Can't you read?" Bellowed a male voice from inside before a throaty female laugh drifted out the open windows beside the door. "It says do not—" The door was yanked open.

Max planted his hand flat on the door. "Consider yourself disturbed." He shoved through, feeling, rather than seeing, Allie trailing behind.

"Who do you think you are?" Kent Devlin secured the tie on the spa monogrammed robe, slick dark hair falling over frantic, uncertain gray eyes.

"Your girlfriend's brother-in-law. Gemma!" His sister-in-law all but glided from the bedroom. Barefoot, with thick blond hair flowing tousled around her shoulders, Gemma poised her fingers just below the plunging V of her matching robe, her shining, cornflower blue eyes both guarded and hostile.

Gemma smirked overfilled lips. "What brings you by, Max? Joe have you doing his dirty work now?"

"Not even a pretense of shame." Max kept an image of Hope in his mind as he set his anger aside. "You really are a piece of work."

"I don't do pretense." Gemma padded across the polished wood floor and poured herself a glass of champagne. "It was just a matter of time before he figured it out. Probably would have sooner if he'd taken his head out of that computer of his."

"Gemma, what's going on?" Kent swiveled as if he were a spectator at a fast-paced tennis match. "What's this all about?"

"The end of my marriage apparently." Gemma let out a dramatic sigh before she walked right past Max and cast a suspicious glance in Allie's direction. "Didn't expect you to bring mental health backup. Is she here for me or you?" She flounced onto one of the two plush sofas and crossed her legs. "I'd bet on you, given your difficult year."

"Where's Hope, Gemma?" Max couldn't stand her casual attitude any longer.

"Why are you asking me?" Gemma let out that laugh of hers that made his stomach revolt. "Aren't you her babysitter now? Besides, Joe's the one dictating her schedule these days. I don't have a say, remember?"

"You're saying Hope isn't with you." Allie touched Max's arm again, this time in a reassuring gesture that made him grateful he'd brought her along. She did have a way of setting him at ease. Even as she unsettled him. "You didn't come back to Sacramento last night and pick her up at the Vandermonts'?"

"What?" Gemma rolled her eyes in Devlin's direction even as her boyfriend inclined his head, eyes going dim. "Of course not. We've been far too busy here to even think about—"

"Your marriage and child?" Allie cut her off and had Max arching an impressed brow. "Yes, we can see that. I'm going to take a look around."

"You most certainly will not!" Gemma bolted off the sofa, sloshing her drink over the edge of her glass as Allie darted around her. "This isn't any of your business, you—"

"Shut up, Gemma," Kent snapped. "What's this about Hope?"

Max blinked at the intensity in Devlin's voice. "She's

missing." Whatever strength Max might have felt coming into this place drained in one big whoosh. He'd been wrong. Hope wasn't here. She wasn't anywhere. "She was at a sleepover with friends. When they got up this morning, she was gone."

"Oh, please." Gemma trailed after Allie, who disappeared into the bedroom. "She's probably just taken off again for attention. You know how she gets."

"This isn't that," Max said. "The police have been brought in. They've issued an Amber Alert..." He trailed off as Devlin retrieved his phone from the kitchenette counter. He clicked open the screen, scrolled down. Lifted wide eyes to Max.

"It's true." Devlin carried the phone over to Gemma, who, finally, seemed to be getting the message. "Why would you think Hope was with us?" Devlin asked as Allie returned.

She stood in the doorway of the bedroom, looked Max straight in the eye and shook her head. "She's not here."

"Of course she's not. She's supposed to be with you!" Gemma snatched Devlin's phone out of his hand. "So what have you screwed up now?"

Max ignored the verbal assault. Assign blame and deflect. Classic Gemma.

"Hope wrote about the two of you in her journal," Allie said as Max struggled to find the words. "She also wrote about how you threatened her, Gemma."

"Threatened her? Gemma, what did you do?" Devlin asked.

All this time, from the moment he'd read Hope's journal, and during the drive, Max had thrown himself completely into the belief that Hope was with her mother. That this was all some huge custody play on Gemma's part made to appear as if...

"Oh, God." Max's legs went weak. Devlin reached him first, helped guide him to one of the matching chairs before heading over to pour him a drink. "I thought you'd taken her. I thought—"

"You thought wrong!" Gemma threw the phone on the sofa. "And I don't know what she wrote in that stupid book of hers—"

"Enough, Gemma." Allie appeared at Max's side, standing next to him, a hand on his shoulder. She squeezed, the small kindness giving him all the comfort and reassurance he needed. And reminding him the pretty doctor had been right from the start.

His head buzzed. This wasn't about the custody battle at all.

His niece had been taken by a stranger.

He accepted the drink Devlin pushed into his hand, swallowed the finger of Scotch fast so he could embrace the burn.

"If you think you'll be able to use this against me in court—" Gemma said.

"Gemma!" Devlin yelled and made Gemma jump. "Don't you hear what they're telling you? Your daughter is missing and you haven't even asked about her!"

"Don't *you* criticize my parenting skills." Gemma curled her arms around herself, her face going tight as her lower lip protruded. Max stared at her, unable to decide whether the reality of the situation was truly sinking in or if she was trying to figure out a way to make the situation pay off for her.

"Then allow me." Allie stepped forward when it was clear Gemma was planning to play the victim. "You told Hope if she said anything about your affair that you'd take her away from Joe, that you'd make certain she'd never see him or Max again. You've had her living in fear, driving her deeper into depression because of your secret. Mr. Devlin, I assume you can confirm Gemma's claim that she hasn't left here long enough to be responsible for Hope's disappearance?"

"I can." Given his sallow skin, he clearly wished otherwise. "We, um, checked in about ten days ago. My wife is away with our kids." His face drained of color. "My kids." He scrubbed a hand across his forehead and swore. "What have I been doing?"

"No offense," Max said as his determination returned, "but I'd rather not be witness to your moral epiphany. If Hope isn't with you, I need to get back. To her father. To help with the search. Gemma? Do you want to ride back with us—"

"Come with you?" Gemma blinked. "Why would I do that?"

"And with that I think I can declare the custody battle is officially over." Allie planted a hand on Max's chest. "For the record, Gemma, Joe has known about your affair for the better part of a year. He chose not to share that information with the court to spare Hope the truth, but you didn't extend her the same courtesy, did you? Joe went out of his way to protect your daughter while you seeded her with fear and distrust. This was never about keeping custody. It was all about money."

"Money I earned! And I don't need some nosy doctor telling me anything about my life," Gemma spat. "I'll get there on my own. Tell Joe I'll be there—"

"I'm not your messenger boy." Max got to his feet. "But I am his. He emailed me before we got here to say he's had new settlement papers drawn up. They'll be waiting for you when you get home. You're going to sign them, Gemma. Without question or negotiation. You will relinquish all custody rights of Hope effective today. If you choose to fight, and honestly, I really hope you do, he will send copies of the investigator's report to the court and to the media." To Devlin, he added, "You need to get ahead of this with your family. She's not known for her altruism." The man gave him a shell-shocked nod.

"You're lying," Gemma protested. "Joe wouldn't do this to me. He loves me."

"He loved the idea of you. And if he doesn't release the report, I will. That's a promise you can bank on. We'll see you at the house." Max took hold of Allie's arm and they headed to the door together. "Unless we don't. In which case everyone will know exactly what kind of woman and mother you are."

"Max, you need to pull over." Allie gripped the edges of her seat as Max played bob and weave with his oversize truck. Any second his tense muscles were going to snap. The Napa scenery flew by at an alarming speed, fast enough she'd triple-checked her seat belt since climbing inside. "Max?"

It took every ounce of control she had to keep her voice calm. Horns blared around them. Brakes screeched, muted shouts of anger and frustration echoed against the confines of the cab, but his foot didn't ease up. His knuckles remained stark-white around the wheel.

"Can't stop." He shook his head, his shaggy hair brushing against his collar. "Have to get back."

Allie pursed her lips. Everyone had their limits. Clearly Max Kellan had slammed face-first into his. Getting both of them killed, however, wasn't going to do anyone, especially Hope, any good. Sometimes Allie really hated being right.

"Max, stop the car." She placed her hand on his arm. He tensed, felt his muscles quiver as she shifted closer. "Please, Max. You're scaring me."

She might not have been able to read everything about him, but she'd seen enough to know that at his core, Max was the kind of man who prided himself on protecting others. If his career as a fireman hadn't indicated that, watching him with his brother, seeing how he was with Gemma would have proven it. Her plea for him to stop the car wasn't part of any plan. Not entirely.

She had to find some way to break through the panic surging through his shocked system.

The truck slowed, not much at first but enough to prove to Allie that Max had heard the concern in her voice. She didn't push harder, didn't say another word. Nor did she remove her hand as he swerved to the side of the road. The gravel popped under the tires as he ground the vehicle to a halt.

Allie released a breath she hadn't realized she'd been holding. She sagged in the seat.

"I'm sorry." He stared out the windshield, barely blinking, barely breathing. His hands continued to clutch the wheel. "I didn't mean to scare you. Again." He squeezed his eyes shut. "The entire drive down here, I thought, I really believed…" He couldn't seem to catch his breath. "Now I can't stop wondering where she is. Who she's with. What he might be doing to her."

"I know." She did know, because her heart was

breaking, too. "It's okay. It's natural. And I'm fine." But she wasn't. She recognized the signs of reality crashing in, of losing hope—in his case literally. "Let's take a walk." Before he could argue, she hopped out of the car and made her way around to his side. The rocks and gravel dug through the thin insoles of her shoes, bruising her feet. She pulled open his door, reached in and pried his hands off the steering wheel. She stood there, holding his hands in hers while he looked at her as if he'd never seen her before. "Come outside, Max."

When he dropped out of the car, she caught him and wedged herself under his arm as she nearly fell over. "I'm beginning to think they call you Bull," she panted as she led him around to the front of the truck and dropped him onto the bumper. "You are not a small man, you know that?" She stepped away and righted herself from head to toe.

"Not Bull." The ghost of a smile, exactly what she'd been waiting for, appeared. "I get another question."

"Save it for later, fire boy. Take a few deep breaths." She stepped to the side as traffic continued to speed past them. "You do manage to keep surprising me, you know," Allie told him. "That was one of the more unique panic attacks I've ever been witness to."

"That wasn't panic." Max shook his head. "That was rage."

Tempered with more than a touch of fear. "That was you coming to terms with the fact you can't fix what's happening just by force of will alone." Allie dropped down in front of him, balanced herself by holding on to his knees so she could angle her eyes to catch his gaze. "You convinced yourself this would all be over by now. That we'd be driving Hope home."

"But you knew better."

She shrugged.

"Leave it to a shrink not to utter the words *I told you so*. Sorry." He leaned back and closed his eyes. "I won't call you that again. I was so sure she had her."

"If there's anything good that comes out of today, it's that Gemma will be out of Hope's life for good."

"You think?"

"I know. Devlin was right. She never once asked about her daughter. She was focused on how the situation affected her and her payout. And as I was there in a professional capacity and as I'm still listed as the consulting medical professional when it comes to your brother's custody case, I can assure you, Gemma won't be coming anywhere near Hope again if I have anything to say about it."

His lips quirked. "Remind me not to tick you off, Doc."

"Keep calling me Doc and you'll see how ticked I can get." Seeing that he was coming out the other end of despair, she returned to the truck to retrieve one of the bottles of water she'd bought with their coffee. "Here. Drink. Hydrate." She twisted off the top and handed him the bottle.

He drank the entire thing, arching his neck as he swallowed. Allie wondered if she'd ever seen anything quite so enticing before. The way he focused on the simple task, the gleam in his eye when he looked at her. Feeling suddenly exposed, she hugged her arms around her torso and glanced away.

"Do I get my question now?" he asked.

"Fire away."

"What are you going to do once we're back in Sac?"

He toasted her with the empty bottle. "And don't tell me you're going to take root in my brother's living room until this resolves itself."

The truth couldn't hurt in this case. At least she hoped not. "I'm going to go home and go over my files regarding Hope's sessions. Then I'll consult with two friends of mine, probably over vast amounts of wine. Eden and Simone and I, we have some experience working cases together. Not kidnappings, per se, but…" She paused and backed away from the fine line of the truth. "They think outside the box, especially where police investigations are concerned. Eden, especially."

"Like the police are going to share what they're doing with the three of you."

"Well, one of them won't have much of a choice. Jack's partner is married to Eden." She shuffled her feet into the rocks to ease the pressure pain. "If we don't pull it out of him, Simone's fiancé will. He's a P.I. and probably loathes the system more than you do."

"I don't loathe the system," Max said. "I just don't particularly enjoy the restrictions it puts on me."

"Yeah, I'm not letting you anywhere near Vince or Eden." She could feel them bonding from here. "None of you need another bad influence. You feeling better?"

"I'm feeling functional." He pushed to his feet, reminding Allie just how much space he took up when he was around her. "In case I didn't say it before, thank you for standing in the way of my truck. I don't know that I could have dealt with Gemma without you. And because I've been wondering about something."

Before Allie realized what was happening, he reached out, caught the back of her neck in his hand and hauled her to him. He bent his head and covered her mouth with his in one fluid move, so fast, so effectively, her mind spun.

She gasped, her mouth opening under his as she reached up, hands poised to push him away as warnings of unprofessionalism and conflicts of interest reared up only to be vanquished by the urgent insistence of his lips on hers. He tasted of Scotch, warm and welcoming and, for this moment, she couldn't get enough.

She moaned. Or was that him? She couldn't be sure, but she rose up on her toes, falling into him as she matched his kiss. Every synapse fired to life as the emotions of the day—terror, panic, uncertainty—melted under his igniting touch.

When he lifted his mouth, it wasn't by much. When she blinked open her eyes, it took a few seconds to focus, and when she looked at him, it wasn't humor she saw on his whisker-roughened face, in his curious brown eyes. It was her own confusion and uncertainty reflected back at her.

"That only raised more questions than it answered." He barely moved and the heat of his fingers brushing her neck may as well have branded her. "Suffice it to say this is something we might need to pursue once we work our way through this nightmare."

She swallowed hard, tasting him on her lips. "I've been known to be a fan of experimentation," she managed. "In theory," she added, "just so you know, you're totally not my type."

"Back at ya, Doc. But you know what they say. Opposites attract."

Attract? Allie stumbled as soon as he let go of her. She lifted trembling fingers to her lips, her half smile faded as she realized how far they had to go before Hope's kidnapping resolved itself.

One thing was certain as far as Max Kellan was concerned. Opposites didn't just attract.

They combusted.

Chapter 6

Would his kiss-declared truce hold up?

Only time would tell.

Max pulled his truck into one of the few empty spaces at the end of the block, unwilling to maneuver through the mess of cars and vans that had piled into the neighborhood in the hours since their excursion to Napa.

The expression of disapproval on Allie's face as she stared out the windshield at the TV news vans plunged Max into that ocean of uncertainty he'd been trying to break free of. "Do you think Joe's appeal to the public is going to work or will it do more harm?" He killed the engine and followed her gaze. He wasn't a fan of the media himself, and while he had to admit they had their purpose, being on the other side of a news story—for the second time in as many years—he had to consider that Allie was, yet again, on the right track.

"There's no predicting what's going to help at this point." Allie gathered her things and glanced over at him. For the first time since they'd met—had that only been this morning?—he noticed how tired she looked. Her eyes had gone heavy, she was moving almost in slow motion, and her shoulders had slumped, which had him wondering exactly what was weighing on her. "I'm going to check in with Jack and your brother, see if there's anything they might need me for before I head out. I'm sorry finding Gemma didn't turn out the way you'd hoped."

Max flinched. "Should have realized it wouldn't be that easy. Especially where Gemma is concerned."

"She could surprise you, you know. She could turn up to support Joe."

"And in related news—" He leaned over and pointed skyward. "Oh, my bad. No pigs flying overhead."

Allie gave him a sad, tired smile. He was glad she liked his sense of humor. "You don't have much faith in people, do you?"

"Low expectations means I can't be disappointed. In my experience, people always let you down. Especially the ones you think you're closest to." He narrowed his eyes, peered closer as he saw a light flash in her eyes. "Well, that was sneaky, Doc. You got yourself into my head after all, didn't you?"

"Mmm." Allie shrugged. "Maybe a little. I don't like that you think that. I can't imagine how different my life would have been if I'd never met Eden or Simone or—" She broke off and flinched before she glanced out her window. "I would have been so incredibly lonely without them. So I guess I've had the exact opposite experience as you."

"Really? Lonely? Even with your—what is it? Twenty-seven siblings?" He had trouble choking that number out, let alone imagining what growing up with all those kids had been like.

"Now who's playing shrink?" She hugged her bag against her chest like a shield. "Believe me when I say you can feel utterly alone in a crowd. And for the record, that would be twenty-seven *foster* brothers and sisters, most of whom I haven't seen in years. My parents took that 'embrace life and experience everything possible' speech to heart from the second they got married. I think they always expected to have more kids of their own, but I was their first and only. So they filled up the house in other ways. When they weren't traveling the world trying to save it."

"Must have made for an interesting upbringing." He'd bet every penny in his meager bank account she couldn't hear how sad she sounded talking about her childhood.

"So how many questions are you up by now? Do I get some free nickname guesses?"

"Have at it." He recognized a sore topic, not to mention a diversion, when he heard one. "You get three."

"I could go through the seven dwarfs. Dopey, Sleepy, Bashful...oops. Nope. I retract the last one." Her face brightened, her cheeks went pink and she smiled at him, lightening what he only now realized was his very heavy heart. "You're definitely not bashful."

"Truer words. Allie?" Was that the first time he'd said her name?

"Yeah." She hugged her bag tighter.

"Tell me we're going to find her." It was the question he didn't want an answer to. It was the only question that mattered.

"I hope so." That Allie didn't hesitate bolstered his flailing hope, but he heard the defeated tears in her voice as she reached for the door handle. "I really hope so."

He watched her get out of the truck and head inside, physically pulling herself together as she slipped her sweater back on, hitched her bag over her shoulder and walked up the path to his brother's front door.

During the drive back, most of which had been done in silence, he'd replayed every minute of the day in his mind. Recalling Allie's behavior, statements she'd made, her reaction when she'd removed the cap on that perfume bottle. That wasn't disgust he'd seen on her face as she'd claimed. That was fear, pure and simple.

As a man who listened to his gut first and his brain second, he had no doubt Dr. Allie Hollister knew far more about Hope's kidnapping than she was saying. As she wasn't being forthcoming, he was going to have to get creative about uncovering the truth.

Creative and cunning.

He got out and locked his truck, pocketing his keys as he followed behind her, glancing at her car as he passed. She'd left it unlocked.

Max stopped and pulled out his cell phone in case anyone was watching him. He pretended to check his messages as he circled around and popped open her driver's door. The trick to getting away with doing something wrong was to act as if everything was perfectly normal.

He would have slid in behind the steering wheel if the seat hadn't been so far forward he'd have crushed his ribs. Instead he braced his hand on the seat, leaned over and released the glove compartment latch. No surprise here. Neat and tidy, even in the glove box. All he found was the owner's manual, a tin of mints, a flashlight and…aha!

Her car registration.

Even as he pulled out what he'd been searching for, he winced. Women, especially single women, shouldn't keep their registration in their cars, especially if they had a…yep. He flicked open the compartment between the seats. Garage door opener. He made a mental note to suggest she change her habit as he took a picture of her address.

He closed her car back up, left it unlocked despite his desire not to, and made his way through the dozen or so people milling about with cameras, microphones and various other media-friendly devices aimed around the property. He narrowly avoided colliding with a svelte, older woman in loose-fitting clothes and a red baseball cap. When someone shouted his name, he pretended not to hear and picked up his pace.

Let Joe take the lead on the public communications aspect. His brother was the brains of, well, everything. Max was the brawn. Always had been, always would be.

Even when—especially when—it came to the people he loved.

Allie stood away from the crowd while Joe Kellan sat on his living room sofa and answered the questions lobbed at him by a group of local reporters. In the hours she and Max had been gone, the Kellan house had transformed into a hub of activity that Allie wasn't nearly as comfortable in.

If she closed her eyes and let herself, she could remember being nine years old with a camera and microphone shoved in her face on her way to school. With Simone's absentee parents out of the country at the time and Allie's parents' lackadaisical attitude regarding Chloe's death, it had been Eden's parents who had stepped up and taken Allie and Simone into their home, into their hearts. Finally, a place where she felt wanted, cared for. Loved. Until years later, when Eden's parents had been killed by a drunk driver, throwing them all off-kilter again.

It was a miracle the three of them could even define *normal*.

Allie's lesson had definitely been learned, however. Alone she didn't have to worry about loss, didn't have to worry about disappointing anyone or, for that matter, feeling invisible. Case in point, she was anxious to leave, to connect with her friends and to see what progress, if any, they and their significant others might have made.

Allie stepped into the corner of the foyer, the sturdiness of the wall bracing her as Jack caught sight of her. After a quick word to Lieutenant Santos, who handed Jack an envelope, the detective headed her way. The strain of the day lay heavy in his weary eyes; the wrinkles in his shirt told her even his clothes were exhausted. Wanting more privacy than a corner would provide, Allie led the cop down the photograph-lined hall to Joe's office just as she spotted Max walking into the house.

She closed the door behind Jack, keeping her voice low, her desire to put some distance between her and

Hope's uncle more intense than she would have liked. "Any news?"

"Not since you texted me twenty minutes ago." Jack braced his hand on the polished door. "And not from anyone who might have abducted Hope. Are you okay? I spoke with the officer from Napa who was on scene when Kent Devlin left. Said there was a nasty scene between him and Gemma Kellan in the parking lot."

"Sounds like we missed a show, but I'm not surprised," Allie muttered. "First time I've ever seen a man sprout a conscience before my eyes. Gemma showed her true colors and none of them were pretty." She tried not to feel discouraged that no word of Hope had come. "What about the perfume vials I found in Hope's room? Any word from Quinn?"

"He went to the local offices to check in on the lab, or maybe just to get some air. So far, all we know is the vials you found are from the mid- to late-1990s. You can still find them in novelty shops and online auction sites. They're big with collectors, which could lead us somewhere. Going to take some time to track down any sales, though."

"If they even mean anything," Allie finished for him. "Go ahead. You can say it, Jack. You're still not convinced this is connected to Chloe." She rubbed two fingers against her temple to interrupt the headache trying to take hold. Right now, she wasn't sure about her own convictions. "Jack?"

"They took a closer look at the plant you found up at the girls' campsite."

"That doesn't sound cryptic at all." Allie crossed her arms over her chest. "Out with it already." What possible news could he give her that would make things worse?

"They found this in the bottom of the pot under the dirt." Jack flipped open the envelope and withdrew a plastic evidence bag. "The lieutenant brought it for you to confirm…"

Allie didn't hear him. She gripped the plastic bag in her fingers and examined the weathered, beaten-up photograph of her, Simone, Eden and Chloe, taken the Christmas before Chloe disappeared. All four of them, arms around each other, smiling faces grinning into the camera, the sun shining down on them, an odd sunspot or glare in the bottom right corner of the picture. "Confirm what?" Allie choked out.

"Any idea where he—or she—might have gotten this? It's not like you've left childhood photographs lying around town in the last twenty years."

"Same place he's found the stationary Simone used as a kid, or the perfume Chloe loved?" She was the one who was supposed to have the answers or, if not, at least a good guess or two. Instead all she ended up with were more questions.

"We can't keep this connection quiet much longer, Allie," Jack said. "At some point it's going to break. Something will leak, a reporter's going to get too close or this maniac is going to let something slip—"

"He won't. That I'm sure of." The weariness that had been creeping up Allie's spine vanished. Until this moment, she had let herself have the slightest doubt that she'd been wrong. That all of what had happened was a horrific coincidence. But seeing her best friends' childhood faces on the same day she'd sat beside three other little girls who were missing their friend was almost too much to process. "It's his game. His rules. If he wanted to make this a public spectacle, he would have."

He'd gotten his kicks with Eden by saving her from a serial killer with an anonymous call to the police; then with Simone by sending her photographs the most practiced of stalkers would have been proud of. He'd been watching them—all of them—for weeks, months. Maybe years.

The very idea made her sick to her stomach. "This isn't about the three of us anymore, and it's not just about Chloe. This is about Hope and doing everything we can to bring her home." She tilted her head as the thoughts coalesced. "I'm tired of hiding, of cowering behind the what-ifs. We know what those ifs are now. He went after someone I care about. He expects us to retreat." It's what they had been doing, she realized. And it hadn't protected anyone.

"If that's the case, we need to do what we can to control the spread of information," Jack said. "Otherwise the department is going to face all kinds of accusations we don't have the time to deal with."

"You already came to this conclusion, didn't you?" Allie asked.

"The LT and I might have discussed it. He has some ideas and connections we can use to soften the blow, but you're right. We've moved beyond Chloe at this point. Are you three going to be able to get on board with this?"

"We'll have to." Allie swallowed hard. This case had been so personal to them for so long, it didn't feel right to turn it loose to the masses. But if they were going to bring Hope home... "Yeah, okay." She couldn't stop looking at the picture, at her past. And imagining the future that might have been. "I'll talk to them. Honestly, I don't think it'll be a hard sell. How long do you think you can give us before the story breaks?"

"Twelve, maybe twenty-four hours?" Jack shrugged. "Depends if we get any tips from the interviews Joe's been giving."

"Okay."

"That means upping the protection details on all of you."

"Figured." A complete waste of manpower as far as Allie was concerned. Whoever took Hope had only come after Eden the one time and even then she wasn't the one who got hurt; another FBI agent had. Special Agent Simmons had survived—and subsequently retired—but every threat they'd received since had been doled out at an arm's length.

Then again, if Chloe's killer was changing the rules...

"If you wouldn't mind passing that information along to Vince, I'd appreciate it," Jack said. "I don't want it to seem as if I don't trust the P.I.'s ability to catch a bullet in his teeth." Simone's fiancé had already turned her apartment building into Fort Knox.

Allie grinned. "Leave it to you to find the humor in this. Now, if you'll excuse me, I'm going home to change." And try to figure out the best way to impart the truth of the situation to a very suspicious and determined Max Kellan.

Allie handed the picture to Jack as if she were putting herself and her friends' lives under his protection. "Do yourself and me a favor, Jack. Find some means to include Max in the investigation, at least until we can soften the blow. Otherwise he's just going to go off on his own and I don't want him getting hurt in all this."

"Would take a lot to hurt him. Guy's a legend in Florida, Allie. Word has it fires put themselves out to get away from him."

She knew the feeling. He could certainly start a blaze raging inside her with just one kiss. "Anything else?"

"Plenty. Dedicated, determined, tough on his probies, but he got the job done. Bunch of commendations and medals. He had a good career going, too. On his way to a captaincy. Well thought of, admired. Still is."

"What happened?"

"Only know a call went really wrong, two of his men died, a third committed suicide a few months later." Jack shook his head. "He reacted badly. Suffice it to say the department was loath to let him go, but whatever he did left his superiors no choice but to force him out. Retired with benefits and a good severance package that apparently he has no interest in touching. He signed it all over into a trust with Hope as the main beneficiary."

Great. Now Max Kellan could be nominated for sainthood. And here she was lying to him about his niece's disappearance.

"Sounds to me like politics stuck its nose in where it shouldn't have," Jack said. "But what do I know?"

"You know a lot," Allie said. What Max had told her in the truck about trusting people made a lot more sense to her now. Should the need arise, she had a good idea about what buttons to push either to get him to open up or calm him down. "You convinced now that he doesn't have anything to do with Hope going missing?"

"If that's your way of asking if I agree you were right, yes." Jack twisted his mouth in forced offense.

"If I didn't think so after talking to his former boss, I would after spending the day with Joe. As far as he's concerned, his big brother walks on water. Guy stepped up big time when they were teens and their mother took off after their father died. Max worked three jobs off and on to make sure Joe had a completely free ride to college. All that while training for the fire department. Not an easy feat."

"This sounds like the beginnings of a budding bro-mance." Even as she joked she could only imagine the burdens Max had been carrying most of his adult life. Betrayed by his mother, then by the work he'd dedicated his life to? He was a man who did what needed doing even if it cost him something personally. As if being kissed into oblivion by the man hadn't made a big enough impression on her already.

All the more reason for Allie to stay as far away from him as possible. The last thing she needed was a knight in shining armor thinking he could protect her from the world.

"I'll keep you in the loop," Jack promised. "And I'll do what I can to keep the hose monkey occupied."

Allie rolled her eyes. "You guys and your nicknames. I don't suppose your background check into him revealed what his call sign was when he was a fireman?"

Jack grinned. "Maybe. But I'm guessing that telling you might rob one of you of some much-needed fun."

Chapter 7

Following the directions of his cell GPS, Max pulled his truck to a stop at the corner of 38th Street and watched Allie gather her belongings from her car. The narrow streets of the Fabulous '40s—as he'd learned this area of Sacramento was called—didn't allow for unnoticed surveillance and him running on borderline stalker mode.

Of all the areas of the valley Max drove through since he'd moved to Northern California, this extensive neighborhood was spoken about with a kind of reverence, and now he understood why. The homes were older, named after the streets they occupied and ranged in style from Tudor, to Colonial, to California Bungalow. Sacramento was known for its number of trees, third in the world behind Singapore and Vancouver if Hope's latest school report could be believed. He had to admit that there were few parts of the city that weren't cascading with exemplary branches dotted with color, arching like natural canopies protecting the dwellings beneath. Despite the flood of leaves and debris the trees caused, there was also a semblance of peace, an old-fashioned throw-back atmosphere he could see appealing to a woman like Allie.

A community teeming with neighbors. In fact, Max would lay odds he'd get tagged as suspicious by someone if he extended his stay too long. Being accused of stalking wasn't on his list of things to do, which is why he hadn't tailed her directly. Choosing to go by the GPS information allowed him to take his time and memorize landmarks like the various hospitals, clinics and a couple of hole-in-the-wall restaurants.

It took him a minute to realize he wasn't the only suspicious vehicle in the vicinity. One of the dark sedans he'd seen at his brother's was now parked across Allie's driveway. The two male occupants gave no indication of getting out. "Now that can't be a coincidence."

He'd been torn, watching Allie leave, as to whether he should follow his instincts or stick close to his brother's side, but after a short conversation with Joe, he realized he'd bring his brother more peace of mind by being out of the house looking for answers—searching for Hope—than by standing in a corner brooding about how useless he was feeling.

Max feeling useless was not a good thing. For anyone.

He sat back, powered down his window and welcomed the early-evening breeze as it wafted through his truck. He could still smell Allie's perfume, flowery but not overly so. Just a subtle hint of rose that drifted past him as a reminder of how sweet and responsive she'd felt in his arms.

The woman definitely knew how to kiss. Personally, he'd just needed to get the idea of kissing her out of his system. He'd never expected to want to kiss her again. How was that possible when he knew she was lying to him?

Part of him wanted to demand to know where Hope was, but he couldn't come to terms with the idea that she knew something and wasn't saying. He wasn't that bad a judge of people.

Then again.

If there was one thing Max abhorred in this life, it was dishonesty. He didn't care what the reason was behind a lie; the truth was always the best solution. It cut through the nonsense of everyday life, put everyone on equal footing. Showed you exactly who you were dealing with.

He'd put up with more than a decade of his brother being lied to by Gemma. No way was he going to get involved with someone potentially more conniving.

Max frowned. Unmarked sedan. Two inside. Allie obviously knew them since she spoke to them casually before taking the winding path to her front porch and disappearing inside the one-story Tudor house.

"Now why would you need a couple of cops sitting outside your home, Doc?" Max pulled out his phone, took a picture of the license plate. Not that he had anyone who he could check it with, but he'd learned enough as a fireman to know that the more intel you had, well, it could be useful.

From there, he opened up the app and typed out any and all information that had passed between him and

Allie since this morning. Names, locations, thoughts, impressions. His stream of consciousness took over. The sun dipped down. He glanced up occasionally, making sure her bodyguards were still in place, that her car was still there.

Simone and Eden. She hadn't mentioned last names, so he had no idea who they were, but something told him it wouldn't take more than a quick online search to find out. His phone gave that gasping bleep that had him digging around in his glove box for the charger. By the time he found it, he saw a flash of color move from her front door to her car. Two engines started up, the sedan pulled out, then backed up to let her out.

Max flattened himself across the seats, waiting for them to pass, hoping she hadn't taken too much notice of the make or model of his car, though, honestly, he didn't think it was that big a deal he'd followed her home. He was concerned about her, concerned about what she knew. Easy enough to explain.

What wouldn't be easy, he realized, as she and her escort stopped at the corner, was making a U-turn on these streets. Keeping an eye on his quarry in the rearview mirror, he started the truck, pulled forward to turn into her driveway and waited until they were out of sight before following them.

He didn't have any official investigation training, technically—the closest he'd gotten was spending a week with one of his supervisors during an arson investigation, one that had resulted in the arrest of a psychotic career-firebug whom Max had been more than thrilled to apprehend.

Wherever Allie was headed, she was taking her time. The late-afternoon traffic was anything but easy as they drove down Howe Avenue, turning onto Arden, after passing what was considered one of the premier shopping malls in the area, which led them to the Garden Highway.

Max dropped back, keeping at least one, sometimes two cars between him and the sedan. This narrow road wasn't exactly helpful for someone trying to be covert, and it was about to get worse as she took the exit to Crest View Marina. Yeah, that would be a hub of activity.

Max followed as close as he dared, watching as her red SUV and the sedan disappeared down the darkening lane.

"Well, this has been a waste of time." Max sighed. Not to mention it was proof of her dishonesty. She'd told him she was going to meet her friends and here she was at a marina? She probably had a weekend yacht or somewhere she spent her downtime. "Curiouser and curiouser."

But they were a good distance from her house. He wanted answers, answers he wasn't convinced she'd give him if he came out and asked, so that left him one option.

He pulled a U-turn and headed back the way he'd come, making a quick detour through a local burger drive-through on his way to Allie's house. If she wasn't going to be forthcoming with what she knew, he'd just have to find out what she was hiding himself.

"I'd offer you some wine, but I'm afraid it might put you out for the night." With her thick, newly strawberry-highlighted blond hair twisted into a knot on the top of her head, Eden couldn't have looked more at home on *The Cop Out* if she was first mate. Which, Allie admitted, Eden pretty much was since she'd married the captain. In her cutoff denim shorts and oversize T-shirt, the barefoot reporter turned blogger turned police consultant motioned Allie down the steps into the fancy cruiser's main cabin.

"That's probably a good idea." Allie grabbed hold of the brass rail and ducked into the depths of her best friend's home and Cole's pride and joy. She hadn't enjoyed the armed escort, but there were prices to pay for their plan of action. At least her protective detail could commiserate with Eden's, who, once Cole and Vince arrived, could leave their posts at the end of the dock and return to their cars. "Have you heard from Cole?"

Eden nodded and then ducked into the galley kitchen. She pulled open the fridge door, grabbing herself a beer. "He's on his way down the hill. Picking up dinner on his way. You want a soda?"

"Caffeine sounds great, thanks." That should be enough to stave off the headache building in the back of her skull. "As anxious as I am to hear what you found out in Portland, I'm happy to wait until Simone gets here." And decompress, even a little.

"Good. It's not something I want to go through twice." Eden grabbed Allie's bag and tossed it on the floor before she curled herself into the corner of the sofa. "Suffice it to say, for now, that we might finally get a handle on this guy."

"Guy?" Allie sat at the other end, cold can in her hand. She had to admit, Cole had done wonders refurbishing this 1960s Gentleman's Cruiser. With the elegant wood cabinetry, marble countertops, planked flooring and practical yet stylish furniture, she found it a little difficult to believe she was on a boat. Cole and Eden had really made a go of this place, especially now that it included Eden's touches like the butterfly trinket box Simone had given her and the photographs of Eden's family. Then there was the large whiteboard leaning against the wall and the small table in the corner housing Eden's laptop and piles of cold-case files. "Then we're sure it's a he."

Eden shrugged. "Catch-all phrase. I can tell you the names I've pulled out of the system from California, Oregon, Nevada and Washington are predominately male. Lots of digging to do."

"Fun times ahead… Just joking. Are you up to speed on Hope Kellan?"

Eden took a long drink, nodded and pulled her cell phone out of her pocket. "There doesn't seem to be much so far, which I can tell you means Cole is going to be in a foul mood when he gets here. He's already not thrilled I ditched my protection detail on the road. He did send me a copy of the picture they found in the potted violet after I picked up the detail again at the station." She took another long drink of her beer. "Pretty much eliminates any doubts I might have had that Chloe's and Hope's cases are connected."

As if either of them had doubts. "Yeah." Allie popped open her soda but didn't drink. She didn't dare with the way her stomach was jumping around. "Now we know."

"Stop it, Allie." Eden leaned forward and poked a stern finger into her arm. "I know that look. This isn't your fault. Even great psychologists like you can't read the mind of a possible murderer."

"I keep telling myself that." Allie lifted uncertain

eyes to her friend. "But I'm not sure it's true. What if we forced him into this? What if something we did—?"

"This. Is. Not. Our. Fault." Eden snapped out each word like she was firing bullets from a gun. "We were nine years old, Allie. Turn on that brain of yours and tell me what you'd say to someone sitting in your office voicing those thoughts. You'd say what I just did. This isn't on us. It's all on him."

Allie shifted on the sofa, kicked off her shoes and tucked her legs under her. "I'm sorry. I've had a really crappy day. You don't deserve to bear the brunt of my bad mood."

Eden responded with an overly bright smile. A smile that blurred behind the tears that exploded in Allie's eyes.

Eden leaped forward. "Don't cry, Allie. I was kidding. Oh, man." Eden went into full flapping mode, something that usually made Allie laugh. Her friend could stare down—and take down—just about anyone, but when it came to tears, Eden St. Claire folded. "Geez, where's Simone? She does better with this crying stuff than I do."

"You do fine." Allie tilted her head to stop the tears from falling. Crying wasn't going to do anyone, least of all herself, any good. "Like I said, it's been a rotten day. I can't stop thinking about Hope out there. With him." Given what these thoughts were doing to her, she could only imagine the internal turmoil Max was going through. She was beginning to understand how frustrated Max must be feeling. She wanted to be doing something other than waiting for information to trickle in. Here, she was stuck in the dark, waiting for someone else to turn on the lights. "We're running out of time."

"Yeah. We are." Eden scooted closer to her on the sofa, wrapped her arm around Allie's shoulders and pulled her into a hug. Exactly the way Willa and Mercy had enveloped Portia this morning. The realization made her heart ache. What were those little girls doing tonight? Were they holding on to each other or had they needed to go their separate ways? "I'm thinking about Hope, too, Al. I got two speeding tickets driving home in order to be here with you. Don't tell Cole," she whispered against Allie's hair. "I might have to mortgage the boat to pay them off."

Allie chuckled. "My lips are sealed." What were best friends for? *Best friends.* Allie squeezed her eyes shut. How could she even think about leaving them?

"We're going to get through this, Al. I promise. The three of us haven't come this far together to let him get away now."

"What if we're too late?" Allie squeezed her eyes shut. "What if—"

"No what-ifs," Eden ordered. "What-ifs aren't allowed on this bucket, do you hear me? We're going to figure this out and we're going to bring Hope home." She squeezed Allie even tighter, exactly how Allie needed to be reassured. "We aren't letting him win this time. We're going to get our lives back."

"I want him dead." Allie loathed the hatred burning inside of her for this unknown person; the person who, twenty years ago, had killed their friend. "I know that doesn't fit with my job. I should want to get him help, make sure he's punished, but I don't. I want him dead and buried and forgotten. And I shouldn't. Maybe I'm not cut out for this anymore."

But what she really wanted, more than anything, remained unspoken. The one thing none of them could ever have.

She wanted Chloe back.

"Dead and buried works for me." Eden kept up the forced humor, one of those comforting signs Allie could get through anything with her friends. "And what job is that? Helping people? It's what you do, Allie. It's who you are."

She'd gone and opened the door, hadn't she? "You ever feel as if you've spent too much time in the dark?"

"It's where I thrive, actually. Is this some kind of psychologist's code? If so, I'm not nearly as fluent as Simone." Eden gave her a considered look. "You want to make some changes, make them. You're under no obligation to do anything you don't want to do."

"And what if that meant leaving Sacramento?"

"I'd ask where we're moving to."

"Not funny." Allie shook her head. Maybe she shouldn't have brought it up. Her friends didn't need to be weighed down with her indecision and growing professional frustration.

"Who says I'm joking. Wait." Eden narrowed her eyes. "A few weeks ago, just after Simone put the Subrov case to rest, you said there was something you wanted to talk about. Is that what this is? You're seriously thinking about moving? Of changing careers?"

"Maybe," Allie admitted. "I've been offered a teaching position at a medical school in Los Angeles. It sounds different." More to the point, it sounded safe. No one else to worry about, no patients to stress over. Or lose.

"Wow." Eden blinked as if she'd been blinded by an exploding star. "Okay."

Allie's stomach tightened. Boy, she'd really stepped in it now. "Wow, okay, as in 'great news, Allie.' Or wow as in—"

"I'm a selfish person, Al. You know it. Thank heavens Cole knows it, so I'm going to stay true to myself and ask you not to go." She ran her finger around the lip of the beer bottle. "But that wouldn't be fair to you. Not if it's something you decide you want to do. I can't imagine not seeing you whenever I want, however. Having you at my beck and call."

"With all that extra time I can take up a hobby," Allie tried to joke. "I would appreciate knowing what you think."

"Would you?" The challenge that sprang into her friend's eyes set Allie on edge. Okay, she probably should have spoken to Simone first and eased into the conversation with Eden. "Well, then, I'll just say this. You shouldn't be making any life-altering decisions at the moment. We've all been living under this plume of smoke that hasn't settled for a while now. Once it clears, once we can finally put Chloe's killer in prison and her death behind us, then you can ponder what mega-changes are waiting for you beyond the horizon."

"I have to admit," Allie said, after a long moment of silence, "that's sound advice. And you're right." She'd just needed to hear it from someone else. "Everything feels in flux right now. With you and Simone getting married and settling into new lives, I see how happy you both are despite everything else. Sometimes it hurts."

"I'm sorry, Al."

"Don't be, oh, please don't be." Allie rushed to ease the guilt washing over her friend's face. "I didn't mean that quite the way it sounded, but you have to admit

I've become a fifth wheel around here, and I certainly don't want to be anyone's obligation."

"Then maybe it's you who needs to start seeing a therapist. You're my family, Allie. Other than Cole, you and Simone are all I have. You're not remotely an obligation. You're part of my life and that'll be the case wherever you live. So be forewarned, if I need to play that guilt card to help convince you to stay, I'm going to."

"Forewarned is forearmed," Allie said. "So. We can put all this aside for now."

"Can we?"

"We don't have a choice. And for now, please, don't say anything to Simone. Not until I've given this some more thought." Eden wasn't the only selfish one. Now hadn't been the time to spring this news on her friend. "We need to focus on Hope." Oddly enough, changing topics to the little girl's kidnapping made her feel more at ease. "Cole told you about having to come clean to the press about Chloe's case?"

"Simone's already in damage-control mode. She went in to talk to her boss this afternoon about what's been happening. The good news is, despite her being on indefinite leave, the DA is on board to give us whatever we need."

Allie sat up, all melancholy thoughts fading. "Vince will come in handy, too."

"Yeah, well." Eden grinned. "If I can't come up with a sneaky way around rules and regulations, our personal P.I. certainly can. So is your confidence crisis over now?"

"Was that what that was?" Allie pouted. "We have something else we have to consider. Max."

"Max." Eden looked at her as if she was speaking another language. "Oh, you mean Hope's uncle Max? I heard that trip to Napa didn't turn out very well."

"Considering he was expecting to find Hope with her mother, no. He's, um—" Allie struggled to find the right words "—Max is different."

"Different how?"

In so many ways, Allie thought. "You know how I'm usually good at reading people? At figuring out how to—"

"Manipulate them? Yes, I'm well aware of that special talent of yours."

"It's not manipulating, not really," Allie argued. "I can't do it with him. And I don't want to. He scares me."

Eden's entire body went stiff. "Scares you how?"

"Oh, please. I've already got two bodyguards out there watching every move I make. I don't need to add you to the mix. I don't mean he scares me physically." Allie bit her lip and scratched a nail down the damp side of her soda can. "I can't explain it. I've never met anyone like him before. Well, I have, of course. He's very, um, overwhelming."

Eden's ferocious glare shifted to amusement. "You think he's hot."

"Geez, Eden." Even as her friend cackled, Allie felt her cheeks warm. As if discussing her future career plans wasn't inappropriate enough. "Now isn't exactly the best time to be talking about—"

"About what? Living? Allie, if there's one thing I've learned in the last couple of months, it's that we've put our lives on hold. We let what happened twenty years ago dictate virtually everything we've ever done. I'm not giving Chloe's murderer another day of my life.

Once this is over, that is. And neither should you. I do find it interesting that you've brought this up just after you've admitted to feeling off-kilter about other aspects of your life. Tell me you have a picture of this Max guy."

"Sure, sure. We stopped and snapped some selfies on our way to look for his kidnapped niece."

"Defensive, too. That's a good sign. About time you stopped living vicariously through me and Simone and took care of things." She grinned and sipped, kicking her legs like a kid when Allie smacked her knee.

"Took care of which things?" Simone Armstrong's long elegant legs made an appearance in the cabin before the rest of her, not surprising considering the curvy blonde turned as many heads as she did stomachs of adversaries in the courtroom. "You know we can hold a police convention out in that parking lot, right? There isn't a safer area in the entire valley. Well." Simone stopped at the bottom of the stairs, a manicured hand planted on one white-skirt-encased hip, all those lush curls Allie had spent years being envious of spilling around her shoulders. "You have had a day, Dr. Hollister." She set her briefcase and purse down and bee-lined for the couch, situating herself on the arm and pulling Allie into a hug that rivaled Eden's. "How are you holding up?"

"I'd really like a do-over." Just like that, bookended by the best friends a girl could ever hope for, Allie felt her world right itself. "But I'll settle for finding Hope and bringing her home."

"Sounds like a plan to me. Vince and Kyla are both running those names you came up with on your excursions, Eden. And you know if Vince can't come up with something, my assistant can." Simone reached across Allie and plucked the beer bottle out of Eden's hand, finished it in a couple of healthy glugs and sighed. "Okay, that hit the spot."

"I've got plenty in the fridge," Eden muttered. "Woman can't even finish her own drink. You want wine?"

"No." Simone laughed at Allie's and Eden's wide-eyed shock. "I'm afraid if I start, I won't stop, and no offense, Eden, but I don't believe you have room for a slumber party on this boat of yours."

"You'd be surprised what we have room for." Eden waggled her eyebrows.

"How did dinner go last night with Patrick and Nicole, Allie?" Simone asked.

"Fine," Allie said. "I wish you both had been able to come. Their new restaurant is amazing. The food's really good. Just this side of frou-frou, you know?"

"Oh, Vince will love that." Simone laughed. "I told him we had to try it out soon. He was not thrilled."

"That's because at the bar he owns he serves food people can afford and don't need a dictionary to pronounce," Eden said. "You did okay with the family stuff?"

Allie assured her she had. "Though it would have been nice to take someone with me and share the evening with them."

"Speaking of such a someone," Eden announced, "Allie's got the hots for Hope's firefighter uncle."

"There's a missing girl, Eden. Now isn't the time to discuss my love life." Her friends cackled. "Ah, man. I just walked into that, didn't I?"

"Our little Allie is growing up." Simone laughed, but when Allie tilted her chin up, she saw understanding and the trace of sadness in her prosecutor friend's face. Despite her reputation as Sacramento's "Avenging Angel," Simone's limitless compassion was one of the things Allie admired most about her.

"Uncle Max scares her," Eden added. "In that *good* way."

"Does he?" Simone gave a nod of approval. "That does sound promising. Guess now we know what it takes to pull your nose out of those research books of yours."

Allie's cheeks warmed. "Before you have us marching down the aisle—"

"Exactly what is it about Max that scares you, Allie?" Simone got up and retrieved a bottle of water from the fridge.

Leave it to Simone to ask the hard questions. "Max is not my type. Not looks-wise, not profession-wise and not personality-wise. He's so physical. And he's got this hair." She made a chopping motion by her shoulder. "It's so long and messy and his beard scratches " She stopped. Pursed her lips. Looked first at Eden and then at Simone. She grinned. "But he's a seriously good kisser."

Eden whooped and then covered her mouth and giggled when they heard male voices coming from above deck. "Food's here. Save the rest of this conversation for dessert, would you?" She jumped off the couch to greet her husband and Simone's fiancé.

"What aren't you saying, Al?" Simone returned to the sofa and sat next to her, plucking the edge of her fuchsia blouse down over her waistband. "You don't scare easily. Or at least you never appear to."

Allie hid a smile behind her hand. After years of

wearing only white, Simone was still getting used to adding splashes of color to her wardrobe. As if pinks and yellows were made out of cholera.

"I never could keep a secret from you, could I?" Except Allie was keeping more than one these days, but Simone and Eden were too distracted to tell. "She's so happy." Allie envied Eden's resiliency, not to mention the changes that had taken place inside her friend since she'd moved forward with her life after putting a serial killer—two of them, actually—behind bars. "With everything that's going on—"

"Happiness doesn't preclude reality." Simone flinched. "And right now, I think it's more of a protective shield against the rage. Believe me, Eden and I understand how personal this is for you. Even if there wasn't the connection to Chloe, we'd have your back. Eden's tempering things, trying to remind herself that there's more to life than chasing our nightmares."

"What happens when we catch that nightmare?" Allie asked, but she watched Simone's eyes light up as Vince Sutton followed Cole down the stairs. The former marine now private investigator and pub owner caught them watching him. He gave them a cautious smile and then winked at Simone.

"What happens is we get to live our lives on our terms," Simone said with a flush of color in her cheeks. "What's bothering you about Max Kellan? And I don't mean romantically."

"I don't like lying to him. About Hope. He still thinks this is a random kidnapping." She took a deep breath and said what she'd been trying to avoid all day. "He needs to know the truth before he finds out in the wrong way."

"Agreed, but what does his reaction matter? There's nothing you can do to change it, nothing you can do to control it. It honestly doesn't affect you, does it?"

Now who was acting like a psychologist? "Maybe I don't like the idea of him thinking badly of me."

"Sounds like Eden's off the mark on this one, then." Simone patted her leg. "You like a lot more about Max Kellan than his appearance. Or the way he kisses."

"He's a good guy." And she knew how very few of them there were. "He's crazy about his niece. His entire face lights up when he talks about her." She couldn't, didn't want to think about that light being extinguished should Hope not come home.

Had all her objectivity disappeared where the Kellan clan was concerned?

"That's so appealing—a man who dotes wholeheartedly on a child. Something you and I have almost no experience with, given our absentee fathers," Simone said. "You're right. You owe him the truth. Only then can the two of you decide if what's going on between you is real or adrenaline-induced."

"Is that what you'd call what happened with you and Vince?" Allie teased.

"That got the ball rolling. Speaking of, let's see what he's brought us for dinner. And then…" She grabbed hold of Allie's hand and squeezed "We'll get back to work finding your Hope."

Chapter 8

For a criminal psychologist with a police escort, Allie had an absolute joke of a home alarm system.

Or she would if she'd switched it on, Max told himself as he closed her front door behind him. Did she really think a sticker in the window and blinking lights on a panel would act as deterrents? Granted, the second deadbolt on the door had been a surprise, but he recognized the brand, knew how easy it would be to bump it with the right leverage—and tools. A flathead screwdriver and hammer from the toolbox he stashed behind the driver's seat did the trick. He was inside in less than three minutes.

His foot kicked a small, padded envelope with Allie's name in big block letters. Something slipped through the mail slot, Max figured as he bent down to pick it up. He stopped. Pulled his hand back. Max glanced over his shoulder. She didn't have a mail slot.

He waved his hand along the base of the door, checking to see if there was enough space to slip it under. There wasn't.

Leaving it alone, he pushed to his feet, pulled out his cell phone and tapped his flashlight app open. He shined it around the comfortable living room. Nothing too pricey. Not surprisingly, she leaned toward the practical. He avoided the large front window, staying close to the perimeter of the room as he looked over the sofa piled high with pillows, the two matching chairs on the other side of the coffee table. She had tiers of candles in the tiled fireplace that was accented with a large gold-framed mirror complementing the crystal table lamps. Bookcases lined either side of the fireplace, shelves packed with a combination of leather-bound collectable books and well-read, dog-eared paperbacks, including a number of titles he'd read himself. What space wasn't occupied with books she'd filled with candles, statuary, and odds and ends.

The hardwood floors barely creaked under his weight. The neutral colors of the house didn't feel stark, but complemented her chosen furnishings. He stepped into the kitchen, where he found metal mesh bowls stocked with fresh fruit, avocados and tomatoes. A pile of mail sat on one edge of the breakfast bar. He shuffled through the bills and junk flyers.

The staircase at the back of the house led up to what he discovered was her loft bedroom. Spacious, with a triangular ceiling and two windows overlooking the street. A cursory look gave him enough of a feel to conclude she didn't bring work up here with her. No computer table and only a small TV in the corner, a stack of books by the padded chair in the corner. A queen-size bed that looked way too big for the likes of her, but she'd added a thick cover and half a pillow store to fill it up. This was her escape, her sanctuary. He could smell her perfume, that same scent that had lingered in his truck all day. Roses and stubbornness, an intoxicating combination.

Max retreated downstairs and found a small guest room and bath before hitting the jackpot with her office across the hall. Laptop on the antique wood desk, matching filing cabinets, wall-to-wall bookcases lined with medical journals, binders and textbooks. More photos. He closed the door, drew the heavy curtains and flicked on the lights. He slipped his phone into his pocket as he got to work. With the fingerprint-protected computer, he didn't get very far, but the one other thing she did lock, the filing cabinet, was easy enough to pick.

He worked his way through dozens of patient files, glancing at their names and bypassing the information. Max wasn't sure what he was looking for, but he had a pretty strong suspicion he'd know it when he found it. Right now, he didn't particularly care if he ended up in jail. If his instincts were right, something in the good doctor's office was going to help him find his niece.

He slammed the last drawer shut with more force than was necessary. The crash echoed through the silence of the empty house.

Max gripped the edge of the cabinet. He knew he wasn't wrong. The doc had secrets. The question was, where did she keep them?

Time to view this from a different perspective. He walked around the desk, sat in her chair and almost lodged his knees into his chest given how low she had the height set. He didn't dare change it, though. Middle drawer was typical junk stuff: pens, paper clips, high-lighters. He sat back, perused the top of her desk. It was the photographs that caught his attention next. Two of them, framed. Nice frames, he noticed. Expensive.

This was where she spent money. Displaying the people she cared about.

The picture on the right was of her and two other women around the same age: a stunning, blue-eyed blonde in a tailored white suit and a spunky-looking redhead who had a defiant twinkle in her expression Max could relate to.

And then there was the doc. Small, bright eyes, short dark hair, the gleam of happiness on her face that was something he personally hadn't been witness to. The three women reminded him of those advertisements for girlfriend getaways, the bonds of friendship evident in the way they clung to each other, laughing at whoever was behind the camera.

"Nice to meet you, Simone and Eden." He set the frame down, picked up the other.

Four girls this time. Simone and Eden were instantly recognizable as neither had changed much. Allie had, however. Her eyes were the same; the dimple in her left cheek was just as pronounced. Allie's hair, however... Max blinked. Was he seeing this right? She'd been a redhead? Long hair, nearly down to her waist and the same distinctive bright red color as the girl on her left.

A young redheaded girl with long straight hair, freck-les dotting her nose and a crooked gap-toothed smile.

"Hope." Max's heart skipped a beat. He flipped the frame over, pried open the prongs and ripped off the back. He read the faded writing on the back. "Simone, Eden, Allie and Chloe." The date? Twenty years ago.

He pulled out his phone and accessed the picture Hope had sent him last night. He held it up beside the photo of Allie and her friends.

The two girls could have been identical.

Max tensed. This was like trying to assemble a puzzle when you didn't know what the final picture would be. Too many pieces, none of them corners to give him any boundaries, any guidelines.

He wrenched open the other drawers of the desk, nearly pulling the handle off when the bottom right one wouldn't open. Max dropped to his knees, grabbed the letter opener off the desk and jammed it hard into the space between the drawer and desk. He didn't care about damage. When the lock gave way, he sat back on his heels and stared down at the thick file.

Chloe Evans.

Max couldn't believe how his hands shook as he pulled the file free, set it on the desk. After staring at it for a long moment, he flipped open the cover.

And began to read.

"You found how many murders connected to Chloe's?" Allie reclaimed her seat on the sofa next to Simone, who was sliding the tiny heart pendant along the thin gold necklace she always wore.

The pasta primavera Vince had brought them from his bar and grill wasn't sitting well in Allie's stomach. Neither were the potential results of Eden's investigation. Allie couldn't seem to stay still. *Shades of Max*, she told herself. He must be rubbing off on her. She was coming out of her shell.

"Three murders, each five years apart. Hope's kidnapping makes it four, and, I hate to say it, but it's right on schedule. But I didn't say they conclusively connect to Chloe," Eden replied. "I said there were specific similarities to her case. I was able to get copies of the victims' most recent school portraits."

Cole finished clearing the table and counter, his spine ramrod-stiff as he listened to his wife explain. Vince, ever the silent observer, stood at the base of the stairs, the muscles in his jaw working so hard Allie could practically hear them pop across the room.

"There are times I really wish Eden wasn't so good at this." Simone kicked off her stiletto pumps and crossed her legs while Eden pinned up disturbingly innocent pictures of the preadolescent girls. "Vince?" Simone called. "You okay?"

"Not even a little."

"No one ever gets used to dealing with murdered children," Allie said.

"I would hope not." The serious glint in Vince's eyes made Allie very glad he was on their side.

"When dead kids stop bothering you, it's time to retire," Cole cut in. Since getting home, the detective had traded in his blazer, button-down shirt and tie for jeans and an old Sac Metro PD sweatshirt. Like his wife, he'd abandoned the idea of shoes, displaying a bit of the carefree attitude Allie had spent many years envying. The complete opposite of stoic, intense Vince. If ever there was a visual example of bad boy meets good guy, they were it. That said, there was nothing else carefree about Cole tonight.

He was right. When the idea of a child being killed didn't make you slightly ill, there was little left to fight for. He'd been in the fight to find Chloe's killer for as long as Simone, Eden and Allie had been; they'd all known him since they were kids. Chloe had been his friend as well; his was yet another life her death had inadvertently impacted.

"Eden, please tell me you're going to limit this photographic display to the before pictures," Simone said.

Allie agreed, although she wasn't overly thrilled at the idea of a board full of Chloes staring back at them. Eden might be able to process and detach from the crime scene photos. Allie, despite her consulting work with law enforcement, would prefer not to challenge herself.

She took her time examining each school photo. Odd. The victims weren't clones of Chloe, unlike Hope Kellan. Two of the girls had curly hair, and the shades of red for each varied. One had blue eyes, two green. The freckles were a common denominator as were their...

"Their clothes." Allie shot to her feet. "They're all wearing quirky, odd clothes."

"That's what I saw first, too," Eden said. "Handmade, uneven, different. Definitely mismatched but not in a cheap, neglected way. Fun, that's what Chloe called it. Then there's this." She pulled out one of the files. "I've got their school records. All the girls were well liked and, in every instance, had a tight group of friends. Inseparable." She pointed them out. "Also, each girl disappeared on her way home from being with those friends. The movies, a school carnival."

"Please don't say camping trips," Simone said.

Eden shook her head, stuck her thumbnail in her mouth as she considered a picture. "No. No camping trips."

Was that good news or bad?

"What about where their bodies were found?" Vince

asked. "Isn't there some theory that where a serial killer leaves the bodies is part of his signature?"

Allie nodded. "That can be a telltale sign of his psychopathy. Eden?"

"They found Alyssa Knight behind a park aviary that was under construction at the time," Cole said by rote. "Shannan McPhearson was found on the banks of a lake but on the other side of town from where she lived. Rosalie Jenson's body, however, was left behind a strip mall."

"You committed all these cases to memory?" Allie asked him.

"Given who I live with, I didn't have much choice."

Allie appreciated the affection in the cop's voice despite the dark revelation. Eden didn't make things easy on anyone on a good day. She was, at times, unlikable. But she had a big heart. Sometimes too big. Allie could only imagine what Eden was like to live with when she was neck-deep in investigating and blogging about one of her cold cases. Then again, she didn't have to. She'd witnessed it often enough over the years.

"I'm still waiting on copies of the coroners' reports for two of the girls along with the crime scene photos of where the bodies were left. Small towns shut down on the weekends," Eden said. "I'm hoping Lieutenant Santos will be able to speed up the process for me tomorrow. In the meantime, I found these notations on the one file from Nevada. The first officers on scene with Shannan McPhearson said they thought they smelled something sweet on her body. 'Cloying,' one of them called it."

"Sweet as in cotton candy?" Simone glanced at Allie.

"Possibly." Eden flipped the pages. "No perfume

bottles were found, though, and while there was mention of an odd scent in Alyssa's file, the doctor who performed the autopsy wasn't exactly up to the job."

"Why weren't any of these deaths in the news?" Vince demanded. "Why didn't anyone pick up on the similarities?"

"We're talking about three deaths over the span of fifteen years in three states. No one was looking," Cole said. "And the first was five years after Chloe was murdered. Add in the small-town aspect and limited resources for the local law enforcements." Cole drew his wife to him, wrapped his arms around her waist. "You can't blame the cops, Vince. Sadly, these are some of the realities of the world we live in."

"Tell that to Hope and Joe Kellan," Vince said.

"I'm not arguing, man." Cole held up a hand in surrender. "I get it."

"Well, we're on this now," Eden said. "I've spoken to Alyssa's parents up in Oregon and Rosalie Jenson's on the phone. They've moved their family back east. Couldn't deal with staying where it happened."

"Not many people can," Allie said. "What about Shannan's family?"

"I phoned, left a couple of messages, but no one's called me back. We were thinking about driving up there tomorrow, see if we can speak to them in person," Eden said.

"Harder to slam a door in someone's face than not pick up a phone," Simone agreed. "I can go, too."

Eden set her file aside and leaned into Cole. "You want to drive?"

"Yes," Cole answered for Simone. "She does. Someone else has already reached her lifetime limit of speeding tickets."

As she observed the newly married couple, an odd pang of envy chimed inside Allie. She had been lying before. She did wish she had someone—someone like Max, maybe—who had her back. The change in Eden since she'd fallen for their lifelong friend was astonishing. All those harsh edges that cut deep had been smoothed and rounded. Once upon a time, it would have taken an act of Congress—or maybe a lit stick of dynamite—to blast a file out of Eden's hands and a case out of her head. These days, all it took was a well-placed touch and murmured word of encouragement from the man who loved her.

"What about Chloe's parents?" Vince asked. "Is there any reason to reach out to them? Anything you don't know?"

"I don't think there's anything they know that we don't. We lost touch a long time ago," Simone said. "Her death broke the family apart. Parents divorced and her older brother moved away with his mom. I haven't—"

"Her mother and brother live in San Francisco." Allie swallowed the lump in her throat and tried to ignore the stunned surprise on her friends' faces. "I check in with him, usually on Chloe's birthday, sometimes Christmas. Lunch a couple of times a year. Nothing much, just a quick catch-up and a memory or two. Something to remind each other we haven't forgotten her."

"Why didn't you ever tell us?" Eden left Cole's arms and stepped forward.

"Allie?" Simone actually looked hurt.

"Because that would mean discussing Chloe and she's the one thing we don't talk about." When neither Simone nor Eden responded, Allie took advantage of their discomfort along with the opening. "We don't talk about her and when we do, it never feels good. We all know when we're thinking about her, though. She's become this ghostly presence that we never acknowledge out loud. I'm not blaming you," she added when Eden grimaced. "There's no right or wrong way to process what we had to deal with and I say that after spending half my life studying the human mind. We've all coped differently." *Some in more self-destructive ways than others.* That was one of the reasons she'd gone to medical school. She needed to understand, to fathom what had happened to them. Allie ducked her chin. "Sometimes I just need to talk about her with someone else who loved her."

The silence that followed made Allie wish one or both of her best friends would yell at her, scream at her, get angry, do anything that would make her sound less pathetic than she felt. Less guilty. They were the closest thing she had to family; she loved them like sisters and yet, somehow, keeping this secret felt like she'd betrayed them.

"I go to her grave." Simone took hold of Allie's hand and squeezed. Hard. "A few times a year. I take a lunch and a bouquet of those baby-pink roses she loved so much and I talk to her while I eat."

Allie blinked back tears. "Simone." She wasn't the only one? She lifted uneasy eyes to a ferocious Eden as her friend bolted. She disappeared into the smaller bedroom under the stairs that had become her office. Allie jumped at the sound of a drawer slamming shut, not entirely sure what Eden held in her hand when she returned.

Eden stopped in front of them, held out a small

leather-bound journal. "I don't talk about her. I can't. Because I'm afraid once I start, I'll never stop." Tears clogged her voice. "I write about her. Here." She pushed the book into Allie's hands. "Take it. Read it. One of you, both of you, it doesn't matter. It's about all of us."

Allie accepted the book and clutched it against her chest like the treasured possession it was.

"Even when you think you're alone in something, you're not," Simone told Allie.

"Returning to the topic at hand…" Vince cleared his throat. "Do you think Chloe's brother might have any new information that would help with the case? Is this someone else we should talk to in person?"

Allie hesitated.

"Out with it, Al." Eden planted a hand on her hip and glared at her. "No reason to stop now."

"You don't have to go to San Francisco." Allie took a deep breath. She really didn't enjoy being on the other side of Eden's interrogation tactics. "Chloe's brother is here. Cole's already spoken with him. He goes by Eamon Quinn now." Allie waited a beat to let them catch up. "FBI Special Agent Eamon Quinn."

Chapter 9

The headlights of Allie's SUV flashed through her curtain-draped front window and jarred Max out of his self-imposed stupor just after ten. He blinked, refocused his eyes in the darkness of her living room and took a long, deep breath. Times like this he almost understood why people took up meditation.

He got up from the chair by the fireplace, set the file containing the information on Chloe Evans's unsolved murder on the coffee table and walked to the front door.

He made sure to step around the envelope that still bugged him. Chances were it was something she'd dropped on her way in or out, but given everything that had been thrown at them today, he wouldn't bet on it.

The second pair of headlights was the unneeded reminder of her police escort. Hopefully her detail would be more effective than the nonactivated security system that had allowed him to spend the majority of his night perusing her home.

He heard the voices of Allie and two men as they headed up the walk. He flipped the locks and pulled open the door. Stunned silence, wide-eyed surprise and two drawn weapons greeted him as he stepped onto the porch, hands raised. "Evening, Doc."

"Don't move!" The older man shouted as the second familiar officer placed himself between Max and Allie, his Glock pointed directly and steadily at Max's chest. "Bowie? You good?"

"I've got him, Sarge." The young officer who had been at Joe's house this morning fixed sharp, trained eyes on Max.

Max remained still as the older plainclothes officer reached the bottom stair, grabbed Max's wrist and spun him around. Max turned his head at the last second to avoid breaking his nose against the front of the house. He felt the cop's hand firm between his shoulders, heard the distinctive slide and squeak before he sensed the metal of the cuffs lock around his wrists. "Allie, I've had a bad enough day. I'd appreciate not being arrested."

"You should have thought about that before you broke into my house." Disbelief and irritation mingled in her voice. "And for the record, *I* don't appreciate your nihilistic intention of trying to get yourself shot on my front porch."

"Not the first time I've been accused of that." He grunted as his captor cranked the cuffs tighter, turned him around and pushed him solidly against the siding. "Easy, big guy." Max looked up into beady, intense black eyes situated in a face of stone. "I mean no harm. The lady knows me. So does your partner."

"Allie?" The sergeant glanced at her over his shoulder. "Bowie?"

"He's Hope Kellan's uncle," Bowie said.

"Which means you can take the cuffs off me now." Max met Allie's defiant gaze beyond the two cops. He'd definitely unnerved her, but he'd also gotten exactly the information he'd needed. The Sac PD were not messing around when it came to her safety. And it had nothing to do with Hope being missing. "Now, preferably. We have some things to discuss."

"It's okay, Bowie." Allie pushed the younger officer's arm down so he could holster his weapon. "Can we start with how you got into my house?"

"It's not that difficult when you don't use your alarm system," Max said.

"Wait, what?" Even in the dimness of her porch light he saw the color fade from her face. "I turned it on before I left. Sergeant Tomlinson, you can uncuff him."

"Not a chance."

Max stumbled as Tomlinson shoved him forward to sit on the porch stair. "If I wanted to hurt her, I would have waited until she was inside."

"Hang on. We'll check the place out," the sergeant said before he waved at his partner to follow. "You, stay." He pointed at Max before he drew his weapon again. "Don't make me call for backup." The officers disappeared into the house.

"Someone left you a gift." Max jerked his head toward the door. "Envelope on the floor there. I nearly tripped on it when I went in."

"And when was that exactly?" Allie stood in front of him, arms hugged tight around her waist, her bright mint green outfit almost blinding in the darkness of the night. She glanced nervously toward the door.

"After I followed you to the marina." He grinned, not because he found the situation remotely humorous but because he knew it would annoy her. "About six? I thought you were going to *consult* with your expert friends."

"I did." She looked taken aback as her head dropped to the oversize bag under her arm. "Eden and Cole live on a boat."

"Oh." Well. That explained that.

"Let me guess," Allie said. "You assumed I lied so I could go on some kind of girls' night out while your niece, one of my patients, is missing?"

There she went, playing mind games with him again. Max winced. Okay, it sounded better as a theory when he wasn't looking directly at her. "I have trust issues, remember, Doc? They don't get better when people keep things from me."

"Let's you and me get one thing clear right now." She stepped forward, leaned over and peered directly into his eyes. He could feel her breath on his face, feel the anger radiating off her, anger that reassured and surprised him. "I am not your sister-in-law. I'm taking what's happened to Hope very seriously. More seriously than you could ever understand."

"Because of what happened to Chloe Evans?"

Bingo! Max might have let out a whoop of triumph at the way she shot up, but the inclination died the instant he saw the flash of pain cross her face. Pain he couldn't let matter. This was his niece's life they were talking about. He couldn't let his emotions get in the way. And he wasn't about to let Allie Hollister's lack of them prevent him from finding Hope.

"You've been lying to me, Doc. You've been lying to me and my brother about Hope's kidnapping. It's part of something bigger, something even more insidious. Don't you dare try to deny it. I saw the pictures on your desk. Hope could be Chloe Evans's twin." He shifted and tried to work some circulation into his fingers. "Either you tell me exactly what's going on or I'm going to hit social media hard first thing in the morning with everything I've learned in the last few hours."

Allie glared at him. Funny how she could pack a punch with a mere glance. Chills raced down his spine, but not ones born of fear or intimidation. Chills bred of full-blown, unwanted desire.

"House is clear, Allie." Sergeant Tomlinson returned to the doorway and pointed at the envelope. "Aside from that. Someone cut the power line to your alarm system. Knew what he was doing, too, because it's one clean cut, no fumbling around. Bowie's down in the basement now seeing if it can be repaired. Unless lover boy here is lying and he did it?"

"I didn't touch your alarm system, Allie. Lover boy?" He angled a glance at Tomlinson before refocusing on Allie. Max tamped down on the anger that had been set to simmer the instant he'd located that file. The pressure built inside him. There would come a time and soon that he'd let loose, but that time wasn't now. At least not while he was cuffed and being looked at as if he were a threepeat felon on his way back to solitary. "There's a nickname you haven't tried out yet, Doc."

"And yet somehow it never occurred to me, Sparky," Allie muttered as she stomped past him and into the house. She stared down at the small padded envelope. "It's okay, Sergeant. I'll take it from here." Bowie joined them on the porch. "Max will be staying the night."

"He is?"

"I am?"

Both Max and the two cops asked their questions at the same time.

"We'll be fine," Allie said. "We have a lot to discuss and when we're done, we'll be *working*."

Both officers looked at Max as he hoisted his cuffed hands up an inch and set his shoulder blades on fire. "Nice to meet you."

Sergeant Tomlinson swore and tossed his keys to his partner. "This is the hero Jack was raving about today?" he asked Allie as if Max didn't possess ears.

"Jack MacTavish raved?" The idea made Max break out in a cold sweat. He wasn't anyone's hero. If he were, three of his buddies might still be alive. "I'll have to thank him when I see him."

"You want to keep the cuffs just to be on the safe side?" Tomlinson asked Allie.

Max grinned and shook the feeling back into his hands as he got to his feet.

"Maybe we should bunk in the guest room," Bowie offered.

"There won't be room with Max in there. Besides, I'm going to call Vince and have him drive out to check my security system tonight. You guys are heading off shift in a bit, right?" Allie asked.

"We'll take off as soon as the second team is on-site at midnight. We'll be back with you at noon tomorrow."

"Thanks. For everything." Allie placed her hands on their backs and propelled them down her steps. "I promise I have all you guys on speed dial. And if something or someone comes at me tonight, I'll throw Max in their path." She shot Max a warning look. "Don't think I won't do it."

Max held up his hands.

"You." She pointed at him. "Inside. Now." She marched ahead of him, giving the package on the floor a wide berth as she flicked on the lights. He closed the door, welcoming the silence, mainly because he wasn't entirely sure what to expect when she started talking. He followed her into the kitchen, watched as she retrieved a pair of plastic gloves from the recessed desk in the corner.

"You moonlight with the crime scene unit?" He meant it as a joke as she took inordinate care picking up the envelope and returning to the kitchen.

"I get where humor is a pressure release, Max, but tonight I find it incredibly annoying. Zip it."

The care with which she pried open the seal scraped on his last nerve.

"Okay, I was wrong. The silence is bugging me." She tilted the envelope upside down and gave it a quick shake. A smartphone dropped onto the counter. "Grab me a large plastic bag in the pantry over there and tell me what inspired you to break into my house."

"You lied to me."

"Did not." She pressed her lips into a thin line and dropped the envelope into the bag. "I didn't tell you everything."

"Same thing."

"Semantics." She gripped the edge of the counter for a moment before she retrieved a pencil and pressed the eraser against the On button. They waited in forced silence as the phone chimed, flashed and opened on a screen with a digital clock set to zero.

A video flickered to life.

And then Hope was there, on screen, talking to them.

"Daddy?" The little girl blinked squinted eyes, as if the light from the camera hurt. She sat on a chair in complete darkness, illuminated only by the dimness of what had to be a cell phone. Max's entire mind went black. He could see she was wearing the star-emblazoned sleep shirt he'd bought for her on their most recent trip to the mall, could almost hear her teasing laugh when he'd offered to buy himself a matching one. "Uncle Max? The man said to tell you that Dr. Allie and her friends know why I'm here. That it's their fault." Tears glistened in her eyes, stained her face. She swiped at the tears and for an instant, her eyes went cold, as if a spark of defiance caught before she thought better of displaying it.

Allie must have seen it, as well. She gripped her hand around Max's arm and squeezed, but nothing dimmed the roar settling in his head.

"I want to come home, Dr. Allie. Please. Tell my daddy and Uncle Max I miss them. And—" Hope leaned forward and it was then Max realized she was reading from the card "—please don't make me go and meet Chloe."

The screen went blank.

The digital clock reappeared.

Seventy-two hours.

"What's it counting down to?" Max barely recognized his own voice.

Allie looked at him, the silence, her cool detached expression the only answer he needed. The only answer he didn't want.

The clock was counting down how much time Hope had left to live.

"I need to call Cole. Don't touch!" She snapped off her gloves and left the kitchen.

"I wasn't going to!" Except he wanted to. He wanted to play that video again and again, if only to remind himself that Hope wasn't dead; this maniac hadn't killed her. At least not yet.

He could hear Allie in the other room, but it felt farther away than that—almost like another universe.

When she returned, she stood in front of the counter, stared at the phone and took a long, deep breath. "All I want to do is play that again."

Max absorbed the punch of guilt like a pro. She'd been thinking the same thing as him, wanted the same thing: Hope home safe.

"But we can't," she cautioned. "There's no telling what might happen to the phone if we do."

"What? You think this guy booby-trapped it or something?"

She used the plastic bag containing the mailing envelope to flip the phone over, then covered it. "I think this guy is familiar enough with me that he knows my routine. It's also a great way to get surveillance into my house, isn't it?"

"Because this is all about you," Max said. "You and your friends."

She flinched. "Since you've already read through Chloe's file, why don't you ask whatever lingering questions you might have while we wait for the cavalry?"

What was there to ask? As angry as he was, as disappointed that she hadn't confided in him—then again, why would she?—he wasn't so cruel as to make her rehash, probably for the millionth time in her life, how her friend had gone missing from a girls' campout one night, her strangled body found in a field a few days later.

He'd seen the photos and the newspaper clippings, read the interviews and crime reports. He'd found himself looking at a black-and-white newspaper photo of Allie and her friends, arms wrapped around each other, staring stunned and devastated where their friend had been left.

"Here's a question for you," Max said, watching in stunned disbelief as she walked over to the fridge and pulled it open. Next thing he knew, she was pulling out food. "Do you approach all your cases with this cool detachment or is Hope a special case?"

"What?" Allie stopped, a confused expression on her face.

"Some unknown person was in your house late this afternoon, a potential child killer. He's left physical evidence of my niece's kidnapping—proof of life, even—and here you are, making what? An omelet?"

"It was going to be vegetable fried rice. You're a vegetarian, right?" She looked down at her arms filled with the eggs, vegetables and a plastic container she'd grabbed, and shook her head. "Cooking helps me to relax. I thought you might be hungry. Unless you already raided my kitchen while you were waiting."

"Unbelievable." Max walked over, took the items out of her hands and clunked them onto the marble kitchen island. "Did you hear anything I just said?"

"I heard every word. What exactly would you like me to do, Max? Yell? Scream? Break down sobbing in your arms because the same psychopathic murderer who killed my best friend is currently stalking me and my other two friends and, for whatever demented reason, took possession of your niece before sending me what in his mind amounts to a 'don't forget me' greeting card?"

The spark of anger that ignited in her eyes ignited something deep inside him. "I don't expect you to break down," Max said. "But this is the first time I've seen anything close to an actual emotion from you."

"Did it ever occur to you shutting down is *my* coping mechanism? Yours seems to be barreling full steam ahead, consequences be damned. I don't work like that, Max. I can't. Because the second I lose control, the second I let myself give in to the fear, I might very well never come back. And I will not give him the satisfaction. He's taken enough from me."

He reached out and slammed the refrigerator shut with more force than necessary.

"What was that for?"

"Because you're shivering." The next thing he knew, he'd moved in, wrapped his arms around her and drew her to him. "And don't tell me it's because you're cold."

"I'm always cold," she mumbled, standing stiff in his arms. "I've been cold since I was nine years old."

The shudder that ripped through her vibrated through him. Why did he always think the worst of people? Especially people who were doing their best to help him?

"Fear is paralyzing, Max. It's mind-numbing and I can't afford that right now. I have to do this however I have to do it and I don't need you judging me for it. But don't you dare think I don't care."

"Okay." He rubbed his hands up and down her back, waiting, willing her to soften, to relax, to trust him, even a little. But how could she when he'd made it clear he didn't trust her? "Okay, you're right. Not everyone's the same. We don't all deal with things in a similar way."

There. A fraction of change. Her clenched posture eased and she slipped her arms around his waist. "This isn't me breaking down," she whispered.

"Of course it isn't." He rested his chin on the top of her head. "I'm sorry I broke into your house."

"No, you're not."

"No." He pulled back, caught her face between his hands and looked into the eyes that had captured his attention so fully. He shouldn't care this much, not about her, not about how she dealt with Hope's kidnapping. But he did. And not just because she was his best chance at getting his niece back. But because now that he allowed himself to, he could see just how much this was ripping her apart. "I'm not sorry. How did you know I'm a vegetarian?"

She laughed, the sound oddly light and foreign to his ears.

"Your brother's been gone for a while, but his fridge is stocked with fruit and vegetables, protein powders. Tofu." She tilted her head. "Tofu? Ugh. There wasn't a burger in sight. So." She shrugged. "Vegetarian."

"You're that observant and you couldn't see me well enough to trust me with the truth about Hope?"

Another shrug.

"I don't appreciate being kept in the dark." It occurred to him that perhaps some honesty on his part would make a difference. "If you need to keep whatever it is you know from Joe, fine. If you think it's best we don't show my brother that video of Hope, that you need to convince me of. It's proof of life he can see with his own eyes, but I'll find a way to deal. I can help you, Allie. I can help all of you. I'm not so broken that I'm useless. Please, let me in."

"Is that what you've been thinking? That I think you're useless? That you're not capable of helping?"

"It doesn't matter what I think."

"Sure it does." The momentary weakness she'd surrendered to vanished. In its place he saw that irritable determination he was coming to appreciate more than he should. "What on earth happened to you in Florida that you lost faith in yourself?"

Max froze. Was that what had happened? "I didn't listen to my gut." The ghostly sound of bagpipes echoed in his memory, accompanied by the image of flag-draped coffins being lowered slowly into the ground. "And three men died because of it. But this isn't about me." And he didn't want it to be. Ever. If he was going to dig his way out of this hole of a depression he'd fallen into, he'd do it on his own. "Tell me the truth, Allie. Tell me why Hope was taken from the Vandermonts'."

She stepped away, but he shifted his hold, gripped her shoulders and held her steady. "We can't be sure."

"You must have a theory. Hope was kidnapped in the same way as your friend Chloe was, what, twenty years ago? What do you think they have in common? Who's behind all this?"

"We don't know who he is." And there it was, the desperation he'd been wanting to see, afraid to see. Because now he knew she didn't have any more of an idea about what to do than he did. "We don't know why he killed Chloe and we don't know why he's come back. As far as your other question goes, there's only one thing both of these girls have in common." She pulled away from him and hugged herself in that way she had that he now realized was for self-preservation.

"And what's that?"

"Me." She inched her chin up. "The one thing Chloe and your niece have in common is me."

Chapter 10

"That'll be Cole and Vince." Allie pushed her half-eaten plate of rice away when she heard two car doors slam outside. "You need to be on your best behavior."

Max gave her that grin of his that turned her insides to Jell-O. "I'm always on my best behavior."

"Yeah, that's what I'm afraid of."

"You cook a mean midnight meal, Doc." As she rose, Max tugged her close and kissed her. One of those quick reminders of a kiss that brought all sorts of inappropriate thoughts. "And FYI, you and I aren't nearly done talking about what I found in your office. But I can wait until your friends leave."

"Assuming they do leave." Now it was her turn to tease. "You kiss me like that in front of them, they're going to put you through questioning that might make the Spanish Inquisition seem like a picnic."

"I'm a big boy." He scooped up a carrot. "I can take it."

"Uh-huh. Keep thinking that." Allie hurried to the front door, not only to prevent Vince from charging through it but to put some distance between her and Max Kellan. She did not need to be activating this dormant part of her life. Not now.

And yet, somehow, Max's presence was making the situation easier to cope with. Had she been with anyone other than Max when she'd watched that video, she may very well have lost it.

"Hi, guys." She stepped aside to let Cole and Vince inside. Only then did she notice Simone and Eden bringing up the rear. "Really? You had to tell them?" She planted her hand on her hip and stared at the detective and P.I.

"I'm not inclined to leave Simone alone these days." Vince looked anything but apologetic. "Besides, when I took her on, I took on the two of you, so, sorry. You're stuck with me. Alarm box is down in the basement, right?"

"Um, yeah. Just, um. Hi, Eden."

That was as far as she got before Eden grabbed her arms and squeezed. "You're really okay? You aren't hurt?"

"Whoever it was was long gone before I got here." She closed the door behind her friends and gestured for them to follow her into the kitchen. "You didn't have to come out, you know."

"Please," Simone said. "Basically we've all sworn off sleep until we get Hope back in her own bed and—" Simone stopped short in the doorway. "Now this is a surprise. You must be the uncle we've heard so much about. I recognized you from the…" She waved a hand by her own hair.

"From what?" Max flashed too-innocent eyes from Simone to Allie.

"Where? He's here? Let me see." Eden ducked under Cole's arm to jump in front of Simone. "Oh, yeah. Okay, I get it." She sent Allie one of those smiles that made Allie's blood pressure surge. "Totally get it."

"Oh, please," Allie mumbled when her cheeks went hot. "Who wants coffee?"

"Me." Max held up his empty mug. "I'm going to need it to get through this first meeting of the Justice League. I've met Bat—"

"Oh, that is such a dead-on accurate description of Vince I can't stand it," Eden said. "I'm Eden St. Claire. And you're Max Kellan. Firefighter extraordinaire and super uncle to Hope."

"Yeah." Max suddenly appeared as if he was going to choke. "That's me."

"Eden, don't." Simone offered her hand to him. "Hello, I'm Simone Armstrong."

"Don't what?" Eden demanded. "Just want him to know we know about him. And for him to—"

"Eden." Cole's controlled voice seemed to do the trick as he brushed his hand over his wife's shoulder. She sagged.

"We're going to find your niece, Max," Eden said in that special way she had of speaking to those affected by violent crimes. She might be one of the most abrasive, sometimes obnoxious people Allie had ever known, but there were few people who understood Max's current situation better than her friend. "I promise you, we're going to get her back."

Max glanced at Allie and then at Eden. "I think maybe for the first time I believe that. Thank you, Eden."

"You're welcome. Now, coffee, Allie? And tell me you have some of those chocolate chip cookies of yours lurking in the…aha!" She reached into the ceramic fruit basket of a cookie jar and pulled out three. "Nice."

"Not to break up the meet and greet," Cole said as his wife chomped on sugar, "but, Allie, where's the package and the phone?"

"Right here." Allie pointed to the phone covered with the bag. "Examine it all you want, but I'm not turning it over for evidence."

"I'm sorry, you're not what?" Cole blinked in confusion.

"You'll understand when you click the screen on," Allie explained. "He meant for me to have it as long as Hope's missing. I'm not giving it up."

Cole said, "Eden, use my phone, record everything I'm doing then we'll get the phone information and send it to Eamon. I'm betting the FBI can get things through faster than our lab can."

"On it." Eden reached into her husband's pocket and pulled out his phone.

Allie stood off to the side, trying to block out the haunting sound of Hope Kellan reciting chapter and verse of what her captor had given her. At least now they knew replaying the video wouldn't dismantle the phone.

When Cole was done, the countdown clock returned. Almost an hour gone.

"Well, that's just freakishly creative," Eden muttered as Cole flipped the phone over, slipped open the back, and took a picture of the SIM card and serial number.

"I wore gloves when I opened it," Allie said. "In case you could get prints off it."

"I've got a kit in the car," Cole said. "I'm happy to dust it, but I'm not holding my breath. Max, why are you here?"

"Me?" Max finished his meal, picked up his plate and carried it to the sink, where he washed it and set Allie's heart to pattering. "Oh, I broke in while Allie was meeting with you all on your boat. Brought myself up to speed on Chloe's case since no one was interested in filling me in. Then waited for her to get home."

The stunned silence of her friends had Allie scrambling forward to provide protection for Max. "He's kidding!" She forced a laugh. "It's a joke. He has a very inappropriate sense of humor."

"Uh-huh." Simone nodded slowly, her long hair brushing against the soft fabric of her yellow T-shirt. Allie blinked to try to process her friend's continuing fashion transformation. "I really don't think that was a joke."

"If I hadn't broken in, you all would be having a different type of night," Max said. "I bumped the lock just after six. The alarm panel was dead from the start. No lights. That envelope was on the floor. Seeing as Allie led her protective entourage off to the marina around five, whoever broke in before me had an hour window. Might be worth checking with the neighbors. Personally, I wasn't surprised to see the system not working. I figured she just hadn't been using it since she doesn't lock her car doors."

"Criminy, Allie, still?" Eden sounded more irritated at her than she did at the idea of Max Kellan breaking into Allie's home. "Didn't my experience in that parking lot last summer teach you anything?"

"Yes, it taught me not to go after serial killers all on my own," Allie snapped and glared at Max. "And you, not helpful."

He shrugged. "How do you think I found out where you live?"

"Because Allie keeps her car registration in the glove box," Cole said. "Wow. Now I know what to get you for Christmas. Someone's going to take self-defense classes."

"*Someone* can already kick your butt," Allie said, grumbling. "When did this little get-together become a referendum on my personal security? He's the one who committed a crime." She jabbed a finger at Max.

"I'd like to point out that arresting him isn't going to do much for your relationship," Eden countered.

Relationship? Allie scoffed and added coffee to the coffeemaker. "Vince, back me up here." She turned to the P.I. as he came up the basement stairs. One glance at his normally unreadable face had her insides shifting in dread. She leaned against the counter as the room fell silent again. "I know that expression, Vince. You found something."

"Did you go down in the basement at all?" Vince asked Max.

"No. Didn't even think about it," Max said and surprised Allie by moving closer to her. Instead of being irritated by the protective gesture, she found herself leaning into him. "Why?"

Vince nodded as if processing the information. "Follow me."

"As loquacious as ever," Eden mumbled as she took the lead and headed downstairs.

Allie's heart pounded in her chest. Darn it! Now she was going to have to explain what she kept in the basement. She went last, trying not to imagine what was going through their minds.

"This doesn't disturb me at all." Simone examined the expansive basement that had been designed to Allie's specifications. When she'd first been looking for houses, she hadn't taken only the number of bedrooms and bathrooms into consideration; she hadn't particularly cared how decked out the kitchen was. She'd wanted her space, her private area that allowed her the luxury of working out her frustrations in as many ways as possible.

"You women and your basements." Cole pushed his fist against the free-standing punching bag while Vince circled the nearly five-foot-tall body opponent she'd named Steve. "First Eden with her psycho room—"

"Research lab," Eden corrected. "Something we've all used, remember?"

"I don't have a basement." Simone circled the sand bag hanging in the center of the space. "But now I know where to come if my treadmill breaks down. Allie? Something you want to share with the rest of us?"

"I'm pretty small, in case you hadn't noticed." Allie watched Max and Vince admire her collection of gloves, rubber knives and other equipment. "I need every advantage I can get." She didn't think they were up to hearing the news she'd increased her one-on-one training sessions with a former Navy Seal turned self-defense teacher in the last few weeks. Taking a page from Max's humor manual, she added, "You aren't going to find me hanging in a meat locker."

"Now that's just rude," Eden said.

"Good to know there's a sparring partner in the family for you, Vince." Simone dipped her chin, a wry smile on her face.

"If anything, this setup convinces me you're capable of taking care of yourself," Vince said. "Over there. By the open transom window." He gestured around the corner from where the power box for the alarm system was situated on the wall. "Not exactly the best place for growing flowers."

The group moved toward the potted violet, which was twice the size of the one that had been left on the Vandermont property near the girls' tent.

"I'd like to go on record that if you ever bring me flowers, I'll deck you," Eden said to Cole.

"Noted." Cole moved in to examine the window. "We're going to have to get Tammy out here to dust for prints. May as well have her do the phone, too."

"What's the use?" It wasn't defeat that coated Allie's words but frustration. When were they going to catch a break? "Lab techs won't find any, except mine. I'm sure we can all agree this guy hasn't stayed hidden for twenty years by leaving prints behind. He didn't where Simone's pictures were concerned, he didn't up at the Vandermonts'." Chloe's killer—Hope's captor—may as well be a ghost.

"No, he hasn't left anything, has he?" Vince said. "But then, as Eden's learned, he hasn't been hiding for twenty years, either."

"What are you talking about?" Max asked. "Allie led me to believe…"

Allie squeezed her eyes shut. When she opened them again, she no longer found friendliness and affection displayed on Max's face. She didn't flinch. Not when his beautiful eyes narrowed. Not when his jaw clenched.

"Chloe wasn't the only one, was she?" Max asked.

"No." Eden came up behind Allie and dropped a hand on her arm. "She wasn't."

"Eden found evidence Chloe's killer didn't go dormant," Allie clarified. "We think she's found at least three more victims."

"Three?" Max gave a very slow, big nod. "Three other murdered girls. Tell me again why I should trust you?" He swung on Allie. "You're still keeping secrets from me. Still lying to me."

"I thought you told him." Vince cringed, regret shining in his sharp eyes. "Sorry, Allie."

Allie waved off his concern. This wasn't his fault.

"Don't be," Max snapped. "It's not as if it's my niece's life we're trying to save or anything. You said three *as far as you know.*" Allie flinched when he turned his back on her to address Eden. "How long do we have?"

"According to that clock on the phone, less than seventy-two hours." Eden didn't hesitate. "For what it's worth, Allie planned to tell you. There just hasn't been much—"

"Time?" Max drew himself up. "From where I'm standing, you all have had twenty years—"

"They were kids when this started," Cole cut him off. "Nine-year-olds don't exactly have access to police files and investigations."

"That isn't what I mean and you know it," Max blasted. "And what's with this violet thing?" He waved a dismissive hand to the beautiful, toxic plant. "Clearly he's trying to say something, so what is it? I'm guessing nothing murderers like this do would be on the spur of the moment. Everything means something."

The violets. Allie flinched, as if the flowers had smacked her in the face. Violets. So simple in their basic terra-cotta pot, their deep, dark purple petals elegantly displayed. Lush leaves, plump stems. Someone had cared for this plant. Nurtured it. Almost as if it was more than a reminder of where their friend's body had been found.

"He's right. I can't believe I didn't think of this before." She pushed past Eden and raced up the stairs to her office. She was tapping on her computer when they joined her. "When were the girls found? What months?" Allie asked as she skimmed the information in the search engine.

"Two in late May," Eden said. "The other three in late July or early August. I can get you exact—"

"That's violet season." Allie flipped her laptop around. "Which is sometimes longer depending on the weather. Like it was this time twenty years ago. That field of violets bloomed late into August. You told us where all the bodies were found earlier, Cole. A park and a lake for two of them. It's another connection— a natural one. Flowers in particular. I need to look at those crime scene photos when you get them, Eden. We need to examine exactly where each body was left and what was around them."

"Don't forget there was also a strip mall," Simone added.

"It's the oddity." Cole shook his head. "An outlier."

"Three out of four isn't a coincidence," Eden said. "This gives us something to go on."

And isn't that what they'd all been hoping for? A real starting point?

"Not to be a pest," Max asked from the doorway. "But I don't suppose this epiphany of yours gives you any idea of where to look for my niece, does it? Because, if not, I'm going to follow through on Allie's idea starting tomorrow and start banging on every door in this city."

"Give us a few hours to work this through, Max," Vince told him. "If nothing pans out, I'll join you. Right now we need to address something we're probably choosing to ignore subconsciously. Whoever took Hope has spent a good part of his day focused on Allie. I see that as a good thing."

Allie nodded. "It means his attention's divided."

"But he could kill Hope at any time. Or she's already dead." Max's simple statement sent a chill down Allie's spine.

"I refuse to believe that," Allie snapped. "She was alive to make that video and that's what I'm going to cling to. Vince is right. He's had his fun with Eden and Simone. Now it's my turn. He'll want to draw this out as long as possible. I say we take complete advantage of that and keep the focus on me."

"What are you thinking?" Cole asked.

"She's not thinking," Eden said. "She's already thought. You have a plan, don't you?"

"All these years we thought killing Chloe was his only crime," Allie said. "Now we know different."

"Know. Can't prove," Cole corrected.

Allie waved away his criticism. "*We* know. Jack and

Lieutenant Santos think it's time we expose the connection between Hope's disappearance and Chloe's case. With these other cases, we have more information than the killer probably realizes. Let's throw everything out there and see what happens. What better person to present that information to the media, what better person to twist the knife, than the psychologist with a personal interest who's also consulting on the case?"

"So your solution is to paint a big bull's-eye on your chest and hope his aim sucks." Simone arched a brow. "Forgive me if I vote nay."

"My *solution* is to see what sticks. And I wasn't asking for anyone's permission." If anything, Allie's decision brought her an odd sense of peace. "Cole? Can you make this happen?"

"Yeah, Cole?" Eden swung on him, hands planted on her hips. "Can you?"

"The married part of me is thinking I should say no," Cole said after a pause. "I hate the idea of you putting yourself out there as much as Eden and Simone do, Allie. He's been building up to this for decades. You could very well be his endgame."

"You all could," Vince added. "There's nothing saying he's stopped focusing on Eden and Simone. Maybe he's just added you to the mix."

"Except it was Allie's patient he abducted," Simone said. "And it was Allie who received the phone."

"And if it's going to come down to the three of us, I'm happy to take point." Allie pushed to her feet. "You two finally got what you always wanted with these two." She gestured at Cole and Vince. "I'm not letting anything interrupt your happily-ever-afters."

"Funny." Eden looked down at her tennis shoes.

"I don't remember putting on my glass slippers this morning."

"Do I look like a fairy-tale princess?" Simone flipped her long blond hair behind her shoulder.

"I'm going to go out on a limb here and suggest no one answer that," Max said. "I agree with Eden and Simone, Allie. Your plan is too dangerous. And while I don't appreciate you all playing keep-away with the truth, you should know I'm not going anywhere until I get Hope back. Whatever it is you're going to do to get this guy, I want in."

"Third time's the charm." Eden's claim had a hint of annoyed acceptance. "We each have wound up with our own bodyguard. Now it's your turn, Allie. If you want to do this, then Max sticks with you 24/7. That's the only way I'll agree."

"Your agreement is not required. And absolutely not," Allie said. Why wasn't anyone listening to her? "I'm doing this to keep the two of you out of the line of fire, not make more targets."

"That's nice, Allie, but I don't see it like that. Your child killer made me a target when he took my niece. So I'm in," Max said. He crossed his arms over his chest and looked to Cole and Vince. "Suggestions?"

"Given what I saw in the basement?" Vince reached out and slipped his hand into Simone's. "Wear protective gear. You're going to need it."

Chapter 11

Max stood at Allie's living room window and watched the parade of cars carrying her friends away. Tomlinson and Bowie had taken off a while ago, replaced by another duo who, as far as Max was concerned, weren't much different. They parked their not-so-inconspicuous sedan strategically across Allie's driveway, ensuring she couldn't leave without them. Not that she was going anywhere at—he glanced at his watch—nearly one thirty in the morning.

In the dark room alone, the night pressed in on him, ringing in his ears as if a silent reminder of the nearly twenty-four hours since Hope vanished.

He swallowed hard, doing his best to shove the growing fear aside. Every second that passed, every minute they didn't hear, was both good news and bad. It had only been a day for him and yet, somehow, Allie, Simone and Eden had dealt with the aftereffects of their friend's murder for over two decades.

How? he wondered as exhaustion crept over him like a cat stalking its prey. How did anyone ever deal with something like this? As selfish as it sounded, he did not want to find out.

"I put fresh towels in the guest bathroom for you." Allie's voice was quiet enough that she didn't surprise him. How could she when he felt the air charge whenever she was around him? "Guest room is all ready."

He nodded, unable to form the words around the paralyzing grief threatening to take hold. She moved in behind him, brushed timid fingers over his arm. "You're completely justified being angry at me."

"Good to know I have your approval." He saw her eyes glint in the dim light cast from the kitchen. "No head games tonight, Doc, please."

To put some distance between them, he walked over to the small sofa, sat where he'd waited hours earlier for her to come home. How had so much happened between now and then? How had so much changed?

She'd changed. Her clothes at least. Gone was the bright spring color of soft fabric. Instead she wore a pair of striped pink flannel pajama bottoms and matching top. If possible, she appeared even younger than she did normally, with her face displaying that freshly scrubbed glow. She tucked her feet under, curling into a ball in the corner of the sofa, close enough for him to feel the warmth of her body radiating toward him. Close enough to smell the freshness of the soap she'd used. "I could make you some warm milk. If you think it might help you to sleep."

"I don't sleep, remember?" But he wanted to now,

more than he had in he couldn't remember how long. He slumped down, rested his head on the back of the sofa, stretched out his legs. What he wouldn't give for a few hours of oblivion, a few minutes of not dwelling on what might be, on what could be happening to Hope. On what would never be the same. "I appreciate the offer."

"Personally, I could do with a fifth of Scotch, but Cole finished mine the last time he was here."

Small talk. The doc was making small talk with him. Why? Because she was nervous? Or because she felt guilty about having lied to him from almost the first moment they'd met. Or because maybe none of this would be happening if it wasn't for her and her friends? "One of us should be coherent for that press conference tomorrow, Doc. You should go to bed."

She leaned her chin on her arm, which she'd braced on the back of the sofa. "Too wired. Too much going on up here." She tapped a finger against her temple. "But I'm choosing to focus on that look on her face in that video, Max. She's a smart girl. And she's angry. Both are going to work to her advantage."

He stared at her, jaw tightening. Hope shouldn't need an advantage like that.

"Max, if your thoughts weren't spinning out of control, I'd be worried."

"You should have told me about Chloe," he accused.

"Why?" She nodded as if contemplating her answer. "Would it have made your day easier? Would it have made anything better?"

"No." The only thing that would have made his day easier was to hear Hope had been found safe. Found alive. "But I might have liked being able to trust you. That trip to Napa was a complete waste of time."

"You needed to feel as if you were doing something."

"But it took you away from doing your job."

"There isn't anything I can do for your brother, Max. And from a purely selfish perspective, you were as much a distraction for me as Napa was for you. I needed something to focus on to keep me centered."

"Always the analysis with you docs."

"Why do you hate us so much? Doctors?"

"*Hate*'s a strong word," Max argued. "Where you're concerned, anyway." He could definitely think of a few other words that described his feelings for the doctor. "My issues are my issues, Allie. They don't involve you."

"Maybe I want them to involve me." She stretched out her arm and touched his shoulder. "You know what I hate? I hate seeing people I care about in pain. And it's written all over your face, Max. Or should I call you…" She squinted, leaned closer. "Smokey? Sparkles? No, that sounds more like a unicorn. How about Captain Fireball?"

How had she made him smile when it was the last thing he wanted to do? "Not even close, Doc. My turn." He lifted his hand and slipped his fingers between hers, reveling in the sensation of her skin touching his. "From a purely analytical and statistical perspective, what's a more effective tonic for sleep? Hot milk, Scotch or sex?"

"From a medical standpoint?" Her face barely flickered except for a spark in her eyes, bright enough, quick enough, for him to think he'd imagined it. "Chemical reactions in the lactose that take place during the warming process have been proven to—"

He arched a brow, folded his fingers around hers.

She returned the favor as she unfolded herself out of the corner.

"Scotch, of course, would come in right behind it, as long as one drinks enough to make passing out a viable option."

His stomach muscles clenched as exhaustion faded. "And option three?"

"I believe that would require some experimentation to prove the theory." She closed the distance between them, pulled her hand free and straddled him, her knees pressing into his hips. "You know what other theory might be worth exploring?"

"What's that?" He bypassed her hands, smoothed his own down her sides, over her hips as he went rock hard.

"The theory that animosity between potential partners makes for invigorating copulation."

"Mmm." He gripped her hips and smiled up at her. "Talk dirty to me, Doc. Who knew medical lingo would turn me on?"

She smiled and then gasped as he shifted. She caught her lower lip in her teeth and let out the sexiest moan he thought he'd ever heard.

Now she moved, slightly, just enough to make him wish she'd stop. Or not stop. Allie leaned over him, grasping his shoulders before slipping her hands up along his neck, cupping either side of his face. "There's also evidence that the endorphins produced by rigorous sexual activity stimulate brain waves and thought processes."

"It certainly stimulates something." He arched off the sofa, ran his hands up her spine so he could draw her to him. He wanted to, needed to kiss her. To find out for certain if the explosions she'd set off inside of him on the side of the road had been a fluke or if there was something more.

As if reading his mind, she brushed her lips against his. Eyes wide open, she stared into his, her knees tightening around him, her hips pulsing against him. She stroked her fingers over his mouth, licked her lips and then, as if answering his every desire, she kissed him.

The urgent demand of her mouth emptied his mind. Her tongue invaded, dueled, stroked and threatened to drive him out of his senses as he met her, action for action. Max slipped his hands up under her shirt. The bare skin of her back felt electric under his fingers. She curved around him, rocked against him, as she took and gave in equal measure.

He pushed her shirt up, drew his hands around to cup her breasts. She tore her mouth free and leaned back as he tweaked her nipples with his rough, calloused hands.

"Max," she gasped as he let go but then pressed her onto her back on the sofa. She curled her legs around him, locked him against her as he bent his head to feast on her breasts.

A faint jingling echoed in his mind. An odd tone, one he remembered hearing before, but not one loud enough to break through the Allie-induced fog in his brain.

She went stiff in his arms, and not, Max realized, in a good way. "That's my phone." She planted her hands on his shoulders and shoved him aside. "I'm sorry, I have to…it could be about Hope."

He sat up like a shot as she rolled off the sofa. She tugged her shirt down and covered herself as she wobbled into the kitchen. Part of him took pride in her semi-intoxicated stumble out of the room. Only when he heard her strained voice on the phone did he come crashing down to reality.

No, no, no...

He scrubbed his hands down his face as he tried to get control of his breathing. What was he doing? Getting hot and heavy with Dr. Allie Hollister when his niece was out there all alone, probably terrified. Wondering if she'd ever see her family, her home, again? He swore. What kind of man did that?

Max got to his feet and made his own unsteady way to the kitchen where he found Allie sitting at the breakfast bar, scribbling on a notepad. "No, Eamon, it's fine. I was still awake. I'm glad you called." She turned hooded eyes on Max and bit her lip. "Yeah, the press conference is scheduled for ten a.m. We'll see you there?"

To distract himself—in a way that didn't include divesting Allie from her clothes—Max went to the fridge and pulled out a beer, a close-enough choice to option number two when it came to knocking himself out for the rest of the night. "Is Eamon coming tomorrow?" he asked her when she hung up.

"No." Allie shook her head. "He hates press conferences more than the rest of us put together. He's going to go back up to the Vandermonts' place, talk to the girls again."

"Was that why he called?" That pang of jealousy that struck him when he'd first seen Allie and the FBI agent greet each other hit again.

"No. They found two sets of prints on one of the perfume bottles from Hope's bedroom. Hope's, of course. And Chloe's."

"Chloe's?" That was the last name he expected to hear. "They're sure?"

"They ran them twice to be sure. I swear the deeper into this we get, the less anything makes sense." She rubbed her face as if to erase the exhaustion he saw there, but it didn't help. Allie looked positively drained.

"Did Eamon have any other information?"

"No. He's going to wait at the lab to see if anything turns up on the envelope Cole brought him. He just wanted to give me an update before he headed to his hotel," she added.

"Sure." He tried to shrug it off. "Makes sense."

Allie's cheeks went pink after she looked at him. "About before—"

"I'm sorry," Max cut her off. The last thing he wanted to talk about was how wildly inappropriate and callous his actions had been. "I was out of line. Not thinking straight. Cloudy. It won't happen again."

"Oh."

Her disappointment crashed through him and nearly finished him off.

"Okay." She nodded, as if trying to convince herself. "You're probably right. Heat of the moment and all."

"I can't let myself think about anything other than Hope right now." Why did he feel the need to explain, to ease what she was clearly seeing as a rejection? "She's all that matters, Allie. Maybe, once this is all over, if—"

"I understand, Max." She drew herself up and, he noticed, curled her arms around her torso as if locking herself off. "You're absolutely right. Hope has to be our main focus. We can't afford to let ourselves get caught up in something…else."

So other distractions were acceptable not just…the

something else. He nodded, drank half his beer. "I'm going to bed." Although the idea of that cold, lonely guest room held little appeal. "You good?"

"Mmm-hmm." She nodded with a tight smile. "Perfectly fine. I'm heading upstairs myself so, um, good night." Allie moved toward him, stopped as if she thought better of it and gave him a cursory wave. "I'll see you in the morning."

She flipped off the light as she left and plunged him into the dark, the dim table lamp in the guest room his only guide. But what he saw on her face the instant before she disappeared had him wishing that something—everything—was different.

"Way to go, Allie." Allie slipped into bed and clicked off the bedside lamp. Sitting back against the pillows, she shut her eyes briefly and tried to push the impatience and frustration away. "Nothing like trying to seduce a traumatized family member to cement your reputation as a therapist." What was wrong with her? She'd never lost her objectivity like this before. Then again, she'd never met anyone like Max Kellan before.

She took a deep breath and then another. She'd been thinking he seemed lost sitting there on her sofa, defeat and doubt replacing the barely there optimism that had brought her comfort most of the day. No one had ever looked at her the way Max Kellan did; or if they had, she'd certainly never felt the overwhelming urge to do something about it.

Allie flexed her fingers, repeating the ghostly memory of sinking her hands into that glorious thick hair of his, the feel of his mouth under hers, his hands roaming her bare skin as his slightest touch set off tiny explosions of desire inside her.

She shook her head as if she could dislodge the thought and curled up onto her side to stare out at the dim streetlamp. He was absolutely right. They had to focus on finding his niece and making sure her abductor—and Chloe's killer—was locked away for good. Whatever either of them might want shouldn't matter, couldn't matter.

Except it did.

She flopped onto her back and stared up at the ceiling. It was physical, she told herself. That's all it was between her and Max. He was everything she never thought she could have, all those teenage daydreams and fantasies come to life. Sex had never been high up on her priority list and now she knew why.

No man had ever made her feel as wanted, as desired as Max Kellan had. The feminine power within her had exploded, maybe for the first time in her life. She wanted him.

But, as Allie knew, you don't always get what you want.

Chapter 12

"Hey, Max."

Max started when a foot kicked his. He sat up in his chair, blinked himself into consciousness and gazed uncertainly at the steaming paper cup of what he hoped was very strong coffee.

"It's almost showtime." Detective Jack MacTavish jerked his head toward the window of the second-floor office in the courthouse that had been turned into command central for the press conference. "You good?"

"Yeah, good." He accepted the coffee even as he longed to escape into the fitful twenty minutes of sleep he'd managed to catch. Twenty minutes on top of the unexpected five hours last night. Most sleep he'd had in months. "Thanks." Afraid he'd drop back off if he didn't move, he got up and searched for the least invasive path to the window and tried to stay out of the way.

The conversation that filled the room was subdued and intense. The constant clicking of keyboard keys, the murmured orders and comments bouncing across the conference room table were muted, but Max could see all these people doing whatever they needed to do to bring his niece home, and it helped to slow to a thin trickle the mounting doubt he'd been struggling to keep on top of. Max pinched the bridge of his nose. He felt as if he'd been caught on a hamster wheel and no matter how hard he tried, he couldn't jump off.

The half-dozen techs ranging in age, sex and size had gobbled up nearly every inch of space in the room, buzzing like a beehive, humming in cooperation and understanding. Between the laptops, surveillance equipment and electronic devices, he felt as if he'd stepped into a briefing room at the CIA. "Everything set for the press conference?" Max asked the detective before he drank. "Okay, that's awful." He shook his head as if he could dislodge the taste from his mouth.

"Mmm. Drink more than a cup and you won't blink for a week." Jack nodded and took a solid stance by one of the three windows. Video cameras had been set up in each one, their narrow lenses barely peeking through the slats, each aimed in a different direction toward where the anticipated crowd would gather outside. "We've got two vans set up on either end of the block monitoring anyone coming and going. These guys will be running a new facial recognition program on the onlookers who stick around. We've got eyes and ears on all involved, including Allic and Simone, not that I think this guy would be brazen enough to try something with news cameras filming."

"If he even shows." Max wasn't entirely convinced

this was the best course of action, but if it had even the slightest chance of working, there wasn't a choice, was there?

"The DA and my lieutenant have been promoting this event since last night. They even got the mayor to say something in his morning briefing," Jack said. "Your brother made sure to include it on his social media and that's been picked up by national news sources."

"Great. More press."

"Could be great, actually. Or not." Jack pinned him with that practical, no-nonsense, straight-shooter expression. "More attention could drive this guy deeper into hiding or it could shine a light on wherever he's hiding."

"And all we're gambling with is my niece's life," Max grumbled.

"I guess it seems that way." Jack took a long sip. "Allie wouldn't have suggested this course of action if she didn't believe it had a shot of drawing him out."

Wouldn't she? "Tell me something." He figured Jack was a safe and objective person to ask. "What's foremost in Allie's mind and her friends' at the moment? Finding my niece or finding whoever killed Chloe Evans?"

"You make it sound as if the two are mutually exclusive." The sharp female voice had Max looking to the door as Eden St. Claire entered. "Come and get 'em, guys." She set stacked trays filled with oversize paper cups on the table, pulled two free and made a mad dash around the stampede of officers diving for digestible coffee. "Figured you could use something drinkable, too, Max. Ah! Not there." Eden kicked out a foot to stop Max from setting his cup of swill on the closest desk.

"Trust me. No liquids near the computer equipment. Right, Officer Castillo?" Eden blinked too-innocent eyes at the young female officer nearby.

"I'll take a cup of coffee near my system over you any day, Eden." Was that a smile on her face or a grimace? The way she said it, combined with the snort that emanated from Jack, told Max there was a story behind the exchange.

"Don't suppose you brought us any food?" Jack asked as he dumped his coffee into a sad, sagging potted plant in the corner.

"Coffee now. Food later." She beat her way through the crowd to grab the last cup. "How's our team looking?"

"I'm about to go check," Jack said. "Simone seems fine. Allie, I'm not so sure. Ten minutes and counting. You waiting up here?"

"I have no interest in becoming part of the story until absolutely necessary." Eden sipped and cringed. Max felt safe in assuming the expression on her face had nothing to do with the exceptional caffeinated liquid. "My former colleagues aren't high up on my Christmas list," she explained to Max. "Especially that one." She stabbed a finger through the slats at the crowd of reporters and interested onlookers gathering in the courtyard beneath oddly gnarled, leafless trees. "The sallow, scrawny, gerbil-looking guy next to that woman in the baseball cap?"

Max inclined his head, appreciating her way with words. "Gray suit? Squinty eyes?"

"Benedict Russell. That charmer was after my job for most of the time I worked at the *Sacramento Journal* and, wouldn't you know it, I ended up giving him one of the best stories of his career." She aimed a tight smile in Max's direction. "Karma works both ways. You hanging in there? How's your brother doing?"

"Not great." Max hadn't liked the defeat he'd heard in his brother's voice this morning. If the information Max gave him about his faith in Allie and her friends eased Joe's mind, Max hadn't been able to tell. "He seems torn between staying hopeful and preparing himself for the worst." Just like Max.

"There's no right way to deal with a missing child," Eden said in that clipped, matter-of-fact way she had. "But now isn't the time to lose faith in people. Allie knows what she's doing," she added as if Max needed clarification about whom she was talking about.

"Because you're so objective when it comes to your friends."

He got a smile out of her—a genuine one this time. "I like you, Max. For the most part, at least. I can work with that."

"I'm flattered."

"You should be. I don't like a lot of people." She tugged the hem of her faded rock T-shirt over the waistband of her jeans. "And a lot of people don't like me."

"I'm sure they have their reasons," Max countered. "Whether they're good or not—"

"The reason I bring it up," Eden continued as if he hadn't interrupted, "is so that I can tell you that Allie's different. She honestly cares about everyone she meets. She just doesn't show it. She can't. That shield she wears is the only thing that helps her function."

Max nodded. He did know. Not only because Allie had admitted as much last night, but because he'd been doing something similar for most of his life.

"That emotional-distance thing she's supposed to have when it comes to her patients?" Eden went on. "Yeah. She's flirted with that line since she was a grad student working with vets and troubled youth. Has she told you anything about her family?"

"A little. She told me her parents took in foster kids, a lot of them."

Eden smirked. "Mistress of understatement, that's Allie. Intentional or not, Sitara and Giles Hollister did a real number on her. If I didn't know firsthand the damage they'd done, I'd be inclined to think they were saints based on how they've cared for other people's children. Their own?" Eden shrugged. "Not so much."

Max had trouble correlating the Allie he'd met, the Allie who had trembled in his arms last night, with that type of emotional upheaval. Then again?

Max shifted his attention out the window, his gaze landing on Allie and Simone huddled together just outside the press's view. "They didn't set out to hurt her, did they?"

Eden shrugged. "No. But being ignored and pushed aside most of your life, being expected to take care of yourself well before kindergarten? That's a special kind of neglect to my mind. To her credit, she hasn't cut them off, which is why Simone and I tend to stick close when we can where they're concerned. I'm not telling you all this so you'll feel sorry for her. And if you tell her we had this conversation, I will string you up by your...thumbs."

Max grinned behind his cup.

"Allie and Chloe were close," Eden continued. "Inseparable from the second they met. The four of us, actually, but there was this bond between the two of them

Simone and I could never quite break through. And that was okay. Allie felt protective of her, even though she didn't need protection. At one point, she asked Simone if she knew someone who could dye her hair red so other kids would stop teasing Chloe about hers. Allie needed to be someone's protector, like we'd been hers. She needed to be needed. When Chloe was killed…" Eden paused and took a long breath. "It broke something inside of each of us. We didn't go back together in the same way. I got angry and some would say cruel. I'm still angry. I don't see that changing even after we get this guy. I'm lucky Cole understands that and somehow still loves me."

He must, Max thought. Why else would he have married her?

"Simone got smart," Eden said. "I wanted to make people—criminals—pay for what they'd done in any way possible. Simone wanted them to be held accountable within the confines of the law."

"And Allie?" Max was almost afraid to ask.

"Allie needed to know why. If she can figure that out, then maybe she can stop it from happening again. And yet here we are, dealing with not only another child abduction but one that strikes closer to her heart than she'd ever admit. Hope is hers, Max. She was from the second she stepped foot in Allie's office. Even if her disappearance wasn't connected to Chloe, Allie would be doing exactly the same thing. If you can't see or understand that, that's fine. But don't judge her for it." She took a slow drink and gave him a glance. "Don't judge any of us for it. Lecture's over. I'm going downstairs to find Cole and bug him."

He watched Eden leave, her words clearing the confusion hovering around any thoughts of Allie. Eden was right. Allie was more than what he'd seen of her in the last day. She was a product of a path not so dissimilar to his own and Joe's, and yet she hadn't let it define her to the point of losing herself. She'd exploded beyond her potential, beyond her circumstances, just as Joe had, just as Max had tried to.

And here she was waiting to publicly reopen a wound that anger, reason and time hadn't been able to suture. In fact, Allie was taking it one step further by putting herself in the kidnapper's sights in the hopes of luring him to her. Daring him to come after her, to make a mistake.

All in order to bring his niece home.

A sacrifice Max would never, ever be able to repay.

"Stop that." Simone grasped Allie's hand and pulled it away from her lapel, where it had been smoothing the pin the surveillance team had tacked onto her egg-yolk-yellow jacket. "Since when do you fidget?"

Allie pinched her lips tight. "Nervous energy." Energy that had nothing to do with the press conference and everything to do with finding Max in her sunlight-bright kitchen this morning making her breakfast. They couldn't have been more polite to one another if they'd been having tea with the Queen of England. "Long night."

"I'll bet." Simone leaned over to peer around the oversize planter to where the reporters were gathering. "Your Max looks as if he'd be very attentive to detail."

"He's not *my* Max." Allie shuddered against the sweet memory of Max's hands slipping up her back, sliding around to her— "Nothing happened."

Simone stood up straight, looked slightly disbelieving as she arched a perfectly drawn brow. "If you say so."

"Nothing much happened," Allie corrected and resisted the urge to roll her eyes. "Did it occur to you that this topic is completely inappropriate given everything that's going on?"

"Has it occurred to you sometimes life presents you with certain opportunities at the absolute worst time? Take advantage of it or don't, but don't wallow about it."

Allie shook her head. What was it with her friends' accusations of wallowing? "You don't understand."

"You want to try that again?" Simone moved to stand in front of her, blocking Allie's view of the podium, and nailed her with that big-sister stare she'd perfected in the last twenty years. "You think I didn't feel guilty when Vince and I got back together? That I didn't realize the timing was—as you put it—completely inappropriate? One second we're watching them drag Natalie Subrov's body out of the Delta and then the next I'm wondering what future I might have with him."

Allie didn't like the disappointment she saw on her friend's drawn face.

"I did feel guilty, but I also still had my life to live," Simone said. "I still had possibilities ahead of me and she didn't. It took some time to get used to."

"Natalie wasn't murdered because of you," Allie said.

"Geez. Eden's right. We need to send you to a support group. Listen to me, Allie." Simone ducked her chin, took a deep breath. "You're not to blame for what happened to Chloe. Did it ever occur to you that you and Max need each other? If it grows into something more, all the better. I've always thought you were brave, Allie.

Don't bail on me now claiming you're afraid to take a chance on something potentially wonderful because you're afraid of…what? How it will look?"

"That's not what I'm doing," Allie snapped. "I need to focus on Hope. I can't afford to be distracted—"

"That's my point, Al. He doesn't have to be a distraction. He can just be. Unless you're just scared and using Hope's kidnapping as an excuse to avoid any confusing entanglements. You've never let yourself get serious about anyone. Until now. And whether you realize it or not, whether you want to admit it or not, you are serious about Max."

How Allie wanted to argue, but she couldn't.

"You don't need anyone's permission other than your own to be happy, Allie. But if it'll help, you have mine and Eden's."

The double glass doors to the courthouse opened and what looked like a suited army of judicial power emerged. Lieutenant Santos headed their way as DA Ward Lawson, dressed in tailored blue perfection, took his place at the podium. "You ready, Allie?" the district attorney asked.

"She's ready," Simone said. "I'll be right behind you." She squeezed her hand around Allie's. "Whatever you do."

Allie welcomed the anonymity of a crowd; it was her safe place, where she always felt most comfortable. Probably a result of feeling ignored and invisible most of her early years and then later because of the strength she'd found in friendship.

Yet here she was, hours after the press conference had ended, hours after the reporters and bloggers had stopped shouting questions at her and her fellow speakers, holed up and dwelling on all the things she'd said, what she wished she'd said. And waiting. For what? What exactly was she waiting for?

Being alone allowed the doubts to creep in and settle, eating away at her professional and personal confidence until she was that shy, five-year-old girl on the school yard having her ball stolen. Only this time Eden couldn't beat up the playground bully for her; Simone couldn't hold out her hand and welcome her into a new reality.

This was her reality; in the next day or so they'd know if Hope had a future. Or if Allie had made such a huge tactical error that she cost a young girl her life.

She could hear the replay of the press conference echoing through the station room in the offices of the Major Crimes unit. Her own voice scraped against her ears as she answered question after question flung at her by voracious reporters eager to sink their fangs into a potentially career-making story.

Had she given them anything they could use? Anything that would help find Hope? Had her cool examination, explanation and accusations made any difference?

She didn't have the answers. So here she sat, in one of the small interview rooms, staring at the life-altering cell phone and its countdown clock.

Allie swallowed hard, tried to stop the tears from forming in her eyes. If she'd failed this child, if somehow she'd done something to endanger her even more…

A knock sounded on the door. Before Allie could respond, it opened. Max poked his head inside. "There you are."

Allie forced a smile. "Here I am." She sat up, suddenly alert. "Has there been word—"

"No." He stepped in and closed the door. "No, nothing yet. I went to Joe's for a bit, checked up on him, but all we could do was stare at each other in silence. So I came back. If I'm going to stare at anyone, I'd rather it be you."

Allie wished she could force herself to smile at his attempt at humor. Somehow, in the last few days, he'd become more of a coping mechanism than her self-imposed shutdown. She liked having him around, teasing her, throwing out completely inappropriate statements or comments that both mortified and amused her.

Simone was right. Maybe the universe had put them in each other's path for just that reason.

"I didn't mean to interrupt whatever this is."

"Oh, this?" Allie waved her hand over the phone. "No, Simone and Eden would call this wallowing, but it's actually me second-guessing every decision I've made since this whole thing started."

"How exactly is that different from wallowing?"

This time her lips twitched.

"Well, then, I've found the right place." He took a seat across from her as if they were about to engage in interrogation. "How about I offset that with an apology."

"For what?"

"For blaming you. For accusing you of being responsible for what's happened and not thinking about Hope. She's being used against you and has been from the beginning. That isn't your fault and I should have seen that sooner. You were amazing at that conference. I don't know how you do it, remain so calm and seemingly detached."

"Remove me from the equation and none of this would have happened, so there's no apology necessary. But I appreciate the sentiment."

"Removing you from the equation means we never would have met." He placed his hands on the table, palms up. "As much as I hate what's happening with Hope, as much as I'd do anything to change that, I'm grateful for you and everyone who's trying to help."

Because she wanted to, because she needed to, she put her hands in his. "I thought by now he'd have responded," she whispered. "I thought I read the situation well enough—"

"There's no reading this situation, Allie. There's only doing what we can do."

Another knock sounded on the door. Bowie pushed it open. "Hey, Allie. There's a Nicole and Patrick Goodale here to see you? If you have time. They're down in reception."

"Oh." Allie pushed to her feet, a bit unsettled at the idea of her two worlds colliding. "Thanks, Bowie. I'll be there in a second."

"Your foster sister and brother?"

Allie nodded. "I would have thought they had their hands full with the restaurant and all."

"They're probably worried about you."

Allie shrugged. "I should probably go."

"Are you planning on teleporting?" Max asked when she didn't move.

"No." Allie forced a laugh. "No, actually, I was just… Would you mind coming with me? I know it sounds silly—"

Max stood and held out his hand. "You want to take

that with you?" He inclined his chin toward the phone as she rounded the table.

"Unfortunately." Allie slipped it into her jacket pocket. "Thank you. For—"

He kissed her. Not like he had before on the side of the road. Certainly not the way he had on her sofa. No, this kiss, while it conveyed affection and the slightest note of passion, felt more like his version of a warm hug but with added benefits. "Sometimes you think too much, Doc," he murmured against her lips. "How about you ease up on the throttle and go with the flow?"

Unaccustomed to feeling speechless, she nodded and together they walked to the elevators.

She spotted Nicole out of the corner of her eye when the doors slid open on the first floor. Tall and thin, with jet-black hair and pale porcelain skin, Nicole Goodale had always reminded Allie of Snow White. Nicole wore a forest-green suit today, elegant and refined, and the furrowed brow told Allie her foster sister had been watching the news.

"What is going on?" Nicole asked in an odd, whispered tone. "Patrick and I were having brunch at the restaurant when we saw the broadcast. I'm sure you're busy, but we wanted to come by and—"

"Are you all right, Allie?" Patrick, graced with the same features and coloring as his slightly younger sister, cut her off. The tension in Patrick's eyes seemed pronounced; there was a heaviness in his face that couldn't be blinked away.

"I'm fine." Allie glanced between the two of them. "It's my patient who's missing. I'm just doing everything I can to help find her. You didn't need to come down here."

"I told you we'd be bothering her," Patrick admonished Nicole, who moved in and wrapped her arms tight around Allie. "I'm sorry, Allie. Nicole was worried all this would bring up memories of Chloe."

"I always have memories of Chloe." Max squeezed her hand as if warning her about her irritation-tinged tone as she struggled to breathe in Nicole's hold. "Oh, sorry. Max, this is Nicole and Patrick Goodale." She used the introduction as an excuse to pull free. "They lived with my family for a while when we were kids. This is Max Kellan."

"Kellan?" Patrick's eyebrows vanished under the sweep of dark hair edging his eyes. "As in Hope Kellan, the missing girl?"

"She's my niece," Max said.

"This entire thing is terrible, just terrible." Nicole tapped restless fingers against the base of her throat. She moved to stand beside her brother. "Please tell me if there's anything we can do to help. Do you need to hold a fund-raiser or have a meeting place for community outreach? We'd be happy to offer our restaurant."

"Not at this time, no," Max said. "But I'll be sure to tell my brother about the offer. Allie was saying you've only recently come back to town. Must be nice to reconnect after all this time."

While Max's effort at small talk seemed appropriate, something in his tone didn't ring true.

"It's been wonderful." Nicole reached into her purse and pulled out a business card to give him. "So many lost years and family is so important. I'm sure Allie's told you all about her dinner the other night. Allie, we didn't realize you were seeing someone. You should have brought him with you."

"We only just—"

"Got serious," Max cut Allie off. "But I'll keep the invitation in mind for the future."

Patrick's cell phone chimed. He gave his sister and Allie an apologetic look. "I'm sorry. My crew is putting the finishing touches on the restaurant. It's a lot of hand-holding." He moved outside to take the call.

"What is it that Patrick does at the restaurant exactly?" Max asked.

"A little bit of everything." Nicole said with a glimmer of pride. "He's my partner, my right hand. Keeps me steady and focused. Also doesn't hurt that he can make or fix anything. It's saved us a fortune on reconstruction and upgrades. It's a nice change for him after all the years he spent in construction as a contractor."

Allie just smiled.

"We're bothering you, aren't we?" Nicole blinked obsidian eyes at her. "I'm so sorry, Allie. I just wanted you to know we're here for whatever you need. Has there been any word on Hope? Any idea who's taken her or why?"

"Nothing we can talk about yet," Max answered before Allie could.

"I think you need to take that as your cue, Nic," Patrick said as he returned to the lobby. "I need to do some damage control myself back at Lembranza. Allie, hopefully this will be resolved and Max's niece will be home soon."

"Well, let's hope we can put all this behind us and enjoy your parents' party, Allie," Nicole said with a restrained smile. "Max, I assume you'll be joining us?"

"Afraid we'll be playing things by ear." Max backed

away, giving Allie an excuse to follow. "It was good to meet you."

"You as well." Nicole waved at them as she and her brother headed out the door.

"Well, that was odd," Allie said.

"Glad to hear you say that," Max muttered. "You didn't tell me your foster siblings were vampires."

"They've always been on the eccentric side," Allie admitted. "It's not uncommon when kids have the erratic and unstable upbringing they did. From what I remember, it was pretty rough. They mean well. Well, Nicole, at least. I've never really been able to get a good read on Patrick. He's always been quiet."

"How long did they live with you?"

"Off and on for nearly three years. There was a hard cycle of their mother being committed, being released, going off her meds, getting readmitted," Allie said. "It's not atypical of patients with her level of mental instability. My parents were convinced she'd find a way to get well so she could have her kids back. Eventually, she did."

"That's why you hadn't seen or heard from them for so long?"

"Yeah. The last time Mina was released she showed up in a loaded van ready to leave town. That was the year after Chloe was killed, so it's a bit foggy." She didn't remember a lot of what happened in the ensuing months. "I think Nicole kept in touch with Ma over the years, but until they moved back to Sacramento, I hadn't seen or spoken to them in ages."

"And you don't think it's strange they wanted to reconnect? That they came back here?"

"The Goodale family and strange go hand in hand,"

Allie admitted. "Patrick and Nicole were a lot older than me and while Nicole had her big-sister moments, I got along much better with their younger brother, Tyler."

"There's another one of them?" They entered the elevator and he pushed the second-floor button.

Allie jumped when the phone in her pocket vibrated. She pulled the phone out and grabbed Max's arm. "It's doing something." She dived at the doors the second they slid open. "Cole! Jack!" She raced through the squad room, dodging officers and detectives, who were smart enough to move out of her way. "Something's happening with the phone!"

"Here!" Jack waved her over to his desk where they had a bunch of electronics set up. He motioned for her to hand the phone off to one of the techs, who plugged in the cord so whatever displayed on the phone projected onto one of the laptops.

Allie stood back, arms folded across her chest. She felt Eden and Simone move in beside her, but it was Max's gentle grasp on her hip that brought her any semblance of comfort.

Allie's own face flickered on the screen, stuttering, like a film reel trying to catch hold.

Images began to flash—photographs, pictures not just of Allie but of Simone and Eden, different from the surveillance pictures that had been taken of Simone weeks before. She noticed Eden holding out her cell phone to record. The back of Allie's neck prickled.

Hope's face appeared, followed quickly by those of her friends, Peyton, Willa and Mercy, slowing to a merged image of Allie and her friends, transposed with Hope and hers.

"Cole," Allie warned. "Find out where Hope's friends are. Now."

"I'm on it." He snatched up his desk phone and dialed.

"I can't begin to fathom how this guy's mind works." Simone's sentiment had most everyone nodding in agreement. "Why doesn't he just come out and tell us what he wants? If it's not money and he has Hope—"

Digital blood dripped from the top of the screen, pooling at the bottom until it completely obscured the pictures.

The clock blinked fifty-seven hours and powered down.

"What did you do?" Max demanded of the computer tech who had plugged the phone in. "Where did it go?"

"It's rebooting," the tech said. "It did it on its own. It has its own operating system, its own program."

"Great," Max muttered. "Now this guy's a tech genius."

"No." Eden shook her head. "No, I don't think he is. Jack, remember that case a few years back, that hacker group you busted in one of the abandoned warehouses down by the rail yards? Didn't you confiscate a bunch of computer equipment and cell phones that had been wiped and reprogrammed?"

"Right," Jack replied. "They did custom burners for all sorts of groups to fund their other ventures. Installed specially written programs and apps for everyone from live-action role-players to drug dealers. They found similar phones down in San Diego, where one of the hackers was from."

"I knew I'd seen this before." Eden tapped her own phone and replayed the video. "Here." She paused it, placed it on the table. "That. It's like a watermark behind this picture of Allie and Hope. It's a flash of something, like a logo, maybe a bit of code?" She backed away as the tech replayed the recording on the laptop. "Anyone recognize it?"

"The Vandermonts were way ahead of us." Cole hung up his phone. "They've hired private security for the family and Mercy and Portia until all of this has been resolved. They haven't seen or heard anything unusual, but they'll let us know if they do."

"Can't play this too safe," Max said.

"Here's the image from the corner enlarged." The tech typed on his keyboard and brought up the logo.

Allie blinked. "Is that an owl?"

Simone leaned over. "An upside-down one."

Cole and Jack looked at each other. "Strix."

"What's a strix?" Allie asked.

"Local hacker. Sneaky. A bit squirrely, too," Vince spoke up and shrugged when the two detectives smirked. "What? You have your contacts. I have mine. You know where to find him?" he asked. "If not, I can find out."

"Probably faster than we can," Jack muttered. "Go. We'll be ready."

Vince was pulling out his cell as he walked away.

"What does all this mean?" Allie asked.

"It means we find out who hired Strix," Cole said. "It should lead us to Hope."

"Phone's coming back on," the tech at the desk said.

The screen went dim, flashed once. The digital clock returned.

Twenty-four hours.

"I cost her thirty-three hours." Allie's heart beat double time. She should have expected it. Maybe she had, but seeing the consequences of her arrogant action had her second-guessing everything. Max's fingers flexed against her waist. "He's punishing us. Punishing me for talking to the press and going public."

"He's playing you," Max said. "If this phone was programmed, the countdown reset was already installed, which means he planned to use it. It wouldn't have mattered what you said or did, or even if you did nothing. He's trying to get under your skin and scare you."

"It's working." She let herself lean back, half expecting Max to move away from her, but instead, he moved in, rested his other hand on her shoulder and squeezed. "Eden, did you get those other forensic reports about the murdered girls yet?"

"Kyla is running off the last of them at Simone's office."

"I'll give her a call," Simone said, referring to her invaluable assistant. "Even though I'm officially still on sabbatical, the district attorney told me the office and resources are at my disposal as far as this case is concerned. Anything else we need?"

"I want to see everything in one place," Allie said. "Everything you have, Eden, from all the cases."

"Thought you might. It's in a box in Cole's car. Cole! Keys!" She yelled at her husband across the room and caught the keys when he tossed them to her. "Give me a few minutes."

"Allie, claim your space and let's get to work," Simone said.

"Got him!" Vince spoke louder than Allie had ever heard him do before, but it was necessary given the sudden explosion of activity in the bullpen. "My source says Strix is holed up in the back of a defunct travel office off Broadway. You want to do this official-like or my way?"

Cole glanced at his LT.

Lieutenant Santos moved out of earshot.

"How about we ride to Strix's rescue?" Cole suggested. "Jack, you don't mind if Vince plays the heavy, do you?"

"It's what he does best," Jack said with a bright smile.

Allie caught Cole's eye, inclined her head toward Max.

"Kellan?" Cole called on his way to the elevator. "You're with Vince."

Allie felt Max's entire body tense before he gave Allie a reassuring squeeze and ran to join them.

"It's like he was just asked to play with the cool kids," Allie said to Simone, who was pressing buttons on her phone.

"Well, he kind of was." Simone gave her an encouraging smile. "Only there's a lot more at stake than who scores the first touchdown."

Chapter 13

When the muted strains of classical music drifted through the black sports car, Max wondered if he'd been transported to an alternate reality. Vince Sutton didn't strike him as a fan of Bach, Beethoven or Mozart. He'd have thought heavy metal, maybe hard-rocking country, but strings and flutes?

Max pulled out the card Nicole had given him in the lobby of the station. Something about those two Goodales didn't sit right with him. Even Allie thought their visit was weird, but was that because of the timing or was it more than that? The conversation had felt forced, as if the siblings had been digging for information, waiting for the right time to ask questions or…

Or what? Max shook his head.

"I can hear you thinking from over here," Vince said as he shifted gears. "Out with it."

Max couldn't very well voice his confusion to Allie, not without either offending or alarming her, and she had enough to worry about without adding more family drama. "Have you ever met Allie's foster siblings?"

"No." Vince's jaw worked. He glanced into the rear-view mirror. "Simone's told me a little about Allie's family. Doesn't sound like it's something she's fond of talking about. Wonder how long Cole and Jack are going to give us alone with Strix."

"Not long enough, I'm betting." Max turned to look out the back window and caught sight of Cole's Fed-friendly SUV. "Maybe we can lose them?"

Vince's mouth quirked in approval and he sped up. "What makes you ask about Allie's family?"

"Two of them stopped by the station out of the blue to talk to Allie. Seems like they've been out of touch for a while. Back in town in the last few months. Now they're getting chummy."

"Either you're hedging because you think you're wrong or you want me to land on your suspicion on my own. Speak, Max."

"I don't like coincidences." And the last time he'd ignored his gut, one of his friends died. Allie was a little too close to be objective about the people she cared about. Max, however, was another story. "Last night we all agreed that taking my niece was a personal attack on Allie. Doesn't get more personal than family."

Vince didn't respond. He barely moved as they maneuvered through downtown traffic. Max flicked the card against his hand.

"Never mind. I'm probably projecting." Great. Now he was starting to sound like a shrink.

"Second-guessing yourself is only going to tick me off," Vince said. "Last name?"

"Kellan."

"Not you," Vince drawled. "Nicole and Patrick."

"Oh." He must have left his brain back at the station. "Goodale. Why?"

"Because I don't ever go against a father's instincts."

Father? Max blinked. "I'm not Hope's—"

"May as well be." He tapped the phone icon on his steering wheel and activated the speakerphone. It rang twice before it was picked up. "Hey, Jace. It's me."

"I haven't burned down the bar yet, if that's what you're wondering."

"Good to know," Vince said with a bit more lightness in his voice than Max had heard before. "I need you to do a background check. Nicole and Patrick Goodale. Ages?" He glanced at Max.

"Between thirty and forty?" Max guessed given what Allie had said. "They just opened a restaurant in midtown, Lembranza. Patrick's a former contractor—I'm thinking he was licensed back east." He rattled off the address on the business card. "Allie also mentioned something about a third sibling, Tyler. Younger than the other two."

"Okay to use your computer, Vince?" Jace said.

"I would prefer it," Vince said. "Get me everything you can, kid. Email it to me and me only, understood? ASAP."

"What am I looking for exactly?"

"Crazy," Max said to the voice on the other end of the phone. "You're looking for anything crazy."

"My specialty. Talk soon."

"Let me guess," Max said to Vince. "Kid brother? I've got one myself."

"He's studying to get his P.I. license against his better judgment," Vince said. "I'd like to make him a partner, but he's balking. Thinks he's going to bring down my rep."

"Why would he do that?"

"He's got a record. Armed robbery. Accessory, actually. Just got out of prison a few weeks ago thanks to Simone. As I keep telling him, that gives him more insight into the job, not less. Besides, Jim Rockford was an ex-con."

Max grinned. "There was a time I'd have given my right eye for a trailer like Rockford's."

"You and me both. So, about Strix. Are you a plan-ahead kind of guy or do you just want to wing it?"

"I've always believed in the power of improvisation," Max said. "Put me wherever you think I'll do the most good."

"That particular bank of stores and businesses has an alley for deliveries and employee parking. Let's say you plant yourself back there and be a blockade."

"Should the need arise, you mean," Max clarified.

"Oh, the need will arise." Vince took a hard left and smirked. "Trust me."

"What are we missing?" Allie stood in the corner of the conference room and watched as Eden, Officer Castillo and Jack organized photographs, official notes and forensic results. They'd commandeered every over-size magnetic whiteboard they could get their hands on, three of which had been left blank for now. The rest had been dedicated to Chloe's case.

And Hope's.

"Sorry it took me so long." Kyla Bertrand, Simone's executive assistant and a soon-to-be lawyer, once she passed the Bar, swept into the room, arms filled with files and folders. The radiant young woman was always a breath of fresh air.

Kyla dropped the papers on the closest desk, her ebony curls sliding in front of her eyes. "For once, it's because I had too much information to print out." Kyla let out a sigh of relief. "I've got every piece of paper from all three of the girls' cases. Alyssa Knight, Shannan McPhearson and Rosalie Jenson. How do you want them?"

"In chronological order starting on the board right behind you," Eden ordered in a way that told Allie she'd had too much coffee already.

Allie felt like a computer, absorbing new input, processing the information, but no matter how hard she tried, she couldn't pull herself free of the tidal wave of fear and grief.

"Hey." Simone joined her, leaned against the wall beside her and nudged her with her hip. "How are you doing?"

"Isn't that supposed to be my question?" Young girls' faces were tacked onto the sterile whiteboards, their smiling innocence like an additional knife to her heart.

"You're too close to this, Al. All three of us are."

"And yet Eden's going full steam ahead."

"Eden doesn't have another setting." Simone slouched down, not an easy feat given her teetering heels. "But you're the key to all this. Not because he's targeted you this time around. But because you can see things the rest of us don't."

"You make it sound so easy." And yet when she examined the mounting bits and pieces of information, all she could feel was a growing sense of dread.

"And you're making this too difficult on yourself. Stop fighting whatever's going on in that brain of yours. Embrace the thoughts, the fear. Walk into it, not away from it."

"Where on earth have you heard that bunch of malarkey?"

"From a psychologist I'm very fond of," Simone said without a hint of offense. "I've had to have similar talks with reluctant or scared witnesses. How about you stop trying to force the answers and let the answers come to you?"

Allie nibbled on her lip as she studied the boards.

"Look at this case as if it was about people you didn't know," Simone urged. "Blank out the faces. Look at the details. The small things. What are we missing? What aren't we seeing?"

The details. Allie let her gaze drift over the images and reports, certain words and phrases catching before flitting out of her head. Commonalities, similarities among the victims, beyond the red hair and striking expressions. Beyond the locations and the flowers. Beyond the clothes and the background.

Allie snatched Alyssa Knight's school photo off the board.

The background.

"What is it?" Simone was at her side instantly. "What do you see?"

Everyone in the room stopped, turned.

Allie tapped her finger against the bottom-left corner before double-checking with the other pictures. "YM

Photography. It's the same name on each girl's picture, but the logo has changed."

"What?" Eden came over, took the picture. "Why didn't I see that before?"

"Because you were going off copies of a copy that had been cropped. Not to mention Alyssa's picture is fifteen years old," Kyla said. "I contacted each of the schools and asked them to send me the actual photograph as an attachment. I might have dropped your name, Simone," she added without the barest touch of guilt. "Greased the wheels a bit."

"Brilliant," Eden muttered. "Freaking brilliant. How I wish you'd give up this lawyer dream of yours and come work for me."

"You're always trying to steal her," Simone grumbled. "YM Photography," she said to Officer Castillo, who was already typing. "Let's see what we can find out about them."

"First thing that comes up is Your Milestone Photography out of New Hampshire." Castillo scanned the screen. "Nothing else connects to the YM initials that makes sense."

"There's something else," Allie whispered and turned back to the board. "Something that's here but won't come out." She tapped her finger hard against her temple.

"You need to decompress and stop putting so much pressure on yourself," Eden said. "Where's Max? I bet he's good at depressurization. Oh, wait. My bad. That was Vince, right, Simone?"

"We really need to talk about your sense of timing," Simone told her as raised voices exploded from out in the bullpen. "Why do I have the feeling my significant other has returned?" She walked over to the door and stuck her head out. "Yep. So that must be what they call a Strix."

Allie peeked around Simone, barely catching sight of the top of someone's head bobbing in between Jack and Cole as they escorted him toward one of the interview rooms.

"Ease up, man! I ain't done nothing for you to arrest me!"

"Then maybe you shouldn't have run, Strix." Vince walked past the detectives on his way to Simone. "Told you I just wanted to ask you some questions. You're the one who bolted out the back door."

"Private property, man. You don't just get to come in and shake me down!" As they turned the corner Allie caught a glimpse of Strix's wild expression aimed at Max. "Dude's out of control!"

"True," Vince said. "But he's also not a cop."

"Next time don't play battering ram with someone twice your size." Max brought up the rear as if to follow them into the interview room, only to have Vince steer him away.

"Let them speak to him, Max," Vince said. "Get some ice on your hand before it swells too bad."

"What did you do?" Allie grabbed his hand and ran gentle fingers over the backs of his knuckles. "I thought you went to help, not destroy."

"I was waiting out back, just in case," Max's defense sounded oddly rehearsed. "Vince went in to talk to him. Next thing I know the door busts open and out he flies. So I stopped him. Sexy, huh?"

"We'll see how sexy you feel when you can't move your hand. What does he know?" Allie asked Vince as she dragged Max into the break room to grab some ice.

"We didn't have a chance to get that far. Cole will find out soon enough."

"Don't bet on it." Jack joined them, making the normally spacious eating area feel all the more crowded. "He just lawyered up, which means we're in wait mode again."

"Unbelievable." Max sucked in a breath when Allie pressed a cold towel against his knuckles.

"Let me talk to him," Allie said.

"You can't," Jack admonished. "Right, Simone?"

Simone looked pained. "Technically, as you're a contract employee with this department and the DA's office, that would be correct."

"*Technically* I'm not working for either where this case is concerned. I'm working for the Kellan family."

"Well, we aren't letting Mad Max in there," Jack jerked his thumb at Max.

Mad Max? Was that his nickname? Allie turned expectant eyes on Max, who grinned before he shook his head. "Nope. I like that one, though."

"Give me a second." Allie returned to the conference room, had a short chat with Officer Castillo, who gave her the information she needed. Before she headed into the interrogation room, Allie pulled Hope's picture off the board.

When she opened the door, Strix leaped out of his chair, backed up against the wall and then he sagged like a deflating balloon. "I thought you were him."

"Him, who? Vince?"

"Nah. Vince is all right. No, that grunge-rock-looking dude with all the hair." Strix flinched. "Sucker punched me."

"That sounds terrible." Allie put on her sympathetic doctor's persona and handed him a cool towel. "I thought you could use this. Clean yourself up a bit while we wait for your lawyer. If you still think you need one, of course."

"I got hauled out of my place of business without any cause! Of course I need a lawyer."

"Except I'm not a police officer. I'm a doctor. So how about I ask you a couple of questions and if you answer, I'll make sure you're out of here in less than an hour?"

Strix's icy blue eyes narrowed as he scrubbed the towel over his cheeks and under his nose. "You can do that?"

"I can do that." She set Hope's picture on the table and took a seat, motioned for Strix—whose real name was Reynaldo Soyez—to join her. He wasn't very big, barely five feet tall, and he was dressed more like a grade-schooler than the twenty-four-year-old college dropout she knew him to be. He'd had his share of hard knocks according to his juvie file, but he was whip smart, especially when it came to computers and technology. Though he could also be had for the right price. "Do you recognize this girl?" She inched the picture closer to him when he sat.

"Sure." Strix shrugged, his red-and-black flannel shirt bagging around his shoulders. "From the news and the internet. She's missing or something."

"She is. But that's not where you know her from, is it? Because you've seen her picture in those videos you made."

Strix's eyes darted to the side. He didn't respond.

"Hope Kellan was taken from a friend's backyard early yesterday morning. By the same person you programmed this phone for." She pulled out the phone, tapped the screen to show the clock and set it on top of Hope's picture. "That's how long she has to live, Strix.

According to your own program. That's her life counting down in front of your eyes."

The color drained out of Strix's already pale face. "No way!" He shoved the phone away, shook his head so hard she was afraid he'd start bleeding again. "No way, man. I don't have anything to do with any kidnapping or killing. I just write the program. They asked for a countdown clock—that's what I gave them. What they do with it ain't my concern."

"Except it is your concern, Strix. Especially when you sign your work. We saw the owl and 'Strix' is Latin for *owl*. That's all Vince wanted to ask you about—who hired you. You tell us that, you're free to go."

Strix didn't look convinced. "That's it? That's all you want to know? You're not trying to fit me up for more?"

"All I care about is finding Hope Kellan. I'm betting your client didn't expect you to leave a digital fingerprint like you did, so feel free to give us everything you know about them. Consider it an investment in your future."

Strix's eyes shot from the picture of Hope to the phone and then back to Allie. "It was all done online," Strix said. "Client tells me what they want and I customize it for them. Clock, video and graphics. Shipping and handling included in the price."

"How was payment arranged?"

"Cash. That was weird," Strix said as if it were an afterthought. "Usually I prefer digital currency, you know? Through backdoor channels on the dark web. You know what that is, right?"

"Sure." The internet underground where far more nasty and disturbing crimes went virtually unnoticed except by specialized law enforcement teams. "But this person paid cash?"

"Sent in the mail if you can believe it. Ten grand because it was a rush job. Money arrived with one envelope for both phones. I sent them within forty-eight hours."

Allie inclined her head. "Both phones?"

"Yeah, this program only works with someone on the other end deciding what to code in."

"Like a remote control for a TV?"

Strix appeared impressed. "Yeah, like that. Anyway, once I send it back, I'm done and out. Not my circus, not my monkeys, you know?"

She knew. "Where did you mail it, Strix? Who did you send it to?"

"I don't know off the top of my head." Given his squawking tone she understood where his nickname came from. "That's back at my place."

"Oh." Allie nodded. "Okay, then. I guess I'll let Detectives Delaney and MacTavish know so they can apply for a search warrant. I'm sure your reputation will survive every piece of electrical equipment being confiscated by the police." She stood up and reached for the phone and picture. "Let me thank you in advance for all the unsolved cases you're about to help the Sacramento Metro PD solve, Strix."

"No, wait! Hold up. Um." Strix's knees began to bounce excitedly. "Hang on. The information might be on my cell phone. It was some random company back east. New Hampshire, I think? If I can get my cell back, I can find out the address exactly."

Allie's blood warmed. "YM Photography?"

Strix's expression shifted from stunned to irritated. "You playing me now? You already knew?"

"Not for sure. Thanks, Strix. Someone will be in to take care of you in a few minutes."

"That's what I'm afraid of."

Allie closed the door behind her as Vince, Max, Jack and Lieutenant Santos emerged from the observation room next door.

"Nice interrogation techniques, Doc," Max said.

"Impressive," Santos agreed. "Care to share the relevance of Your Milestone Photography?"

"They took all the murder victims' school photographs," Allie said. "Max? Can you have Joe send you a scanned image of Hope's latest picture?"

"Don't have to. We just got them a couple of weeks ago and I have one on my phone. I'll print off a copy."

"It's my brother. I need to take this," Vince held up his phone and angled a look at Max that had Allie wondering just what had gone on with the two of them while they'd been gone.

"We've got something," Eden announced when they returned to the conference room. "We talked to the receptionist at the home office of Your Milestone Photography in New Hampshire. Turns out they're one of the country's biggest photography vendors with offices all over, but when it comes to smaller and more rural schools, they contract out to local talent. When I asked for a list of contractors for the last twenty years, they started in on the confidentiality spiel."

"Did they?" Simone said. "Give me their number, please."

Eden grinned. "Magic time?"

"You bet." Simone left to make the call. "Stay tuned for that list, Castillo."

"A photographer with access to children makes for good hunting ground," Jack said. "Doesn't explain how he knew where Hope and her friends would be this weekend."

"Actually it might," Kyla said. "I followed a hunch and called Hope's school, asked about the photographer who took the school photos this year. Turns out the photographer was new and hoping to grow her business. She offered substantial discounts on family portraits that included her coming out to the house on the family's schedule."

"She?" Allie frowned. "You said *her* and *she*."

"That's what the school secretary said," Kyla confirmed.

"That's an offer a lot of families wouldn't turn down," Eden said. "Especially with the holidays coming up. Any idea if there were any takers?"

"The school didn't keep track."

"Max?" Allie went out to where Max was waiting for his picture of Hope to print out. "Do you know if Joe had any family pictures taken lately?"

Max shook his head. "Not that I know of. At least not since I've been here."

"We need to check with the Vander—" Allie looked down at the picture. "What's that?" She pointed to the tiny discoloration in the bottom-right corner.

"Don't know. This is the third time I've printed it. Must be on the image itself."

"Yes," she whispered. "On the image itself." Her heart thudded so heavy in her chest she could barely breathe. She ran to the conference room, pushing people out of the way as she searched for the picture that had been left in the flowerpot at the girls' tent. "Where is it? Where's the picture of us as girls? The one we found in the plant at the girls' tent?"

"Here!" Eden sorted through the stack of plastic evidence bags left in the box. "Why?"

Allie grabbed it, peered at it, at the small round discoloration in the bottom-right corner. "It's the same thing. The same defect."

"What are you talking about?" Eden leaned over her shoulder. "What is?"

"That glare or flare or whatever it is. Right there? See? It's on Hope's school picture. Same corner." All those scattered thoughts that had been zinging through her brain began to coalesce. "Jack? Call the Vandermonts again and find out if they accepted the discount offer. If they did, the person's been in their house. He'd know the layout of it and the grounds."

"Right away," Jack said.

Why did it feel as if everything she'd clung to in her past was disintegrating in her hands? "Allie?" Eden said. "I remember the day this was taken. And if I do, I know you do, too."

Allie wanted another answer, any other answer, except the one presenting itself. All the memories that had made her smile, that had helped her get through the rough days evaporated. "Eden, we have to be wrong. He wouldn't have, couldn't have—"

"Who wouldn't have or couldn't have?" Lieutenant Santos's question cut through the noise in the room.

"Allie? It's the only explanation."

"Mission accomplished!" Simone announced upon her return. "Your Milestone Photography will be send-

ing the list of their contractors, along with delivery records of all packages they've received and forwarded
on in the last six months. Don't everyone thank me
at once." She looked around, her spine going ramrod-
straight. "I missed something, didn't I? Honestly, I leave
the room for a few seconds and you go and solve it."
Allie jolted when Simone's gaze landed on hers. "We
know who it is?"

"Enough already." Jack reached out and snatched
the photograph, evidence bag and all, out of Allie's
grasp. He pushed it into Simone's hand. "Who took
this picture?"

"Oh, I remember that. Tyler Goodale did. It was a
couple of days after Christmas the year before Chloe…"
Her voice trailed off before she blinked herself back to
attention. "Tyler? You're thinking Tyler killed Chloe?"
She dropped her hand. "Oh, Allie."

"Tyler Goodale? As in Nicole and Patrick Goodale?
Allie's foster siblings?" Lieutenant Santos asked.

"Even if Tyler killed Chloe, he doesn't have Hope."
Allie trembled, unable to ignore the anger in the lieutenant's voice. "It's impossible."

"Why exactly?" the lieutenant pushed.

"Because Tyler Goodale is dead," Allie said. "He
committed suicide five years ago."

Chapter 14

White noise erupted in Max's ears.

"If Tyler killed Chloe, and Tyler is dead—" he could barely hear himself "—would someone please tell me who has my niece?" The last bit of control Max held on to slipped free. The light faded in Allie's eyes as the reality of the situation hit; the cool, detached doctor reemerged and overtook the determined, passionate woman he needed—they needed—to solve the case.

The room fell into an uneasy silence, punctuated by the occasional tapping of fingers on a keyboard.

"How did Tyler die?" Cole asked.

"Um." Allie scrubbed her fingers across her forehead. "Nicole told me he hanged himself in his hospital room. He'd been hospitalized off and on for years. Same psychotic diagnosis as their mother. I'm not sure exactly. Like I told Max before, I lost track of them over the years."

"Did she tell you he died?" Vince asked from where he stood in the doorway scanning his phone. "Because according to his medical records, Tyler Goodale *attempted* suicide by hanging five years ago. After which he was declared officially brain-dead and subsequently released into the care of his family, one P. Goodale, who had him admitted to a private medical facility near Redding. Although looking at the list of patients currently in-house—" He shook his head. "He's not listed there now. Hang on. I've got more information coming in."

"Why do you insist on breaking the law in a police station and around a DA?" Simone asked her fiancé.

"Because I love the danger." Vince's gaze flickered briefly in her direction before he returned his attention to the phone. "Tyler Goodale was released into the custody of Patrick eighteen months ago. No trace of him since. Strange thing is…" He lifted his phone closer to his face. "Different signatures for Patrick's name. Not even close."

"So Tyler's still alive?" Allie couldn't have looked more stunned if a gang of elephants had just blown through the door. "That can't be right. Nicole wouldn't have lied."

"Not if she holds you responsible for what happened to her brother." Vince walked toward her, held out his phone. "Photographs of Tyler's hospital room taken by the authorities. Seems he wrote *tell Allie I'm sorry* in his own blood before he did the deed."

Max only caught a flash of the image but enough to understand why Allie's face went pale.

"But why? And why would Nicole do that? She's my friend." She turned pleading eyes on Simone and then Eden, neither of whom could explain.

"While Nicole might be many things, she's clearly not your friend," Max said with probably a bit more attitude than was necessary. "She was here only a few hours ago, asking what we knew, if we had any leads. They wanted to know how close we were to the truth."

Allie's eyes cleared at Max's accusation. "Despite what they said, they didn't come here to check on me."

"They didn't have to," Eden said from behind one of the computer techs. "I'm looking at the surveillance footage from the conference right now. Stop it, there." She tapped a finger on the screen. "Nicole and Patrick were in the crowd. There, in the back."

"They're a hard couple to miss," Cole agreed.

"I want a BOLO order on Nicole and Patrick Goodale right now," Lieutenant Santos snapped to the room and his people scattered.

"Check Lembranza first," Eden called to her husband as he left with Jack.

"Hang on," Simone said in an unusually placating tone. "Nicole's lies aside, we're basing this sudden suspicion about Patrick and Nicole kidnapping Hope on a flaw in a photograph from twenty years ago that they didn't even take. That's a huge leap. And who uses a camera from two decades before? Especially in a business?"

"Sentimentality?" Allie supposed. "My father bought Tyler that camera. He thought it would help Tyler bond with his mother, who was also a photographer."

"I don't know."

"You're still not convinced?" Allie asked Eden. "What happened to the pounce-now, ask-questions-later Eden St. Claire?"

"She learned her lesson the hard way."

"So you want to dig deeper?" Allie pressed.

"I want to excavate completely to make sure we're on the right track," Eden said. "And you'd be thinking the same thing if you weren't hurting at the moment. One dot does not prove anything, Allie. Let's find more. Let's be sure."

"What other dots are you thinking about?" Max said even as he tamped down the growing anxiety building in his chest. They were a step closer, even as the clock ticked down.

"Jace finished running background checks on both Patrick and Nicole," Vince said.

"That was fast." Simone frowned at him.

"Not really," Vince said. "I asked him to do it a few hours ago."

"At my suggestion," Max volunteered and flinched when Allie turned blank eyes on him. "Told you I got weird vibes off them. I didn't want to be right."

"It's okay," Allie said, but she wrapped her arms around her waist in that way she had when she closed herself off. "I don't blame you."

She didn't. She blamed herself, not that he could deal with that just then.

"Patrick has a record from when he was a kid. Petty stuff. Stealing, breaking and entering." Vince read off details. "Files were sealed."

"Again, I'm standing right here," Simone said. "If you could stop breaking privacy laws or at least telling me you're breaking them?" She seemed to rethink her stance. "Then again, it wouldn't be a horrible thing if those prints happen to make it to Eamon and the FBI."

"So they can compare them to what?" Eden challenged. "No prints other than Hope's have been found on anything—not on the phone, not on the flowers in Allie's basement. The only anomaly has been Chloe's prints on the perfume bottle, but I'm nowhere near figuring that one out. So, in essence, we have nothing."

"Sporadic school records," Vince went on. "For all three of the Goodales. Moved around a lot every three or four months. The time they were at the Hollisters seems to be the most uneventful—almost three years of nothing. Then they were turned back over to their mother. After that, there's not a lot on record that's abnormal. Community college for Patrick and Nicole. He went to work in construction and Nicole went from state to state. Looks like she was mostly working in the restaurant industry."

"Patrick would have been about seventeen when they left us," Allie said. "Nicole, sixteen. That would have made Tyler fourteen? About the time that particular type of psychosis starts to manifest."

"Why would Tyler have killed Chloe?" Max asked. "Did he know her?"

"We all knew him," Simone said. "We all liked him. He was quiet. Withdrawn but always very kind. Gentle. Especially with Allie. Whip smart. Could fix anything. Toys, electronics, gadgets."

Vince snorted. "So putting together a camera of old and new parts probably wouldn't have been difficult for him. New technology tied to what he knew and loved, what your father gave him, Allie."

"Tyler was lost," Allie agreed. "They all were, but there was something different about Tyler. He missed his mom even though she had been violent with them—with Tyler, especially. He'd have done anything to connect with her."

"Milestone came through," Castillo announced. "I'm running through the list of photography contractors who worked with YM right now. I could use a second pair of eyes. I'm not entirely sure what I'm looking for." The officer's dark eyes darted from side to side as she read. "Twenty years' worth is a lot."

"Keep going," Allie said and leaned over her shoulder. "I'm reading with you."

"Neither Patrick nor Nicole are at the restaurant," Cole said as he reentered the conference room. "No one's seen them since last night when they closed."

"What's that one?" Allie pointed to one of the businesses. "PNT. They have multiple California addresses, including one in the city where Rosalie Jenson's body was found behind the strip mall."

"Why that business?" Max asked.

"PNT? Patrick, Nicole, Tyler," Vince answered.

"It can't really be that simple, can it?" Eden sounded doubtful. "Honestly, it's like someone's laying out the bread crumbs for us. That's either really stupid or very arrogant."

"Well, we know they aren't stupid," Simone said. "And they aren't hiding anymore. Showing up here to talk to Allie proves that."

"That's it. PNT." Allie took a step back.

"You're sure?" Cole circled around to read the screen.

"Look at the listed owner," Allie told him.

"P.G. Ale," Cole read out loud.

"Patrick Goodale," Eden said. "Okay, I'm convinced."

"Me, too," Lieutenant Santos confirmed. "Now let's find them."

* * *

Allie slammed her fist into the heavy bag, taking not one ounce of her usual joy in watching it swing. Another punch, and another. She hopped back, kicked, kicked again until she felt the back of her thigh burn in effort. Sweat poured down her face, ran into her eyes, the sensation welcome as she pummeled her frustration, her anger, her rage out of her system.

The basement stairs creaked, but she didn't stop. Couldn't stop. Every punch she landed, every strike she made, would exorcise the demons gnawing at her insides. Her chest ached; her lungs strained. She embraced the reminder she was still alive. Still breathing.

All these years. Punch. All this time. Punch. Punch. Every day that passed when she'd wondered, every day she'd lost trying to solve a mystery where the answer ended up being closer to home than she'd ever realized.

Tyler.

Punch. Punch. Punch.

All these years and it had been Tyler who was responsible for her nightmares.

Tyler. A sob caught in her throat. Sweet, caring, attentive Tyler who had held her while she'd cried over the loss of her friend. With hands that had choked the life out of that friend.

Punch. Punch. Kick. Kick.

And now Nicole was… What? Taking his place in tormenting her? Picking up where Tyler and his derangements had left off?

Allie turned, meaning to roundhouse the bag, only to have her knee give out. She dropped to the mat like a stone. She swore and slammed her fist into the padding.

"That heavy bag will never harm another person as long as it lives."

She squeezed her eyes shut so tight she saw stars. "Not now, Max."

She didn't want him here, didn't want to hear his humor however he managed to find a way to use it. Not when it was someone she knew, someone she'd trusted, who was responsible for so much devastation. "Don't come down here unless you have something positive to report." Like news that Patrick and Nicole were locked deep in a cell with no chance of escape.

Then she'd get Hope's location out of them. It would only take a minute…

"Depends on your definition of *positive*."

She knew what he was doing by letting the statement linger: daring her to look at him, to engage in a coherent conversation while all she wanted to do was continue to beat the leather bag. The silence stretched, thinned. Grated on her last, frayed nerve.

She surrendered, pushed herself up and stared at him.

There he sat, Max Kellan, wearing sweats and a tank, sitting on her staircase watching every move she made. How could he look at her with such understanding? Such patience? The idea of it reignited the banking rage as she ripped her gloves off. "Don't just sit there. You want in on this?"

"Thought you'd never ask." He pushed to his feet, took the steps to the basement and stood on the other side of the heavy bag. "You want to punch through this first? Or just have at—"

She lunged, striking out, locked her hands around his arm in two places and rotated fast enough to flip him onto his back. Allie moved in, hands still clasping his arm, and pushed her foot against the base of his throat.

"Huh." He blinked those amazing eyes up at her. "You can't see it, but that was my ego you just crushed."

"Get up." She let go and shoved back, hands up, fisted in front of her face. "Go again. This time fight back."

He drew his legs back, rocked up to his feet. He turned as she struck out. This time he dodged and ducked, avoiding the hit, doubling over as her foot found his stomach. He cursed even as he caught her ankle and shoved her back. She hopped, wrenched her foot free and caught her balance.

Readied herself again.

"I don't know if this is doing much for you." He grunted when she hammered out at him. "But I've never had a woman turn me on this hard and this fast before." His eyes narrowed as her vision blurred.

This time when she punched at him, he locked his hand around her wrist, rotated their position and drew her own arm hard up across her neck. She slammed her foot down on his bare one, lifted it immediately with plans to drive it back and into his knee, but he shifted position again, spun her out and then over.

She hit the mat hard on her back, the force driving the air from her chest. He stood over her, feet on either side of her thighs as he planted his hands on his hips. "You let me know when you're done."

"I'm done." She dropped her arms to her side, waiting, watching, keeping her eyes on his as she saw him relax and shift his weight to step away from her. She swept her legs around and knocked his feet out from under him.

He landed next to her, feet by her head, as the air whooshed out of his lungs. "Note to self," he said, groaning and holding up two hands in surrender, "best fake out ever. In related news, you've managed to drain every ounce of testosterone out of me."

"Not yet, I haven't." She launched herself over him, locked her knees on either side of his hips and gripped his hands in hers. Her blood pounded through her veins, like a war drum calling her to action. Never mind the consequences. Never mind what was appropriate or right. "But I'm about to."

She kissed him. Kissed him the way she'd dreamed of being kissed. As if every breath she took depended on it. His fingers flexed in hers as he opened his mouth to her demanding one. She moved forward, sliding her body along his as her tongue dueled with his. She didn't want to think. Didn't want to reason things out, rationalize another thought.

She only wanted to feel something other than pain.

Allie tore her mouth free, far enough to gaze down at him, to make sure he understood. She didn't want words, didn't want platitudes or flowery poems of seduction. She wanted him. Around her. Inside of her.

For once, Allie declared as that mouth of his twitched in amused understanding, she was going to take what she wanted.

"Do it, Doc." He sat up and released her hands. His fingers skimmed down her sides, the heaviness of him pressing hard and urgent against her core and making her moan. He slipped his hands under the band of her sports bra, tugged it over her head in a fluid motion when she raised her arms. "Take what you need."

"I need you." She kissed him again, drew his tongue

into her mouth, teeth scraping against teeth as his hands slipped to her back, pressed her into his chest. The fabric of his shirt rubbed against her nipples, had her making low, raw sounds in her throat until she returned the favor by dragging his shirt over his head.

She felt him tense under her touch as she shifted back, an inch and then another, until he held her hips and flipped her under him. He kissed her, his hands, then his mouth, tracing over her breasts. The whiskers of his barely there beard ignited explosions of pleasure that rocketed through her body.

Allie drew her legs up, cradled him between her thighs as his mouth and hands moved down between her breasts, to her stomach, her navel. His tongue dipped in as his fingers gripped the waist of her shorts. He drew them down, down, and she lifted her hips, impatient to feel him, to have him.

She felt the cool basement air against her bare, slick-with-sweat skin, but wherever he touched her, wherever his body brushed hers, a warmth spread and drove her closer to the edge. "Your turn." His fingers teased, tempted, tantalized until she felt her legs go weak and fall.

"Max," she gasped. "Don't you dare. Not without you." She dropped her hands onto his head, flexed her fingers in the thickness of his hair and thought she'd never felt anything so good, so right.

"Not to worry."

She didn't have to see him to know he was grinning. Her entire body was buzzing, like frayed electrical wires sparking. He shifted up, long enough to divest himself of his pants, only to dive after them when he tossed them almost out of reach.

She lifted herself up on her elbows. "What are you—oh." She couldn't help it. At the sight of the foil packet, she arched a brow. "That sure of yourself when you came down here, were you?"

"I thought I could offer you another outlet for your energies," he agreed. He ripped open the foil, handed it to her. She looked down at him, hard and ready, pulsing. For her. She licked her lips. "I think I'm going to leave it to you. Whenever you're ready, of course." She scooted back, just a little, so she could watch as he covered himself. The second he moved toward her, she lay back, opened herself.

She could feel him, all of him, almost where she needed him. Right where she wanted him. Allie reached up, framed his face in her hands. She kissed him, eyes wide open, staring into his eyes, into him, as he filled her.

She moaned, or was that him? She couldn't be sure. But for a moment—one long, beautiful, heart-stopping moment—they lay there, breathing in unison, joined. And then he began to move.

She couldn't hold on tight enough, couldn't stop meeting him, thrust for thrust. She tightened her thighs around his hips, tried to draw him in farther, deeper, so she couldn't feel where she ended and he began. Her hands fisted against his back, inched down, gripped his hips and drew him closer. His hair brushed around her face as he lowered his mouth, kissed her again as he increased his pace.

Allie felt his body tighten as her own did, and she knew he was—she was—close. She could barely breathe, didn't want to, didn't need to as he drove them higher as one. He looked into her eyes, in that brief second just before, and then they were soaring over the cliff.

Together.

Just as she'd dreamed.

"I never realized just how squeaky these workout mats could be."

The exhaustion that had been blanketing Allie, along with Max, evaporated. Eyes wide, she glanced down and felt an odd sensation at the image of his head resting on her breast as he traced light, chill-inducing circles around her navel.

"Tell me Eden and Simone left before you came down here." She already knew the answer. Knowing one or both of her friends, they would have taken an inordinate amount of pleasure in finding the perfect time to, well, interrupt.

"They left about ten minutes after we got here," Max said. "They said they'll be in touch when they know something."

"You mean when Patrick and Nicole are tracked down." She moved to push Max off her, but he leaned up, stilled her with a look. "Tell me that's not silent speak for round two."

"I only brought one condom down with me. I didn't want to get really cocky." He abandoned her stomach for her lips. "Whatever Patrick and Nicole are responsible for, it's not your fault, Allie."

She couldn't believe her ears. "How can you say that? They kidnapped your niece!"

"I know." And just like that, the afterglow evaporated. He rolled off and lay beside her on his back. "But by now they have to realize we're on to them. Why else would they have disappeared so completely?"

"How completely?" She didn't want to know, didn't want to hear what had been discussed or realized since they left the station.

"They're not at the restaurant or either address listed as residences. Jack and Vince are currently culling through all the different businesses and employers they've worked for and with over the years. If they have property, we'll find it. If we need to lock down a connection between Tyler and one of the other victims, we can now." He hesitated. "The strip mall where the third victim was found had a florist shop in it. And next door was a photography studio."

Allie didn't think she'd feel the next hit when it came, but she did. And it hurt just as much as the previous ones. "PNT Photography?"

"Yes."

She squeezed her eyes shut and shoved the information aside. "We have to do something. Figure the rest of this out. Before the clock runs out." The clock. "Oh, no." Allie rolled onto her knees, scrambled across the mat and grabbed the phone she'd left on the floor. She tapped the screen open. "Fifteen hours." Her stomach rolled. "Until what?" She shook the phone with both hands. "Fifteen hours until what?" She yelled.

"Stop. Allie, stop." Max wrapped his arms around her, drew her into him as she trembled. "We're going to figure this out. I refuse to believe it's going to end as badly as you're thinking. This isn't about Hope. She's a weapon they're using against you. They want you angry, they want you not thinking straight. This isn't about hurting her. It's about hurting you. For whatever reason, Nicole and Patrick want you to hurt."

"Why?" She let him hold her, let him rock her, because for now, in this basement of solitude she'd created, she could surrender. "Why do they want to hurt me? What happened to Tyler wasn't my fault! I didn't even know. I never even visited him." Was that it? Should she have? Was that the mistake she'd made that led to all this?

"You need to come to terms with the fact you might never get the answers you need," Max whispered. "But, in the meantime, did you get enough of a workout that you can focus again?" He cradled her head against his chest. "Or do you need to have me again? Because I'm not adverse to it. I've heard practice actually does make perfect."

"If we practice much more, we might kill each other." Allie managed a light chuckle. She held on to him, her anchor. Her tether. She couldn't imagine going through this without him, could barely remember what it had been like before they met, except now she knew just how lonely she'd been. Now he was part of her, and not just her body. But part of her heart. "I think I could do with a shower, though." She tilted her chin back. "I have a fairly large one upstairs. If you'd like to give it a try."

"I don't know." She couldn't be sure if the uncertainty shining in his eyes was a teasing glint or not. "I don't have the best of relationships with slippery surfaces."

"Then it's a good thing I'm an expert in traction." She popped up and kissed him quickly. "Race you upstairs."

She pushed off him hard enough to have him tumbling back on the mat. Allie took the stairs two at a time, half afraid he wouldn't follow. Equally worried he would.

Her life had always been divided into two: before Chloe's murder and after.

Now the rest of her life would be divided again thanks to Max.

What would she do if there was an after?

Chapter 15

"Either we've somehow hive-minded in the last couple of hours or you're thinking so loud I can hear you." Max tightened his arms around Allie and drew her more snugly against him in her bed. He curled around her. The warmth and comfort of her body pressed into him and brought a sense of peace he hadn't felt, well, ever.

"Sorry." Allie reached for the two phones sitting faceup on her nightstand. He slid his fingers down her arm, through her fingers, and drew her away. "Max—"

"We both know they'll light up the second you get a message or a call." Hopefully not a new countdown clock. Every second that ticked by felt like a stab to the heart. "Let it be, Allie." Even as he wished for her to push all thoughts of Hope and Nicole and Patrick aside, he couldn't. It wasn't Allie's spinning wheels keeping him awake. It was the unending sensation that the ride they were all on had absolutely no mapped-out path. Just twists and turns and motion-sickness-inducing drops. Then again, Allie did possess an amazing capacity for diverting his attention. She wiggled her backside against him and he groaned. "Let that be, too."

In the dim light of her table lamp, he saw her turn her head and smile. She broke his hold and turned over. She rested her head in the crook of his shoulder, draped her arm over his waist. Despite their rather vigorous physical activity, her body was still as tight as a rubber band being stretched to its limits. Max drew light fingers up and down her spine, willing her to relax.

"I'm thinking now is a good time to ask exactly what you have against therapists?"

And there went any hope of him relaxing. "Don't tell me this was all some erotic ruse to get me to open up."

"Hmm." She nestled into him, pushed a leg between his. "Maybe. Why do you hate us?"

"I don't hate all of you." His mind raced, searching for an escape from this discussion. "Just one or two in particular."

"Is this where you tell me what happened in Florida?" She traced lazy circles on his chest. "Why did you get forced out of your job?"

"You mean your supersleuthing friends haven't told you?" Given the background checks that had been run in the last few days, he couldn't imagine one of them hadn't uncovered the truth.

"Jack hinted at some disciplinary issues, which honestly didn't surprise me. But he didn't have any details. At least not ones he shared." She lifted her head and stroked the side of his face. "Your friends were very loyal, Max. No one had a bad word to say about you when Jack reached out."

"Then he didn't speak to the right people." He wanted to make a joke out of it, needed to, but the truth was, even now, despite losing the job he'd loved, he didn't regret what he'd done. He caught her hand in his, brought it up to his mouth and kissed her fingers to soften the truth. He owed her that much. "I assaulted my captain. Well, the interim captain who came in when ours was injured."

"Assaulted how?" She asked the question so casually, it was as if they were discussing what leftovers she might have stashed in her fridge.

He drew his chin back, raised his brows. "You want the how rather than the why?" That didn't quite track with what he knew about her.

"I'll take a wild guess at the why and say he hurt someone you care about. How much damage did you do?"

"Not as much as I would have liked. Enough that I could have faced felony charges." And he would have served his time gladly. "Yes, I know how that sounds. Especially to a shri—psychologist." He corrected himself and earned a grateful smile. "I broke his jaw and his nose. Cracked a couple of ribs. He survived. Can't say the same thing for three of my friends."

She was quiet then, her expression unchanging as she processed his admission. "Tell me what happened."

Was this the therapist talking or the woman he was sleeping with? He couldn't be sure. Did it matter? Apparently not, since his normal trepidation about venturing too deep into this topic had yet to manifest itself and drive him into silence.

"We were on day twelve of fighting a wildfire, trying to get a handle on it. Not easy given the shortage of rain in the last few years. I don't know that there's any way to describe the conditions a wildfire presents, if anyone can ever understand what fighting it entails unless you've done it." He realized how that must sound and cringed.

"No offense taken. Go on."

He wasn't sure if he was relieved or concerned she automatically took his word for things. "When our CO was injured, they brought in a new guy, one of those newly promoted eager beavers who kept being moved up to get him out of people's way. At the time, the fire was pretty well contained so the higher-ups didn't figure he could do much damage. I went to catch a few hours of sleep and when they woke me up—" He could still smell the smoke, feel the panicked hammering of his heart when he'd looked into his partner's eyes and knew, he *knew* something had gone very, very wrong. "Turned out he had negligible experience with wildfires, but he was the only one of rank in the area they could pull in at the last minute. He was only supposed to be in charge for a couple of hours."

She took a deep breath. "I'm beginning to understand already."

"He sent three of my buddies to an area we'd already contained, told them to plow it under even though the wind advisory put that area at significant risk for a flare-up. He ignored the report, ignored the warnings and sent them anyway. We had a skeleton crew, so there wasn't anyone high enough up in rank to challenge him. They were just kids. They trusted him." Max didn't realize how hard he'd been squeezing Allie's hand. He tried to relax, to loosen his hold, but all he could feel were those flames exploding around him as he'd choked on the smoke that had coated the air in a thick, suffocating layer. "The winds can shift on a dime. There's no warning and nothing you can do to stop it. Next thing I remember hearing was their screams."

He squeezed his eyes shut, turned his head on the pillow and tried to shift away. Allie held on, turned her hand in his and gripped harder.

"Go on." Her gentle urging was like a balm to the burns on his heart. "Get it out, Max. It's the only way you can finally start to put it behind you."

As if that were possible. "We managed to pull Bixby free after he dived in to get to them, but he had burns over fifty percent of his body. Solo and Princeton didn't make it out."

"And you blamed the interim captain."

"You better believe it." He still did and the anger burned like a torch inside of him. "Maybe if he'd shown an ounce of remorse or taken the tiniest bit of responsibility, I'd have let it go and settled for doing everything I could to make sure he would never work a fire line again. Instead, at the hearings he chose to play the martyr, blame the communications system, said he'd been given the wrong report and that he didn't know about the wind change until it was too late. It didn't matter three other people testified they'd seen the report both before and after him. What mattered is the committee was loaded with people this guy had worked with for years. I was sitting there, in the front row, listening to him denigrate our unit, my men. My friends. He blamed them for their own deaths and injuries. When he finished, he stood up, turned and looked at me." Max took a deep breath. "Then he smiled."

Anger sparked like flint in her eyes. "That's when you punched him."

"Don't ask me if I regret it because I don't."

"I didn't think for a second you did. Except you must miss it. The firefighting."

"Yeah, well." He shrugged again. There were days when he didn't know what to do with himself. He just felt so useless, and when sirens sounded, his first instinct was to suit up. "If that's the price I had to pay to make sure he would never be in a command position again, it was worth it. That was the deal I struck—go quietly with a severance package in exchange for him being prohibited from ever having any say or oversight again. Last I heard he'd gone to work for a lobbyist in Washington."

"Unless I'm missing something, none of this explains your issues with mental health professionals like myself."

"Not like you." Surprised he actually meant it, Max shifted his focus to her, to her beautiful face, that crop of hair that felt like silk in his fingers. How had she become so important, so vital, so fast? "You listen. You discuss. You exchange ideas, but you don't lecture or tell someone how they're supposed to feel. You don't come in with an agenda but with a curiosity for the truth in the hopes of helping people. You don't presume to understand and placate your patients. Do you?"

"No. In my mind, that would do more damage than good. You'd be lying to them. The patient should always come first."

"Exactly. But Bixby was sent to see a woman who

didn't see anything more than a patient number. I don't think she even tried. She just gave him whatever meds she thought were appropriate. So he changed doctors. Who prescribed more meds. From then on, whenever I saw him, he never seemed to be doing better. And then he just stopped. Everything. Therapy, going out, spending time with his family." He angled his chin down, caught the sympathy in her eyes and, for the first time since they'd buried Bixby, he accepted it without question. "He overdosed a few months ago. On purpose. Left a note for his wife and kids, checked himself into a motel and just went to sleep. In the room, they found six different anti-anxiety prescriptions from four different doctors. None of them bothered to check with the others. They just gave him a bottle and sent him on his way."

"I'm so sorry, Max." Allie moved up and pressed her mouth to his.

"Did they even try to help him? Was there something I could have done, something I should have said—"

"I don't know the answer to that. And I'm sorry to be a realist, but you never will. I'm betting you know that." She placed her hand against his chest. "And that's what's breaking your heart. I wish I'd been there. I wish I could have tried to help. I'm so sorry you lost your friends."

"Me, too." The next breath he took felt clean, pure. Like stepping into a morning rain that washed away the past. "All of it. They were great guys."

"I'm also glad you came out here to start over. With your brother and Hope." She stopped there, as if uncertain what to say. What to admit next as she searched his face for an answer.

He knew the feeling. Things had shifted for him,

completely turned upside-down, and right now, he couldn't imagine being anywhere else or with anyone other than her. "Don't forget about the spunky psychologist who has an amazingly talented—"

She stopped him with a kiss and he felt her smile against his mouth.

"Mind. I was going to say *mind*." He let go of her hand so he could slip his hands into her hair. "I absolutely love your mind." Max kissed her again, rolled her under him and, as she opened herself to him again, he surrendered to the fall, landing be damned.

"Come on, Allie! Over here, hurry!"

Allie opened her eyes against the barely there morning sun, streams of light bursting across the field of knee-high grass and sprigs of wild violets. She turned, searched, listened. That voice. She hadn't heard it in years, for almost as long as she could remember and yet...

She knew that voice.

"Over here, Allie!"

Joy sprung into Allie's chest as she turned and walked toward the giant oak tree that loomed over the field like an ancient guardian. A flash of color—red, almost the color of ripe strawberries—drew her closer and she picked up speed. Began to run.

"Chloe!" She burst across the field, her body singing with excitement and anticipation. Blades of grass and chaotic weeds reached out to catch her, to tangle around her legs, but she kicked them free. "Chloe, I hear you! Where are you?"

Nothing. No response. Allie stopped, lay her hand flat against the rough bark of the tree trunk. Dreaming, she told herself. She was dreaming. That dull pounding, slow, slow, steady beat, was the echo of her heartbeat while her mind projected her heart's one wish.

But it wouldn't come true. Allie pressed a hand against her mouth. It couldn't come true. Chloe was dead. Gone. Had been for two decades. And yet, here she was, in this field where Allie's life had both ended and begun.

"Oh, Chloe." Tears blurred her vision as she lifted her face to the sun. "I miss you so much."

"Here I am, silly."

Allie spun around.

There Chloe Evans stood in the faded overalls and bright-colored T-shirt, her mismatched shoes and crooked pigtails. The red of her hair glimmered in the sunlight. Her smile lit her entire face.

"Chloe?" Allie reached out and grabbed hold, her breath skipping when she could actually feel her friend fold into her arms and return her embrace. "Chloe, I've missed you so much." Allie shut her eyes, afraid for when she opened them and Chloe would be gone again. She stepped back, keeping a hold of the small hands that had clapped and clung and snapped with her own. "We've all missed you."

"I know. But I've always been here," Chloe said in that matter-of-fact tone she had. She grinned, exposed her crooked front teeth. "I've always been with all of you. You and Eden and Simone. You grew up without me."

Allie nodded. "I know. I'm sorry. Why are we here? This was where we found you."

"I had to come show you. Time's running out, Allie. You have to save her."

"Hope? You know about Hope?" Allie swiped the tears off her cheeks. "I don't know where she is. Can you tell me?"

"I already have." She tugged on Allie's hand and led her around the tree. A thick outcropping of bushes stretched and meandered, brambles and branches criss-crossing their way through the wild field. "You don't have to be sad, Allie. Not anymore. Please don't be sad about me."

"I can't help it. You were my best friend." Allie didn't want to walk any farther; she just wanted to sit and talk with her friend. "Where have you been?"

"Right here." Chloe pressed her hand against Allie's chest. "I never went anywhere. But you can stop worrying about me now. All of you."

"It was Tyler who hurt you, wasn't it?" The anger hit her full bore and nearly drove her to her knees. "He was my friend, my foster brother, and he did this to you." He took her from them.

Chloe nodded. "He didn't mean it. He was scared. He knew he shouldn't have taken me, but he was lonely and then..." Chloe shook her head. "He hurt so much, Allie. He was in so much pain." She pulled the collar of her shirt down and displayed red welts in the shape of fingermarks. "I heard him crying when I couldn't breathe. But then I didn't hurt. But he did. And he was so, so sorry."

"But why?" Allie blinked more tears. "Why did he take you?" Bells chimed in the distance.

Chloe pulled her hand free, backed away as she searched the sky. "You need to wake up, Allie. You have to find Hope. Now. She needs you. She's in danger."

Chloe took a step back and then another. And another. Until she faded from sight.

"No, Chloe, wait!"

"Chloe!" Allie shot up and reached for her friend, but found only the early-morning darkness of her bedroom. She put a hand over her mouth to catch the sob as she tucked her knees into her chest. Cold, so cold she shivered. And then Max was there, arms around her as he turned her toward him.

"It's okay, Allie. I've got you."

"She spoke to me," she whispered and grabbed hold of him as if he, too, were going to disappear. "It's the first time in all these years." Even now the dream was fading, but she could still hear Chloe's voice telling her that Allie knew where to find Hope. Except she didn't. She knocked her forehead against Max's chest. "All these years and she spoke to me."

"What did she say?"

Before she could answer, her cell phone rang. She scrambled across the bed, grabbed it and saw the caller ID read *Cole*. She tapped the screen of the second phone. No change, only the same passage of seconds, minutes and hours counting down Hope's time.

"Cole?" She practically yelled into the phone. "What is it? What's happened?"

"Motel manager in Davis recognized Nicole's picture on the news. Local officers have her in custody and they're bringing her to us now. Thought you'd want to be there."

"Yes. We're on our way." She kicked free of the sheets and glanced over to where Max was already tugging on his jeans. "Was there anything else? Any sign of Patrick?"

"No. Nothing yet," Cole said. "You okay to drive?"

"We're fine. See you in a—" Her phone buzzed again. "Hang on, Cole, I have another call coming in." She checked her screen. Her stomach dropped. "Cole?" She turned anxious eyes on Max, who was watching her. "It's Patrick."

"Putting a trace on it now. Keep him talking as long as you can."

"All right." She clicked off, took the other call. "Patrick?"

"Dr. Allie?" The small girl's voice released the pressure from Allie's chest and she sobbed.

"Hope? Is that you?" She held out her hand to Max as he raced to her side.

"It's Hope? Are you sure?" he asked.

Allie nodded, torn between laughing and crying. "Sweetheart, where are you? Can you tell us where you are? Are you okay?"

"I th-think so. But I'm scared, Dr. Allie. A man found me in the room. He said his name was Patrick and that he was your friend. He took me away and put me in the car, but then there was an accident and he was hurt. He gave me his phone, told me to call you. To tell you where I am, but I don't know. It's dark." She started to cry. "My head hurts and I don't have any shoes and—"

"It's okay, sweetheart. We're going to come find you." Allie grabbed the closest clothes she could find. "We just need you to be brave for a little while longer. I'm going to hand you over to your uncle, okay? He's been so worried about you. I want you to tell him everything you told me and I want you to answer his questions. Understand?"

"Uh-huh. But the phone's beeping. I think it's losing its charge."

Allie closed her eyes, pressed her lips together and prayed. "I promise we're going to find you soon, Hope. Just talk to your uncle."

The relief on Max's face as he accepted the phone nearly tore Allie in two as she got dressed. She could hear the forced calm in his voice, the years of emergency training kicking into overdrive. "Where's your phone?" she whispered and he pointed to the nightstand on the other side of the bed.

She grabbed it, dialed Cole. "Cole? It wasn't Patrick. It's Hope. She's out there somewhere on her own. Max is talking to her now."

"We're working on getting a ping on the phone's GPS. Not easy with cells, as you know."

"Her phone's dying," Max said softly.

"I know," Allie said. "Cole, Hope's cell is dying. Do you have anything? Any idea where she might be?"

Muffled voices, shouts and calls echoed through the phone as she waited what felt like an eternity for him to answer.

"We have a general idea, but it's a huge space of land, miles to cover…" He trailed off, shouted something else. "That can't be a coincidence."

"What can't be?" Allie demanded, but even as she uttered the words she knew.

Because Chloe had told her. "It's where Chloe was found, isn't it?" She said to Cole. "That field out near Gibson Ranch?"

"General vicinity, yes," he confirmed. "I'll have squad cars meet us there and get a search going."

"Look for an oak tree. A huge one, Cole. One by it-self. Don't ask me to explain. Just trust me."

"Always do," Cole said. "Eden and Simone will meet us there."

She hung up and found Max sitting on the edge of her bed, staring down at her cell phone.

"The call dropped," Max whispered and turned newly distraught eyes on Allie. "The battery died."

"It's okay." She caught his face between her hands and kissed him. "I know where she is. Let's go bring your girl home."

Chapter 16

"Glad you drove because I don't have the faintest idea where we are." Max gazed out the passenger window of Allie's SUV as she made a sharp left and floored it.

Had minutes passed or hours since she'd heard Hope's voice on the phone? If she couldn't be sure, she could only imagine how distraught Max must be feeling.

"We're going to find her, Max." She took one hand off the wheel to squeeze his. "You just need to hold on a little longer."

"By my fingertips if I have to."

"Sun's coming up. That's only going to help." She swerved back into her lane, distracted by trying to remember every detail she could about her dream. The more time that passed, the more foggy the images became. The spinning lights in the distance bolstered her hope. "They're already here and looking for her. See?"

As if she needed to point it out.

"Hope said she was told to call you," Max said. "Why would Patrick do that?"

"I don't know." Nothing made sense to her at the moment. Nothing would until she knew Hope was safe and home with her father and uncle. "There's Eamon. And Cole and Jack over there across the street."

She braked hard and parked on the side of the road, spotted Lieutenant Santos with a group of deputies and officers on the other side of the patrol cars. Max was already out and running as she yanked the keys free and jumped out to follow. Her energy drained as she drew closer to her friends. She scanned the area for something, anything familiar from her dream, but everything was so different.

She turned in circles, her mind spinning as panic began to mount. Every bit of her training, every bit of her objectivity vanished and left only fear in its wake.

"Allie!" Cole called her over, his brow knitting. "Over here!"

"What's wrong?" Jack asked her as she joined them at the hood of Jack's new SUV.

"I can't explain it." And she couldn't. She couldn't even bring herself to look at Max. She didn't want to let him down, not after everything he'd been through, especially not in regards to his niece. "What do we know? Have you found anything?"

Cole glanced at Eamon, who stood as silent as usual. Stoic, steadfast, stony-faced Eamon Quinn might have looked calm and analytical to anyone who didn't know him, but Allie could see the barely there panic hovering behind the same green eyes Chloe had possessed.

"We found a car not too far in. Patrick Goodale was

the driver." Eamon motioned to the gap in the oleander across the road. "It's totaled from being run off the road. We found traces of evidence of another vehicle."

"Patrick." Relief almost swamped the rage. Almost. "You found Patrick. You have him in custody?"

"He's dead, Allie." Jack tightened the straps on his bulletproof vest as he picked up the conversation where Eamon left off. "Shot twice in the chest. Point-blank."

"Dead?" Allie swayed. "Patrick's dead?" How was that possible? Why…?

"What about Hope?" Max's cool tone meant she couldn't mistake his underlying message. Patrick wasn't the important one. "She said she was taken and put in a car. Is there any sign of her?"

Cole shook his head. "We have deputies and officers searching the area near the car now. The cell phone ping only gave us a general location before it went dead. It's the only reason we found the car. And Allie? There are countless oak trees. We need more to go on."

Allie nodded, determined not to give in to the deflating sensation in her stomach. "Please give me a minute." To what? Magically decipher which tree was the one from her dream?

Max shifted, shoved his hands in his pockets and ducked his head, but not before she saw the frustrated gleam in his eyes. "Just give me a direction to go, someplace to start," he pleaded with Cole. "Please."

"We will in a second," Eamon assured him as he moved around to Allie. "Why here, Allie? Why did you tell Cole to look for an oak tree?"

She shook her head. She didn't want to explain that she'd talked to his dead sister in her dreams. It went against everything she believed, everything she'd studied, and all logic and reason, and yet...

"She was dreaming about Chloe," Max said. "Just before Cole called, she called out her name."

Allie shivered. "I can't explain it," she told Eamon when his expression went flat. "I know it sounds crazy—"

"Tell me what you saw. Close your eyes, Allie." Eamon moved in, placed his hands on her shoulders. "Take yourself back there. Tell us what she showed you."

"I can't—"

"Yes, you can," Eamon snapped and out of the corner of her eye, she saw Max move toward her, only to have Jack grab his shoulder to keep him in place. "Set the fear aside," Eamon continued. "Stop thinking about anything other than the dream. Whether it was Chloe or not, whether she was real or not doesn't matter. You dreamed it. It was in your mind. It's your thoughts. Now focus on them."

His calm rationality settled her. She closed her eyes and jumped when she heard car doors slam in the distance.

"It's Eden and Simone," Eamon told her as he squeezed her shoulders. "Concentrate, Allie. Tell us where to go. Tell us where Hope is."

Allie blanked her mind, emptied it of all thoughts before drawing on the image of the field she'd found in the dream. The sight of Chloe darting around the tree. The tree that arced and spewed its majestic branches high into the sky. She heard murmured voices in the distance as she retraced her steps, felt the weeds and flowers crunch beneath her feet.

And then she wasn't alone. She felt her friends beside her.

"We've got you, Al." Eden's hand slipped into one of hers. Simone took the other.

Grass. Not weeds. Thick grass with tiny explosions of color, the violets that had haunted her for so many years now her guiding force. She angled her head as if she could change her vantage point. She blinked open her eyes, bypassed looking at anyone or anything other than the area on the other side of the barbed-wire fence behind Cole's and Jack's cars.

She pulled free of her friends' hold, walked to the fence that stretched for as far as she could see in either direction. A flicker caught her attention, behind where she'd stood moments before. She ran back, ducked down and pointed to a piece of red fabric off one of the barbs. "Here. She went through this way."

"Are you sure?" Eamon asked as he moved to his car and retrieved a pair of bolt cutters.

Max joined her, reached for the material, but she stopped him before he pulled it free. "It's evidence," she whispered.

"It's Hope's," Max confirmed. "I bought a red sleep shirt at the mall for her."

Allie nodded. "Okay. Through here!"

She started to duck through, but Max tugged her away when Eamon came over to clip the fence apart.

"We go first," Eamon ordered as he dropped the cutters and withdrew his gun. "Cole, Jack, take point. Whoever shot Patrick might still be here," Eamon reminded everyone. "Keep sharp."

"Which way, Allie?" Cole asked.

Allie's gaze landed on the tree in the distance. She pointed. "There."

The morning damp coating the thick grass soaked through her clothes as they waded through the field. The overgrown flora made her feel as if she were swimming through mud. Her feet slipped and slid and she held her hands out for balance as they trudged forward, additional officers and deputies spreading out behind them.

Just when it seemed as if they weren't getting any closer and she again feared she'd been wrong, Cole held up his hand, pointed to the side. "There! I see where someone's cut a path. It's a small one, but it's recent."

"Follow it!" Allie cried as everyone picked up speed. No one said a word as the morning air was filled with the swishing sounds of running and breathing. Allie glanced behind her but found Eden and Simone right by her side, Simone keeping pace even as she knotted her hair at the base of her neck.

And then she saw it.

"This is the tree." She stopped dead in her tracks as she recognized the spot. Eden and Simone grabbed her arms. "You see it, don't you? You know where we are?"

"We know." Eden hauled her forward and into the near clearing where Chloe's body had been found twenty years before. "And we aren't stopping now. Hope!" Eden called and by doing so gave everyone else permission to call for the little girl. But it was Max's frantic call that jolted Allie's heart.

"Hope, answer me!" He disappeared around the tree and she heard him clomping through bushes and shrubs.

"Here!"

They all froze at the sound. "Did you hear that?"

Allie whispered. Her lungs burned, her head throbbed. Simone nodded.

"This way!" Eamon ducked under a tree branch and came into an opening, his flashlight glinting against the green of the flora. "In here!"

"Uncle Max? Dr. Allie?" Hope's gentle voice called out in the semi-darkness and let Allie breathe again. "Is that you?"

"We're here, baby," Max yelled as he dived through a thicket of thorny holly. "We're coming. Hold on."

Allie wrenched herself free and went in after him, her breath catching in her throat as she caught sight of the shadow of a small figure huddled, shivering, at the base of another tree. The dead cell phone was clutched in her hands. The side of her face glistened, and as a shaft of morning sun shone through the branches of the tree, Allie saw the blood.

"Hope." Max's legs wobbled as he approached her. Her long red hair was tousled and tangled, tears streaked her filthy face, but Allie knew, at that moment, she'd never seen a more beautiful sight than Max holding out his arms for his niece. "Hope."

She sobbed and threw herself at her uncle, her small fingers digging into his back with such force Allie could feel it. "I knew you'd find me. I just knew it."

Max sank to the ground, hauled her into his lap and rocked her, much like Allie imagined he had when Hope was a baby.

"She's okay," Max said over his shoulder to Allie. "She's okay."

Allie nodded as tears spilled onto her cheeks.

Simone murmured a quiet prayer while Eden moved

in and wrapped an arm around Allie's waist. "You did it, Al. You found her."

"We found her," Allie corrected. She looked on as Eamon and Vince entered the area. "Eamon?"

Eamon blinked as if trying to pull himself out of a trance and then flinched as he caught sight of Hope and her uncle. His eyes met Allie's for a brief moment, and in that time, Allie's heart broke all over again. He holstered his weapon, gave her a sharp nod and walked away.

"Hope?" Allie approached with as much caution as Max had, only to find herself nearly bowled over as her patient launched herself out of Max's arms and into hers. "I'm so glad you're okay," Allie whispered. She held on tight, unable to stop herself from pressing a kiss to the little girl's forehead. "We were so worried about you."

"She told me you'd find me." Hope leaned back, her arms linked behind Allie's neck. "She told me to hide here and you'd find me."

"Who told you?" The question was out of Allie's mouth before she thought better of it. Before she realized the answer.

"I don't know her name." Hope sat up and scrubbed her hands across her face. "You must have seen her. She looks just like me. Can I go home now, Uncle Max? I really want to go home."

"We're going to take you to the hospital first, make sure you're all right," Max said. "That's a nasty bump on your head."

"Oh." She pushed out of Allie's hold and back into her uncle's as he lifted her into his arms. "It happened when the car crashed. But I'm not sure. I fell asleep."

Max smiled. "I'm betting you get to go to the hospital in an ambulance with a siren and everything."

"Wow, really?" Hope's eyes went wide. "For me?"

"Hope?" Allie asked. "Hope, did you see who took you? Did they hurt you? Touch you? Do anything to you?"

"Not now, Allie." Max shifted Hope out of her reach as Hope ducked her head and hid her face in Max's neck.

"Do you know where you were being—" Allie tried a different tactic.

"I said not now!"

Allie frowned. She needed answers; she needed to know just how involved Patrick was. If Hope had any solid memories or information. "It's best if I talk to her when it's all fresh—"

"You don't get to decide what's best for her. Not now." Max moved around her and gave her a ferocious look that had her taking a step back.

"But we need to know—" She trailed after them like a heat-seeking missile.

"No, *you* need to know," he snapped. "I have what I need, right here." He jostled Hope in his arms. "You can talk to her later if you have to, but right now, leave her be."

"But—"

"She's not your patient anymore, Allie," Max blasted. "She's not Chloe. She's Hope. And she's alive. And if you don't mind, I'd like to keep her that way."

Allie gasped. She wasn't putting Hope in any danger. She needed to do her job. She needed to close this case, once and for all, to make sure there weren't any more Hopes or Chloes. "Max, please—"

"Please don't fight." Hope began to cry. "Not you, Uncle Max. Please don't fight with Dr. Allie. I don't want to hear anyone fight ever again."

"Hush, we aren't fighting, Hope." Max cradled her head against him. "Not anymore." He glared at Allie over the top of his niece's head. "Let's get you taken care of and somewhere safe."

"I'll come with you then." Allie moved to follow only to feel Eden grab her when Max's eyes narrowed.

"Please, don't," Max said. "She's been traumatized enough for now. We'll be fine on our own."

"But—"

"Allie." Simone swooped in and joined forces with Eden. "He's right. She's been through enough."

"Thank you, Simone." But it was Allie he stared at. "For putting my niece first. I can't tell you how much I appreciate that." He turned and walked away.

"You can't blame him for going off the rails," Eden said as she and Simone bookended Allie back at Cole's SUV. The highway had been blocked off, traffic was being diverted, and the crime scene unit had arrived and had taken charge of the scene where Hope had been found. "It's been a pretty rough time for him."

"For all of us," Simone added as she rubbed Allie's back. "He's just worried about his niece, Allie. He's not angry with you."

"I don't care if he is," Allie lied. She'd never seen anyone look at her with such loathing before, as if he didn't know who she was. What she was. "I need to talk to her. I need to know what happened, what she saw." It might be over for Max, it might be over *with* Max, but Hope still had information they needed.

"Let's pray she didn't see all this," Jack said as he joined them by Cole's car. "Whoever killed Patrick did a number on the scene. It's a mess. Almost like they threw some kind of fit after."

"I want to see it. I want to see him." Allie didn't wait for permission. She trudged forward and through the path left by the crashed vehicle. She spotted Tammy by the open trunk taking pictures while her assistant shifted the angles of the spotlights as the sun continued to rise, others placing evidence markers in the appropriate places.

"Allie, you don't have to do this," Eden said in an uncharacteristically gentle tone. "We can look at the pictures later—"

"He was my brother," Allie cut her off, pushing aside any sentimentality. "It might sound strange, and I don't expect you to understand, but I need to see this."

"But—"

Simone pulled Eden away, shook her head. "Let her do this."

Allie left them behind and walked toward the bashed-up car. Both the driver and passenger doors were open, the windshield obscured by spider-webbed cracks. She saw his feet first. The expensive Italian loafers she remembered him dreaming about when they were children. Patrick could spend hours perusing mail-order catalogues, marking off items that one day he'd be able to afford. His tailored black slacks were torn and ripped, the button-down shirt glistening with blood. His pale face, even paler in death, seemed gaunt and stricken, as if he'd died of shock despite the bullets in his chest.

His eyes stared up to the sky, vacant, dull, that same

sweep of bangs brushing the tips of his lashes. Such a waste. Such a horrible, horrible waste of a life.

Allie stooped down, forced herself to memorize every detail. "What did you do, Patrick? Why did you do this to us?"

But Patrick Goodale didn't answer. He never would.

She pushed to her feet, closed her eyes to clear her thoughts and faced her friends.

"I want to talk to Nicole."

Chapter 17

"Max?" Joe burst through the door to the emergency room, eyes frantic behind his crooked glasses. Despite the wrinkled clothes, messed hair and pale skin, a flicker of something akin to happiness shone in his eyes. "She's all right? She's really all right?" The last word erupted on a sob as he grabbed hold of Max's arms and squeezed.

"She's okay." Max could feel what energy he had left begin to drain, as the last forty-eight hours took their toll. "The doctor is still in with her. She has a mild concussion, some bumps and bruises, and they think she's suffering some aftereffects of being sedated." The latter was probably the reason she'd escaped the crash with so few injuries.

Max rested his hands on his brother's shoulders in the same way he'd seen Eamon focus Allie. "She's still a bit scared, but otherwise she's going to be fine. She's already asking to see her friends."

"I called the Vandermonts before I left the house," Joe said. "They're on their way with the girls."

"Mr. Kellan?" A young, scrubs-wearing nurse approached them, a kind smile on her round face. "I'm Debbie and I'll be taking care of Hope while she's here. We're going to get her settled in a room, but if you'd like, I'll bring you to her now. She's asking for you. And her uncle Max."

"Thank you." Joe turned grateful eyes on Max. "I can't thank you and Allie enough for everything you did. You kept your promise. Just like you always do." He smiled and erased the days of suffering from his face. "I'm going to have to make some changes, I know. No more traveling, no more putting business first. Hope is all that matters now."

"What about Gemma?" Max hated to bring up his sister-in-law, but there didn't seem to be a way around it. "Is she coming?"

"Gemma's gone." Joe's expression hardened. "She finally showed up last night, signed the papers, packed her things and left. Didn't even ask about Hope."

"I'm sorry, Joe." Allie was right. Gemma had finally shown her true colors. She didn't deserve Joe Kellan and she certainly didn't deserve Hope. As angry as he wanted to be, he couldn't muster the emotion. "I think for the first time I feel sorry for her. She's going to miss so much."

"Where's Allie?" Joe asked. "I want to thank her in person."

"She's helping the detectives with the rest of the case," Max said even as the words and accusations he'd thrown at Allie struck him. "I'm sure you'll have a chance to talk to her soon."

"At least the man responsible is dead," Joe said. "I couldn't imagine Hope having to testify in court about what's happened."

Max nodded, unwilling to burst his brother's happiness by telling him Patrick hadn't been acting alone.

"You sticking around?" Joe asked as he followed the nurse down the hall.

"I'm here for as long as you need me." He motioned to the seating area near the nurses' station even as he fought the desire to find Allie and explain and apologize. He'd messed up. Big time. "You need anything, you let me know."

"Thank you," Joe said again and clapped his hand on Max's shoulder. "Thank you for bringing her home."

Max nodded as that nagging feeling in his gut returned, the one that told him he'd made a huge miscalculation about Allie. He'd been so worried about Hope, so determined to make sure she was somewhere safe and protected, that he'd forgotten what had started all this in the first place. Even as he'd accused Allie of tunnel vision, of not putting Hope's needs first, he'd done exactly the same thing. He'd dismissed Allie's need for answers as being cruel and callous when they were just the opposite.

Whoever had taken Hope—whoever had murdered Chloe Evans—was still out there.

And he'd bet his entire firefighter pension that they weren't done yet.

"Just got off the phone with the hospital," Simone told Allie as she opened the door to the interview observation room. The smell of stale coffee lingered in the air. "Hope is settled in her room for the night. Minor injuries, but they're keeping her a few days to be sure. The Vandermonts just got there with her friends and her dad is there, so she's being well looked after."

Allie stood, arms crossed tight against her chest, and stared through the one-way mirror at the foster sister she'd once called her friend. "Thanks." In the few hours since she'd left the crime scene she'd attempted to process every bit of information she could, but nothing could cut through the suffocating self-doubt and grief. Hope was safe; that was all that mattered.

"Apparently Max is still there, as well," Simone continued. "He's quite the subject of conversation at the nurses' station. Seems he can't sit still."

"He only stops moving when he sleeps," Allie said.

"Have firsthand evidence of that, do you?"

Allie wanted to smile, wanted to laugh. But the attempt at humor only saddened her more. "Don't tease me about Max. Not now."

"If not now, when?"

When and if he ever spoke to her again? She couldn't get rid of the image of that accusatory, disillusioned look in his eyes. His feelings must have rivaled what he'd felt back in Florida, when his entire world turned against him. She'd put this case first, ahead of Hope, ahead of Max. And why? What was the point? To solve a murder that wouldn't change anything?

Chloe would still be dead. Patrick would still be dead. And Nicole would still be pacing the interrogation room while Allie got up the courage to confront her.

"I can't think about Max right now," Allie said. "I need every ounce of brainpower to talk to her."

"You don't have to talk to her at all," Simone said. "Let Cole and Jack question her. Or Eamon. You know he's dying to."

"Which is why it has to be me. I know Nicole." Or at least she thought she did. "For whatever reason, she sees me as her prey, her adversary. She'll want to keep playing whatever game this is."

Cole strode in, Jack right behind him waving a file folder. "Before you go in there, there's this," Jack said. "Remember during the old Iceman investigation when Agent Simmons got his throat cut by that vagrant?"

"That's a bit difficult to forget," Eden said.

Allie shivered. She'd been sitting in the car with Eden when those shots rang out, watched the color drain from her friend's face as she realized Cole was in danger. There had been no stopping Eden from racing to Cole's side—not Allie and not the threat of getting shot herself. That was love. Allie's heart twisted in her chest.

"You know we went over that scene several times," Cole said. "We found a bullet lodged under the siding of the building. Guess which bullets match that one?"

Allie frowned. "The bullets that killed Patrick?"

"Got it in one. And we've confirmed the surveillance photos left on Simone's windshield weeks ago were taken with the same camera as the one that took the picture of you all twenty years ago. Or at least the same lens. Same defect. Anyone want to lay odds who the new photographer in the family is?"

"We need to find that camera," Simone said. "We need to figure out where they've been holed up, keeping Hope."

"We're going through all the known residences the

Goodales have occupied over the years," Jack confirmed.

"Let's get this over with." Allie smoothed a hand down the front of her shirt. She was ready. Or at least as ready as she was going to be. "What do you think? Do I lead with the fact that Patrick's dead or that we found Hope alive?"

"You'll know what to say when you have to say it," Eden said. "You've got this, Allie. It's almost over."

"It is." Allie looked at Simone slipping her hand into Vince's as Cole slid his arm around his wife's waist. She missed Max. She missed how he boosted her confidence, how he smiled at her. She missed how he made her laugh even in the worst situations. But he was where he needed to be. And that wasn't with her. How could it be when she'd neglected her patient, put her own needs ahead of those of a traumatized nine-year-old? But what was done was done. All the more reason to make sure her relationship with Max didn't die in vain.

She headed for the interrogation room, stopping for a moment to get herself in the right frame of mind before she pushed open the door and walked inside.

"Allie." Nicole sagged with relief. "I've been asking to talk to you for hours! All of this, it's not what you think. I promise, I'll explain—"

"Sit down, Nicole." Allie forced herself to keep her arms at her side. She would not pull into her shell; that's what got her into trouble. And she'd had enough trouble to last a lifetime. "I said sit down."

Nicole jumped at Allie's tone. She took a shaky step to the metal chair across the table and sat. "They arrested me," she whispered. "But we didn't do anything wrong. I promise, this is all a misunderstanding. Patrick and I, we've been trying to stop it!"

"Where's Tyler, Nicole?"

"What?" Nicole couldn't have looked more shocked if Allie had pulled out a gun and shot her. "What are you talking about? He's dead. He killed himself —"

"He survived the hanging, Nicole. You know it. I know it. He may have had brain damage, but Patrick arranged to have him transferred, still, there's no record of him having arrived. Where did Patrick take him, Nicole?"

Nicole shook her head, her black hair cascading around her bloodless face. "I don't know. Allie, you have to believe me—" She reached her hands out and then brought them back when Allie didn't even glance down. She watched Nicole's face, saw the panic fade behind cool, detached realization. "You're not buying it, are you?"

Allie's heart shattered. What she would have given to be wrong. "No, Nicole. I'm not."

Nicole sat back, an overdone pout on her face. "And I had such a good story to tell you. Oh, well. The truth is always so much more satisfying. You take the lead, little sister. Ask me whatever you want." She smirked. "No reason to lie now."

She didn't know, Allie realized. Nicole honestly didn't know that Patrick was dead or that they had found Hope. Alive. "Where's Tyler, Nicole?"

"Dead." She narrowed her eyes, sat up straight and shifted into a position of defiance. "No, he didn't die when I told you he did. He died a little over a year ago. Mom and I buried him near that trailer park we lived in before they stuck her in the hospital. Right by the river, where he used to play."

"So you found time for that while you and Patrick were here looking for your new restaurant location?"

"You do what you have to do for family. Chloe's death drove Tyler insane. Well, drove him the rest of the way." Nicole shrugged. "If he could have just let it go, but no. Because of you, because of your pathetic 'woe is me, I lost my best friend' attitude, he started looking for ways to bring her back. He needed you to like him again, so he could live with you and your ridiculous parents. He was happy there. Then he read some stupid book about flowers with mystical powers and he got obsessed with violets, convinced himself they could bring the dead back to life. So he tried. With a girl who looked just like Chloe. And when that didn't work, he lost himself. Then he came back, tried again. Then again. It never took."

"Imagine that." As much as she hated the monster who had killed Chloe, the idea that Tyler had spent the rest of his life so tortured was almost more than she could bear. "I don't suppose you and Patrick tried to convince him it wasn't possible. That he was only killing more innocent girls." Allie pushed the disgust deep into her belly.

Nicole smiled. "How was I to know it wouldn't work eventually? I thought maybe he just needed to find the right replacement."

"And that's when he tried to kill himself," Allie guessed. "He couldn't have done all that alone, Nicole. He had to have help from you and Patrick. PNT Photography was your way of helping him, wasn't it? Your way of placating him, of controlling him."

"Patrick involved?" Nicole frowned. "Good heavens, no. What gave you that… Oh." She actually laughed. "Mom said that would throw people off. It was the P.G. Ale, wasn't it? You remember my mother, don't you? Mina? Short for Philomina, of course. I do love how moms are always right. Oh, I can't wait to tell her the ploy worked."

Allie hoped her shock didn't show. Patrick wasn't P. G. Ale? "So exactly how is Patrick involved in all this?"

"He's not." Nicole rolled her eyes. "Coward. He got away. For years. Started over. Until I called to tell him Tyler was dead. That's when he knew he had to come back. He knew what would happen if he stayed away. Not that it mattered. Nothing was going to stop it."

"Stop what?" Allie asked.

"Mom blaming you for Tyler's death. The guilt he lived with. Not even that stupid treasure box of things he'd stolen from you all those years ago brought him any peace. Letters and notes and perfume bottles. Barrettes and ribbons and pictures of you and your friends. They were just reminders of what he'd done. It drove Tyler mad. And we knew you needed to be made to suffer for it."

"But why?" Allie's focus slipped as fear settled into her chest. How could they possibly blame the nine-year-old she was for what Tyler had done? "Why do you hate me so much that you'd put the life of an innocent girl, a girl I cared about, at such risk?"

"You honestly don't know, do you?"

It was then Allie realized she was the one being studied. She was the one who'd been lured into this web, slowly wrapped up in Nicole's and her mother's delusions.

Nicole leaned forward, placed her folded hands on the table and gave Allie a slow, evil smile. "Because it was never supposed to be Chloe Tyler took that night." Her eyes narrowed. "It was supposed to be you."

Allie began to shake.

"How I wish I could record this moment of realization for posterity," she went on. "You must remember how similar you and Chloe looked that summer. You'd dyed your hair to match hers. You even started dressing like her because heaven forbid Allie Hollister be an individual. So when poor little Chloe came out of her tent that night and Tyler was waiting to take you with us, he thought it was you. He didn't realize and then it was too late and, well." She tapped her fingers on the table. "We know what happened then. Mom's plan to leave the state with us had to wait because of the attention that was on you and your friends. How would it look if all of a sudden three of your foster siblings vanished? All that planning, all that waiting and then we had to wait even longer. So Mom readmitted herself for a few months. Which meant Tyler was forced to watch, up close and personal, how you moaned about and mourned your friend. Every tear you shed was a nail in his coffin. You drove him to be like that, Allie. And all because you had to try to be someone other than who you are. A weak nothing of a person. Your own parents didn't even want you. They tried to fill up their lives with other children because you weren't enough. And now look where you are. Sad, pathetic and alone."

The door burst open.

Eden launched herself at Nicole, but Allie jumped to her feet and dived between them as Simone grabbed Eden around the waist to keep her away. Allie saw Cole and Jack in the doorway, Vince bringing up the rear, other officers headed toward the room. "Tell her, Allie," Eden yelled. "You tell her or I will because right now I want to knock that simpering smirk off her face."

"As if you could tell me anything that would mar this moment for me," Nicole said. "I've waited years for this, Allie. Years and years and years. How does it feel knowing that your poor, precious Chloe died in your place?"

Allie squeezed Eden's arms, stared her friend straight in the eye before glancing at Simone, who had sympathy and rage written on her face. Twenty years ago, maybe even ten minutes ago, Allie might have believed Nicole. She might have bought into the fact that she was, essentially, alone. But not now. Because she had Eden and Simone. She had Cole, and Jack, and Vince. And Max. Maybe Max.

As right as Nicole was about so many things, she was one hundred percent wrong about this.

"I've got this, Eden," Allie whispered as all hesitation dropped away and the confidence took over. There wasn't anything left to lose where Nicole was concerned. Whatever feelings she might have had for her foster sibling were dead. As dead as Chloe Evans and Tyler Goodale. "I love you, Eden, and thank you, but trust me. I've got it."

Allie leaned on the table and looked her one-time sister in the eye. "You're telling me Patrick did everything in his power to stop you. He had nothing to do with Chloe's murder or the other girls' deaths, or the shooting—"

"Oh, he had something to do with the shooting all right," Nicole said. "He got there in time to stop Mom from putting a bullet in that one's head." She pointed at Eden. "Thanks to him the bullet that was supposed to hit the SUV went wild."

Allie swallowed the nausea. "And the pictures you took of Simone?"

Nicole practically deflated when she sighed. "Are we going to go over every detail? Fine. I took them. It's not like she's hard to track in those white outfits of hers. I would have left them in her apartment, but I have to admit, that security she has is top-notch." She gave Simone an impressed smile.

Simone glared. The disgust in her eyes palpable.

"Let's break this down," Nicole said. "Tyler is dead. So you can't punish him for the girls he killed. Patrick didn't help with any of it, aside from unearthing Tyler's treasure box and doling out to you lot what he found in there. That was his attempt to placate Mom. The flower delivery, the notes, bumping into you on the street with an open bottle of perfume." She jerked her chin at Eden. "He mailed the last one to your little mini-Chloe, Hope. Innocent little tokens he knew would bother you enough to satiate us. And right about now the clock is running down on whatever time poor little Hope Kellan has left." She tapped a finger against her teeth. "You see, I'm the decoy. I'm here to watch every last moment of your misery as you realize there's nothing you can do to save her. And oh, the plans we have for her. Tyler isn't going to be alone for long."

"Because your mother is going to kill her," Allie said as she felt Eden and Simone visibly relax behind her. So that was the endgame. A game they'd put a stop to. "I'm assuming that's who took Hope since she's the only one left alive."

Nicole's gaze flickered.

"Allow me to explain." Allie reclaimed her seat and mimicked Nicole's earlier, superior posture. "You see Patrick had apparently had enough. Wherever your mother was keeping Hope, he found her. He was going to leave her somewhere we could find her. But he didn't get the chance because your mother hunted him down, and ran his car off the road. You know what your brother did then? He saved Hope, Nicole. He gave her his phone so she could call me. And she did. We found her, Nicole. She's safe and back with her family. And you know where Patrick is?" She leaned forward. "He's dead. Because your mother killed him."

"No." Nicole shook her head. "No, you're playing me. Patrick isn't dead. My mother would never—"

Jack came forward and handed Allie a file. She flipped it open and pushed the crime scene photos in front of Nicole.

"Dead." Allie tapped two fingers twice against Patrick's chest. "Two shots. Dead center. Boy, she has good aim. Doesn't even miss when she kills her own son."

Nicole gaped. "This is a trick. No. The plan is still in play. She's supposed to—"

"What? Bury Hope wherever you buried Tyler? Thank you for that bit of information, by the way. We've been wondering where we'd find your bolt hole. Now we know where to start looking. I'm going to leave you now, Nicole. And I'm going to let the police and FBI come in and speak with you about all these murders you've been involved in covering up. And then you know what I'm going to do?" She stood, planted her hands on the table and leaned really close so Nicole could hear her when she whispered, "I'm going to forget your entire family ever existed. I'm not giving you another moment of my life except when I testify at your trial. I will be there every day and I will watch you wither and fade before you're locked away for the rest of your life, along with your mother."

Allie stepped back, held Nicole's gaze, and then turned on her heel and left the room. Eden and Simone followed her lead.

The sound of Nicole's scream was oddly satisfying as Simone closed the door behind her.

The three of them stood there, in the narrow hall of the Major Crimes division, hands clasped together.

"It's over," Eden whispered. "It's really over. We know who and we know why."

Allie nodded as the tears burned. "Yes. Now we know why." And it had been a mistake. A horrible, unchangeable, life-altering mistake that Allie would never be able to undo.

"Chloe can finally rest," Simone added.

Allie couldn't stop the sob that erupted from her chest. "I'm so sorry." She tried to cover her mouth, but they wouldn't let go of her. Why would they? They were her family. She leaned forward.

They did, too.

And then they were hugging each other, holding on to one another as if they'd never let go. Finally. Allie took a deep breath. After twenty years, she'd found her peace, knowing it was over.

"Forget teaching psychology in Los Angeles, Al," Eden laughed. "You should give interrogation lessons. You were ah-may-zing. Pinned her to the wall like the insect she is."

Allie smiled against her friend's shoulder. Such a way with words.

"What on earth are you talking about? Los Angeles?" Simone glanced between the two of them.

"I was offered a job." Allie shook her head. "I'm not taking it." How had she ever thought about taking it? "This is where I belong. With my family." She hugged them again.

"We've put out an All Points for Mina Goodale," Cole said after he cleared his throat. "Sorry to interrupt. Eamon's leading the chase and we'll be backup if he needs it. She won't get far."

"I know she won't," Allie said. "Did you get everything on tape that Nicole said?"

"Yep. And her Miranda rights before you spoke to her. She refused representation, but I'm betting they'll fight the confession unless she cuts a deal." He looked expectantly at Simone.

Simone shook her head. "The Feds can have both of them as far as the DA's office is concerned. They have more to use against her than we do. Multiple jurisdictions, multiple states. I want every book possible thrown at the two of them."

"Hey." Eden gave Allie a squeeze. "Where'd you go?"

"What?" Allie blinked as if coming out of a twenty-year trance. "I think I need to go to the hospital." Being with her friends, her family, meant the world to her, but right now, all she wanted was to see Max again, to apologize. And to hope, that maybe, there was a future for them. "I'm, um, I'm going to go."

"I'll drive you," Jack said. "Could do with a bit of fresh air, and, besides, there's this nurse who works the early-morning shift in the ER—"

"I knew you'd find the right time to move on from

dating Simone," Allie said as she linked arms with his. "Good for you, Jack." To Eden and Simone, she said, "I'll call you two later." She dragged Jack away.

"Say hi to Max for us," Cole called out to her.

"I will." She'd say that and a whole lot more.

"Hey, Allie, we're here."

Allie was confused as Jack shook her shoulder. "What?" She rubbed her eyes, sat up straight. "Oh, man, I fell asleep?"

"For a whole ten-and-a-half-minute drive, yep." Jack grinned and unbuckled his seat belt. "I won't hold it against you. This time. Didn't even give me a chance to seduce you with my seat warmers." He got out and came around to open her door. The parking lot across the street from the hospital was reserved for law enforcement and employees, and it currently didn't have many cars. Allie raised her hands over her head and stretched before she reached into the car for her bag.

She saw movement in the rearview mirror, a flash of color. Time slowed. The image came into focus. An older woman. Dark hair. Beneath a red baseball cap.

Allie turned as the woman drew a gun.

"Jack!" Allie cried, but Jack was already reaching for his weapon with one hand, Allie with the other. She felt his hand lock around her arm.

Bang! Bang! Bang!

Jack jerked and dropped to the ground. His weapon clattered down next to him.

Allie cried out as Mina Goodale moved toward her, weapon raised. Allie braced herself, arms up, hands fisted, and she struck out, ducking to one side as Mina brought the butt of her gun down on the side of Allie's head.

Pain exploded in her temple and down her jawline. Her vision went dark, but she kicked out, punched out and made contact. She heard Mina slam against the car before she backhanded Allie and shoved her into the passenger seat and slammed the door.

Dazed, Allie tried to find the door handle. "Jack," she mumbled. Her fingers went numb as Mina jumped into the driver's seat and jammed the key into the ignition.

The last thing Allie saw through the window was a flood of ER personnel stream out of the hospital door.

"Jack."

And then…darkness.

Chapter 18

Max knew gunshots when he heard them.

He sat up in his chair as ER staff leaped into action, racing for the door, shouts erupting and breaking through the early-morning silence. He followed, pulled by deeply rooted obligation he couldn't shake no matter how hard he tried.

The nurses and doctors ran full steam across the street to the prone figure in the parking lot. Max stopped for a moment, dread pooling thick and deep in his gut as he recognized the hair, the blazer, the weapon just out of reach.

"Jack."

Max plowed ahead, dropping to the ground beside the detective as Jack's eyes fluttered. His breath sounded wheezy, and as the medics pressed against the vest he still wore from earlier, Max felt relief.

"Max," Jack coughed out. Blood pooled in the corner of his mouth, trickled down his face.

"Check his side!" Max yelled as he helped push Jack over. Someone ripped the Velcro free and pulled the vest aside. Blood saturated his white shirt.

"Side shot! Get a gurney over here!" A doctor yelled. "Do you know him?" he asked Max.

"Detective Jack MacTavish with Major Crimes. Jack, hang in there, buddy. Don't you dare check out on me. Not today." He tried to stay out of the way, but Jack flailed his arm at him, waggled his fingers. Max reached out, grabbed hold. Moved in. "Yeah, I'm here, Jack."

"Allie," Jack blinked so fast Max's eyes hurt. "Mina… Allie. Find. Allie."

His hold went slack.

"I've lost a pulse!" A nurse yelled as the gurney arrived. "Get an operating room ready, stat!"

Jack's hand released his. Max backed away as he watched them lift his friend up and wheel him into the ER.

Max couldn't move. He could only stare helplessly as the life of yet another friend hung in the balance. Blood coated the pavement, shell casings lay scattered and a red baseball cap sat nearby. Tread marks… He pulled out his cell phone.

"This is Delaney. Max? Is that you?" The jovial tone in the detective's voice sliced through Max like a sword. "You and Allie make up already?"

"No, Cole, listen—"

"Man, you gotta give her another chance. She knows she messed up—"

"Cole, stop! Listen to me." He waited an extra second. "Jack's been shot. Across from the hospital. Allie's gone, but I think Jack told me who took her. Mina? Does that make any sense?"

Cole swore. "Nicole's mother. Stay where you are. We're on our way. About Jack? How bad?"

Max looked to the ER door. "You'd better hurry."

Allie blinked, expecting the sun, only to find her skull vibrating with pain. They were moving. She tried to angle her head, but every move she made caused more nausea. The space was dark, but she could see a thin strip of light across the top of the car's trunk. Her breath came in short gasps, but she couldn't open her mouth behind the tape. Her hands had gone numb thanks to the plastic cable cord tying them together. She kicked out and heard the denting of plastic and steel as she hit the side of the car.

Car. Jack's car. His SUV.

Jack.

Anger surged. Mina.

Allie kicked again. She didn't care if Nicole's mother heard her. She wanted her to hear her, to come back here so she could do some damage, but instead of the car stopping, the music that had been playing softly increased in volume.

Think, Allie. Think!

She drew her hands up, ready to implement the escape her trainer had taught her months ago, but she stopped. That wouldn't do her any good now. She needed to break free when Mina least expected it. When Allie had an advantage. Which meant she had to wait until Mina got to wherever she was taking her.

The car bounced over railroad tracks. Allie cried

out as her head bounced against the floor. Where was Mina taking her?

Allie replayed every word spoken in her interrogation of Nicole. Nicole who had nothing left. And Mina, who was desperate to finish whatever she'd started. And everything with Mina, Allie knew, began and ended with Tyler.

Tyler.

Allie swallowed and focused on evening out her breathing. Mina was taking her to Tyler. It was her only play, her only option. It was what they'd planned to do with Hope.

It was what Mina was going to do to her now.

Except no one else knew where Tyler was, but they had clues, clues her friends had heard, as well. Dwelling on the what-ifs wouldn't keep her alive; plotting how to get away would.

So that's what she'd do. And put the rest of her faith in her family.

"Any word?"

Max couldn't remember a time he'd seen so many people flood through a door at one time. The endless minutes he'd spent waiting for them had been as bad as watching that stupid countdown clock over the last two days.

Looking at Allie's less-than-optimistic support system had him wondering if he was ever going to see Allie again, a thought that terrified him.

Lieutenant Santos followed behind Cole, Eden, Simone and Vince, along with Officer Bowie and Sergeant Tomlinson and a handful of other officers, who spread out around the ER waiting room.

"Jack's being prepped for surgery," Max told them. "Two hit his vest, broke a couple of ribs. The third went into his side." He motioned to where the straps connected the vest. "He's flatlined twice." He knew because he'd been standing outside the door, watching.

"But he's still alive," Cole said. Eden smoothed her hand down his arm, her expression unreadable.

"What about Allie?" Max asked.

"We didn't see Jack's SUV outside so I'm assuming that's what Mina took off in," Vince said. "We should be able to track his GPS—"

"Unless she's disabled it."

"Did Jack even register it?" Eden asked. "He's only had it a week or so. Cole?"

"I don't know."

"Mina's not in her right mind. Never has been. The last thing she's going to be worried about is a GPS tracker," Simone said. "She had a plan for Hope. She'll have one for Allie. This is about completing her mission."

"What mission?" Eden spat. "Hope is out of her reach. Nicole's in custody and facing multiple life sentences. Who knows what's going on with her now?"

"So Nicole was involved?" Max asked.

"Up to her beady little eyeballs," Vince said. "We need to find that car."

"You won't," Cole said. "Simone's right. She'll have had a plan. Nicole said something about a trailer park in West Sac, near the river. They lived there. It's where they buried Tyler. That's what this is about. Tyler."

"Because he killed Chloe?" Max asked.

"He didn't mean to kill Chloe," Eden said. "He meant to take Allie. It was always supposed to be Allie."

"What are we waiting for?" Max couldn't begin to fathom the amount of guilt Allie must be feeling at that revelation, nor could he just sit around and do nothing while Allie's life was in jeopardy. "Let's get the address and go!"

"We will. But there's nothing stopping Mina from killing Allie the second she sees us," Cole said. "We're going to have to wait."

"Until when?" Max demanded.

"Until dark," Vince said with a slow nod. "Allie's strong. She's smart. She'll hang on."

"And she'll know we're coming," Simone added. "First thing's first. Let's find that trailer park and go from there. Don't worry, Max. We'll get her back."

"We'd better," Max said, determined to make it happen. He appreciated Allie's friend's offer of a strained smile, the only thing he could cling to for now. "No way am I letting her out of this life before one of us wins that bet."

The SUV stopped. Allie had lost all feeling in her arms and legs. It had been hours. At least she thought it had been hours. She'd forgotten how many times she'd fallen asleep and for how long. She was so hot. Sweat poured down her face, stinging her eyes. Her strength was gone. What she wouldn't give for a sip of water, a breath of fresh air, anything to remind her that she was still alive.

That she still had a chance.

The music clicked off. The engine went quiet. The driver's door opened and closed, and the latch on the hatch released. Fresh air swooped in. Allie choked, tried to inhale slowly, deeply.

She blinked into the darkness.

No lights. Nothing but pitch-black in front of her aside from the dim light cast by the taillights. What time was it?

Mina Goodale stood in front of her, her gray clothes as dull as the sallow tint of her skin. Eyes as dead as her son's stared down at Allie, the woman's jaw working overtime.

Allie didn't cry, didn't want to give her the pleasure of seeing that. She refused to give in. Not to the fear and not to this woman who was so far gone she'd murdered her other son.

Mina reached in and ripped the tape off Allie's mouth.

She tried not to make a sound, but she failed. Her skin burned where the adhesive had stuck. Allie pushed herself up, tried to kick out her dead legs only to have Mina reach in, grab her by the front of her shirt and haul her out of the SUV.

Allie turned her head at the last second and took the brunt of the fall on her shoulder. Pain radiated through her entire body, but she welcomed it. She groaned, rolled over and gasped for air as Mina pulled out a knife and sliced through the tape binding her feet.

"Going to end this once and for all," Mina mumbled. "Going to do what he should have done that first night and buried you so deep not even the Gods of the afterlife could find you."

She left Allie on the ground as she returned to the car, pulled a shovel and flashlight out from the back seat.

A calm blanketed Allie as Mina returned. All that was left was her tied hands, and now that she was moving, she could regain enough circulation to snap off the restraints. Depending on how far she had to walk to her grave.

Mina grabbed Allie by her shirtfront again and dragged her to her feet. Allie gasped as her feet prickled to life. She stumbled to the side, leaned against the car before Mina shoved her forward and down a slope.

"Move. Straight ahead," Mina ordered in a tone that made Allie wonder if she was salivating. Madness had overtaken her. She had only one thing in mind and she was going to make that happen no matter what it cost.

She had nothing left to lose.

Neither did Allie.

Mina clicked on the flashlight, and for the first time, Allie could see where they were, could hear the river rushing in the distance. Another field, only she could see trailers and RVs in the surrounding distance. She glanced behind her, spotted the tip-top telltale golden outline of the Tower Bridge. West Sacramento.

She'd been right.

Relief swept through her. "Tyler wouldn't want this, Mina." Allie tried to sound professional and reason this situation out; it was all she could do to try to play for time. "He didn't mean to kill Chloe, which means he wouldn't have killed me. You're getting it wrong."

"Stupid girl. My boy didn't have it in him to kill anyone," Mina said. "Would think you'd have known that given you were all he ever talked about. Allie and her perfect family. Allie and her perfect friends. He wouldn't leave without you. So I said we'd take you with us. I told him to go get you."

"You? You told him?"

"Always was as dumb as a sack of potatoes. Couldn't

even figure out what girl to take. He shows up with that Chloe girl and she's crying and screaming and wanting to go home. Had to take matters into my own hands when he couldn't get her to stop, didn't I? Had to show him what to do. How to take charge."

"You killed Chloe." Tears pricked Allie's eyes. It hadn't been Tyler. And yet all these years he thought he'd been responsible. His own mother had let him believe he'd been the one to kill Chloe.

"Would have killed you, too, so didn't matter who he brought. Didn't expect to spend the next twenty years trying to clean up his mistake. Enough talking. There! I want you right there."

"How do you know—" Allie's foot caught on something solid. She pitched forward, landed flat on her stomach.

Mina walked over and flipped the plywood up and over. "A mother knows where her child sleeps. Get up." She kicked Allie in the ribs.

Allie tightened her stomach muscles, absorbed the hit and rolled up. She scrambled away but not fast enough. Mina pulled out her knife again, and took less care slicing apart the cable tying Allie's hands.

The blade nicked Allie's wrists and set them to bleeding.

Allie pinched her lips together hard.

"I said get up." Mina held out the shovel with one hand as she drew her gun with the other. "And don't go thinking you can use this against me. I'd prefer you to die slow, but I'll settle for quick." She released the safety, cocked the hammer and aimed the barrel at Allie's head.

Allie steeled herself and pushed to her feet, slowly,

as slowly as she could as she counted the heartbeats of life she had left. The headlights from the SUV blinked dark, once, twice. She heard the faint rustle of footsteps.

She stood up straight, held out her hand for the shovel. Moved in.

"Now dig until you find him." Mina circled around and backed up, kept the gun steady on Allie.

"Any idea how long that might take?" Allie asked as she jammed the shovel into the rocky ground. "I had other plans for the evening." Nothing like channeling Eden when she was feeling desperate.

"Snide brat. Never did see what my boy liked about you."

"Too bad you never let him tell you."

Lights burst to life around them. Allie blinked as Mina turned and aimed her gun toward her attackers. Allie gripped the handle of the shovel in both hands and swung up and around. The dull thud of metal against skull echoed in the night as Mina went still.

The gun dropped from her hand as she fell forward, looking at Allie, her eyes glazed over.

Allie dumped the shovel. Maybe she shouldn't have. She swayed on her feet.

The next thing she knew, a crowd swarmed around her, voices familiar, barely breaking through the dull roar in her ears. Simone was there, and Eden, and she heard Cole...

"Jack," she whispered as hands guided her away from Mina Goodale's body and Tyler's grave. She kept her eyes pinned on the mother who had destroyed nearly every life she'd ever touched, and took an odd sense of satisfaction at the darkness pooling around her head. "She killed Jack."

"Jack's in surgery," the distant voice told her. Max's voice.

She looked to her side, found Max there, his hands gripping her arms as he pushed her toward the EMTs waiting beyond the line of lights. "He's alive?" The hope she'd been tamping down surged.

"So far," Max said and pushed her into the waiting paramedics' hands. "Let them look at you, Allie. I want to know you're okay."

"I'm sorry," she whispered as gentle hands pushed her into the back of the ambulance. "Max, about Hope and earlier, you were right, I never should have pushed her. I just needed to know. I needed... Chloe." She blinked and felt tears land on her cheeks. "She killed Chloe, Max. How could a mother do that to a child? Anyone's child?"

He was right. The whys hadn't explained anything. Not really.

"I don't know. And you've nothing to apologize for, Doc." Max bent down in front of her, gripped her hands in one of his as he cupped her face with the other. "We were both wrong and we've moved past it now. I don't want you to give this another thought, okay?"

She nodded as she gazed at his shaggy hair, drawn face. She didn't think she'd ever seen anything more beautiful in her life. "Shaggy." The nickname escaped her lips before she realized what she was saying. She brushed her hand down his hair.

The surprise in his eyes broke through the shock. "Now that was just a lucky guess." He grinned. "Unless someone ratted me out?"

"No rats," Allie smiled as one of the EMTs moved in to check her pupil response and then her pulse rate.

She was hooked up to a blood pressure cuff and then she heard beeps and whines. "You owe me a secret," she told Max when he started to stand up and move away. "Something no one else knows about you." She blinked. Her eyes felt heavy. She could feel the darkness pressing in, tempting her to surrender.

"A deal's a deal." Max stood up, bent over and pressed his lips against her ear. "I love you, Doc. Joe and Hope might have given me a fresh start, but being with you has given me a new life. You're stuck with me." He kissed her, his lips against hers, his glistening brown eyes looking into hers. "Now let us take care of you. And don't worry," he added when she grabbed hold of him, her heart swelling so she could barely breathe. "I'll be there when you wake up."

She smiled. He loved her. Max Kellan loved her. She wasn't alone. Not anymore.

"I love you, too, Shaggy."

His words were enough. His words were everything.

She closed her eyes.

Max stood aside as Allie was moved to the stretcher, an oxygen mask slipped over her face. His momentary panic at her passing out was quickly eased by the EMTs assurances she had done just that. Everything else was reading normal, but they'd take her to the hospital to be safe.

"I'm going with her," Max stated and was told they'd let him know when they were leaving.

"You've had a busy few days."

Max turned his head and found Vince standing behind him, pistol sticking out of the waistband of his jeans, an odd expression on his normally stoic face.

"Almost makes fighting fires feel like a vacation." He grinned. His sense of humor was returning, something that would no doubt be irritating everyone near and far sooner than later.

He looked to where Eden and Simone stood beside Cole and his lieutenant over Mina Goodale's body. His grin faded. "I can't even imagine what they must be feeling. All these years and to finally have closure."

"There's going to be an adjustment period for them," Vince agreed. "They've been focused on this case for twenty years, since they were kids. Now they can start living again."

"We all can." And there wasn't anything he wanted more than to start that life with Allie.

"Speaking of living," Vince inclined his head. "What are your plans employment wise?"

"Nonexistent," Max admitted. "Other than babysitter and chauffeur to my niece. I'm not trained for much outside the firehouse."

"Not true." Vince's expression hardened. "Sounds like Allie was right about your confidence issues. I'd appreciate it if you worked those out before you came to work for me. I know a psychologist who might be able to help."

"Work for you? Where? You mean at your bar?" He could think of worse things than slinging beer mugs and flipping…ugh. Max cringed. Burgers. Ever since he'd worked for a butcher in high school he didn't do so well with meat.

"As a P.I.," Vince said with what sounded like exaggerated patience. "I've been offered a couple of contracts from insurance companies and I'll also be working for the DA's office. I'm going to have lots to keep me busy, probably more travel than I'd like, but I could use someone on the team who understands fire and arson. You're good under pressure and you follow orders. You also have keener instincts than most people I've worked with. I'd need you to get some certifications, of course, and it'll take some study and time. If you're interested that is." Vince shrugged. "Something to think about."

Max's heart hammered in a way it hadn't since he'd decided to become a fireman. It seemed too good to be true, working with people he liked and respected, doing something important and being close to his family. He ducked his head, pinched his brows. "I'm inclined to say yes, but there would be one thing I need."

"Worst case is I say no," Vince urged.

There was little Max liked more than a straight-shooter. "A flexible schedule. I need to stick close to home, to Joe and Hope. There's going to be some adjustments for both of them, too. They're my priority."

"I'd have been disappointed if you'd said otherwise," Vince agreed. "We'll work it out. What about Allie?"

Max frowned. "What about her?"

"You have any plans for her?"

"Oh, I have plans." Max's smile was slow to spread. "And I might just need the rest of you to help pull them off."

Chapter 19

Somehow, thanks to the healing powers of time and understanding, Allie's parents' anniversary party the following weekend wasn't the nightmare event she'd expected. Not that she hadn't been anxious for her planned solitary retreat to the tree house, but it wasn't for the reason she'd been expecting.

Allie stood at the base of the tree, looking up at the house her father had built over twenty years ago. It had been reinforced twice, the wood planks hammered into the ancient oak replaced and solidified. For a moment, she wondered if the opening was big enough for her to squeeze through.

"Only one way to find out." She grabbed hold and stepped up, climbing the ladder until she poked her head into what she remembered as a spacious hideaway.

A couple of sleeping bags and blankets were huddled

in the corner, a stuffed rabbit sagged beside them and a plastic tea set was tipped over on the makeshift table.

Her hideout growing up had been her refuge, her safe place. And for a few years, Tyler had been her companion, sneaking up here at night so they could look at the stars. Later, it was where she went to cry and talk to the friend she'd lost.

Except she'd lost two friends that day: Chloe and Tyler. Tyler, who had been as much a victim of life's tragedies as Chloe.

Whatever guilt she'd expected to feel at having ended Mina Goodale's life never quite manifested in the way she'd thought it would. She'd been cleared of any wrongdoing, which wasn't surprising, since she had at least a dozen police officers and an assistant DA as witnesses, but Allie hadn't been able to shake this odd detachment from what had happened the night Mina kidnapped her. It was almost as if it had happened to someone else.

There would come a time, she supposed, when her mind would be ready to process it all, but she wasn't in any rush. She wasn't in any rush about anything these days.

Well. Maybe there were a few things.

Allie stooped down and looked out the window with the crooked trim that gave her a long view of the backyard. The chicken coop and vegetable garden were still in full operational mode, with her mother and father holding court with their family and friends.

She could still feel the unusual sensation of her mother's arms around her hours after her parents had arrived at the hospital. Allie almost hadn't known what to do when Sitara and Giles had offered a heartfelt apology for how they'd treated Allie.

It was an important step, she admitted, one that had been induced by what she'd only just learned was a rather vehement suggestion from Eden, Simone and Max. How she wished she'd been privy to that conversation.

"There you are." Max poked his not-so-scruffy head through the opening. "Eden said she thought she saw you headed this way. Wow." He glanced around at the tree house and gave an appreciative nod. "This place isn't half-bad. Remind me to bring Hope up here before we leave."

Allie smiled. "I'd love to show it to her."

The little girl was doing remarkably well and had taken it upon herself to drop the "Doctor" from Allie's name. It made sense due to Allie's decision to change the focus of her practice. She'd still work with children occasionally, but hearing Max talk about the difficulties his friend Bixby had gone through, she wanted to work with firefighters, police officers, vets…those who were dealing with life-changing injuries or events. And her consultations with the police department and FBI? She was done for the most part.

She'd given a significant part of her life to criminals and trying to figure out the why—usually to do with the past. Now it was time to focus on the future.

"You doing okay?" Max had to duck his head to stop from bashing it on the roof as he crawled forward. Allie chuckled and sat back, finding herself instantly enveloped in the arms of the man she loved.

"I'm doing okay. Cole stopped in to see Jack en route to the party."

"So I heard. Detective Awesome is going to be okay."

Allie nodded. "Eventually." The bullet that had

missed his vest had done serious damage. It would be six to eight months before he was back to full strength again, although he was already showing signs of his usual crankiness. Another positive. "We'll make sure of it."

When the silence stretched, Max began to shift, as he always did when he sat still for so long. "You want to go?" She looked up at him and then realized he'd been trying to reach into his pocket.

"No, I do not, actually. I just didn't expect such a tight...ah! Fit. Geez." He sagged against the wall and exhaled. "You just never make things easy for me, do you, Doc?"

"Nope. And I don't plan to start." She sat up, a hand on his chest as he held out a small square box. "What's that?" Her heart slammed against her still-sore ribs.

He gave her that grin that made her heart race. "What do you think it is?" He flicked open the box, turned it around so she could see it. "I went shopping with Eden and Simone the other day but didn't really see anything that screamed *Allie*."

"I didn't realize rings screamed," Allie teased, and then, when she looked more closely at the simple, square-cut diamond ring, her throat tightened. Her vision blurred. "That's Eden's mom's ring."

"It is." He lifted his arm from around her and plucked the ring free. "Eden told me how her mom and dad thought of you as one of their own. They loved you, Allie."

She nodded. "I loved them, too." Losing them to a drunk driver when she and Eden were fifteen had been another fracture in her childhood. "They welcomed me into their home from the beginning. They even gave me a key." And she'd never had the chance to tell them how much being a part of their lives had meant to her, how much strength they'd given her.

"So we all know Eden isn't exactly a sentimentalist when it comes to her own life," Max joked.

"Hence the quickie wedding in Tahoe," Allie said.

"She thought maybe you'd like to have it. There's only one catch." He sighed, an overly dramatic sigh that had Allie both laughing and sobbing. "I come with it." Max angled it into the sun and watched it glint rainbows against her childhood refuge. "But the good news is, I've got a job now and I come with a family who loves you almost as much as I do. And I like your friends."

"My family," Allie whispered as she held out her trembling hand. "They like you, too. I think it's a deal I can live with, Shaggy."

"Oh, that's the other catch. I have to get a haircut. And shave." He grimaced. "Vince's rules. I need to look less beach-dude and more professional."

"That might take some getting used to." She straddled him, squeezed her knees around his thighs as she leaned in to wag her fingers in front of him. "Would you please put that on me already?"

"Last chance to change *your* mind." But he didn't wait another second. The white-gold band slipped easily on her finger and settled right where it belonged.

"Yes" hovered on her lips as she heard a giggle beneath the tree house. Allie brushed her fingers over his face, leaned back to look out the window.

There, standing in the tall grass, looking up, was a little girl with red pigtails, a crooked smile and sagging overalls. She kicked up one bright turquoise shoe, did a quick dance before she waved, turned around and skipped off, fading straight into the shimmering sunbeams.

"Bye, Chloe," Allie whispered and smiled when Max rubbed his hand down her back.

"So what do you say, Doc? Ready to start a new life?"

She nodded, tears in her eyes. She'd waited so long for something and someone special to come into her life. No more. She grabbed hold of Max's face, kissed him hard, completely and with every ounce of love she could muster. "I love you, Max. And yes." She took a deep breath, held it and let everything go. "I'm ready."

* * * * *

Don't miss the other titles in USA TODAY
bestselling author Anna J. Stewart's
HONOR BOUND *miniseries:*

MORE THAN A LAWMAN
REUNITED WITH THE P.I.

Available today from www.Harlequin.com!

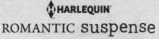

SPECIAL EXCERPT FROM

◈ HARLEQUIN®

ROMANTIC suspense

*One night with billionaire Alastair Buchanan turns
life altering when rancher Halle Ford finds out she's
pregnant. But Livia Colton's reach extends beyond the
grave; will Halle and Alastair survive long enough to
build the family they've come to dream of?*

Read on for a sneak preview of
THE BILLIONAIRE'S COLTON THREAT
by **Geri Krotow**, *the next book in the*
THE COLTONS OF SHADOW CREEK *miniseries.*

"You don't think I can do it?" Her chin jutted out and her
lips were pouty. Not that he was thinking about kissing
her at this particular time.

"I know you can do whatever you want to, Halle. You
pulled me out of a raging river, for God's sake. That's not
the question."

"The river was still by the time I got to you. Tell me,
Alastair, what do you think is the issue? What's your
point?"

"The concern I have is how you're going to make
enough money to not only keep Bluewood running, but to
invest in its future. How will you ensure a legacy you can
leave to our child? That's a full-time job in and of itself."

Tears glistened in her eyes as she bit her trembling
bottom lip. Not that he was looking at it for any particular
reason. "I'll do whatever I have to. It's how my daddy

raised me. Fords aren't quitters. Although Dad always found time for me, always let me know that I was first, the priority over the ranch. He was bringing in a lot more money when I was younger, though. I don't know if the ranch will ever get back to those days." She wiped tears off her cheeks.

"Are you sure you want to take on another full-time job on top of the ranch? With a new baby?"

"That's the question, isn't it?"

"That's part of what brought me here, Halle."

She grabbed a napkin from the acrylic holder on the table and wiped her eyes, then blew her nose. He made a note to order the finest linen handkerchiefs for her, with the Scottish thistle embroidered on them. Her hands were long, her fingers graceful. Would their child have her hands?

Her long, shuddering breath emphasized her ramrod-straight posture. He was certain she was made of steel. She rested her sharp whiskey eyes on him.

"Go on."

"Marry me, Halle. For the sake of our child, marry me."

Find out Halle's answer in
THE BILLIONAIRE'S COLTON THREAT
by Geri Krotow, available November 2017
wherever Harlequin® Romantic Suspense books
and ebooks are sold.

www.Harlequin.com